I looked back at the photographers. "Um…would you believe we just met a few minutes ago?" I said it in a way that was playful, like I was trying to hide the truth.

"Come on," several of the photographers answered. They smelled a story now, with me being not only an unknown with at least some celebrity cred, such as it was, but also trying to evade their questions on Lion's and my "relationship."

"Isn't she great?" Lion asked the group, placing a kiss on the top of my head as the flashbulbs ratcheted up another notch. The questions came fast and furious, but we only stared in each other's eyes.

You're not too bad at this, his eyes said to mine.

I eat assholes like you every day at the table, I conveyed back to him through a loving grin.

Again, he gave a big laugh, and it felt like the first sincere motion he'd made since we'd stepped onto the carpet—which, though small, was indeed red.

"Anna and I are just…friends. Very…very close friends. And I'm delighted she joined me tonight." He then launched into his spiel about his foundation and all the children it helped. I stood by his side until other guests started coming in and he turned to greet them.

He set me off to the side, but gave me a warning look when his back was to the cameras.

"Don't go anywhere. Just look at me adoringly, like you can't wait to get me alone later."

"Oh, I can't wait," I said, mentally calculating how I could destroy him—and embarrass him, *definitely* embarrass him—at the card table.

Huh. Maybe my superhero name should be the Destroyer after all.

AGAINST THE RULES

Anna Dawson Book Three

MARA JACOBS

Published by Mara Jacobs
©Copyright 2016 Copper Country Press, LLC

ISBN: 978-1-940993-12-6

For more information on the author and her works, please
see www.marajacobs.com

To my sisters-in-law—Patti and Gwen.
We're so fortunate that you both joined our family.

One

I SAT IN THE NOSEBLEED SECTION, *way the hell up there, surrounded by fans. I had worn red to blend in, had even worn one of the wigs I owned. A wig I thought I'd never wear again.*

A different wig from the one I'd worn last night when I'd paid a visit to the hotel room of one of the players who was right now, many, many rows below me, missing a free throw.

Easy, *I cautioned him in my head.* Nothing too obvious.

I hadn't brought that up last night when I'd spoken with him and given him the front end of his payment. I probably should have.

When giving pointers to a point guard about how to throw a basketball game, apparently you needed to think of everything.

I hadn't had this problem the only other time that I'd talked a player into outright losing a game in which his team was heavily favored.

But DeShaun Rogers, the player who was now missing his second free throw—stupid kid—was no Raymond Joseph.

Skills, DeShaun had in abundance. Cunning—other than on the court—not so much.

And there was no way, not for any amount of money, that Raymond Joseph would have thrown the college basketball national championship game. He had too much heart.

A heart I had torn from him.

A heart that right now was sitting in my Vegas home, watching this very game. If his name and location hadn't been outed as being connected with a murder case.

The fans around me cheered as DeShaun missed the shots, and I, not wanting to be noticed, cheered along with them.

I'd even sat amongst the opponents of DeShaun's team so as to remove myself yet another degree if possible.

Maybe I could fool the fans around me, hell, everyone in the place.

But I couldn't fool myself. There was no way to distance myself from what was playing out below me.

I had created this farce. Again.

DeShaun picked it up a little bit, and I wondered if I'd misjudged him. His team was up by four now, with three minutes to play. The Wisconsin guard drove down the floor, DeShaun guarding him, not too closely, not wanting to foul.

Would he remember what I'd told him last night? About how to unobtrusively give the kid he was guarding—a point guard with as deadly a three-point shot as DeShaun—just enough of a fake, then take a tiny step back so that the kid would take (and make) a three.

Right at that moment, DeShaun picked his head up, almost as if he'd heard me all the way from the cheap seats. Heard words I'd only thought, not said out loud.

But he remembered, and he did just what I told him. The guard from Wisconsin hit a long three and everyone around me went wild. I cheered right along with them.

It felt wrong, of course, but it was true that I desperately wanted Wisconsin to win.

Desperately as in…the health and livelihood of people I loved depended on it.

Including my own.

DeShaun drove the ball down the court. The Wisconsin guard who'd just drained the three slapped his hands on the floor in a "Hell yes, I'm fired up!" motion.

Raymond Joseph had done that too, in big games. When he'd been allowed to play college basketball.

Before I got my hooks into him.

Before JoJo had.

DeShaun made a hard pass that bounced off his teammate's hands and a Wisconsin player got his fingers on it, tipping it. DeShaun lunged for it, but the Wisconsin guard, never far from DeShaun, got to it first and drove it the length of the floor for an easy layup.

DeShaun was just a step behind him, looking like he was going to chase the kid down no matter what it took. But I knew it was going to be two points for Wisconsin. At least DeShaun didn't foul him. No need for that kind of post-game scrutiny.

Wisconsin was up by one now, and everyone around me was hugging each other and screaming. I even joined in on a high five with the people closest to me.

I'd been moving fast since Saturday when the last four had become the final two. Talking with Raymond back home almost constantly as he paved the way for me to meet with DeShaun.

There would be a lot to deal with in Vegas when I got back. Part of me wanted to stay here in Indianapolis, where the national championship was being held. Nice city. I was originally from Wisconsin (yes, I'd seen the irony of unintentionally ensuring my school would win it all), and had always liked the Midwest, though not necessarily the length of the winters. But Indy was south enough to not have to deal with that, at least not too much.

Yeah, I could move to Indy. Not so much "move to" as much as just never go back to Vegas.

Leave it all behind. The lies, the self-loathing, the threats— both those made to me and by me.

Become lost in Indy. I couldn't remember if all my aliases were blown or not, but Jimmy would be able to set me up with a new identity, I was sure. Jimmy probably knew someone in Indy who could help me out. But I wouldn't want to put Jimmy in the position of knowing where I was and keeping it from the others.

Even if it would be in their best interests for me to disappear from their lives forever.

I didn't know if there were any tribal casinos in Indianapolis, but I was concerned by that thought being one of my firsts when considering—however blithely—relocating.

Relocating, fleeing, whatever.

But if one of my first thoughts was where and how I could gamble in my new home, it was clear that leaving Vegas wouldn't help anything.

Time crept by. The last few minutes of any basketball game can last ten, but this was the national championship, and a very close game. DeShaun's team was only a two-point favorite, so the money line payout—betting on Wisconsin to win outright, not using the point spread to even the odds—was not a huge difference compared to betting them with the spread, but enough to make a difference at the stakes my…employer was betting.

Instead of winning even money, they'd win one and a quarter times their bet. Big deal with a thirty-dollar bet—you'd win thirty-seven fifty instead of thirty.

But when you were betting a million dollars—spread out amongst every casino reachable to not arouse any bookmakers' notice—winning one point two five instead of one was a different story.

And thus, Wisconsin had to win, not just lose by less than two points.

They were up by three now, thanks not only to DeShaun. The Wisconsin guard was putting on a clinic in three-point shooting, even when someone else was guarding him.

DeShaun was taking the ball down the court, only seven seconds left.

Everyone was on their feet (had been for pretty much the whole game); the Wisconsin fans surrounding me were hanging on to each other with banked glee. They knew they were close. They also knew that DeShaun could easily hit a three and send this thing into overtime. DeShaun and his outside shooting was what got 'em to the dance.

He faked a pass to a teammate, but then rose in the air for a jumper three that was nearly poetic. Except I knew there would be no joy in Mudville. I knew that DeShaun had pulled his shot a tiny bit to the left.

The game clock ticked to zero; the buzzer sounded. The Lucas Oil stadium went silent as the ball arced in the air as if in slow motion. It would be shown that way for days—weeks—to come on all sports shows.

ESPN would probably have the damn shot on a loop, interplayed with the cheering Badgers and a disconsolate DeShaun Rogers.

And it was headed that way, every bit of it, as the ball rolled around the rim and out.

Until the whistle blew and the ref called a foul on the Wisconsin guard who had grazed DeShaun's fingertips.

My fellow comrades in red groaned around me. The guilty guard held his head in his hands, unbelieving of the huge gaffe he'd just made. It reminded me of the ending of a game the previous week—a game that set this whole damn thing in motion.

And DeShaun's team tried to maintain a level of composure as he stepped to the line to shoot three free throws with the potential to send the game into overtime.

I did not like the thought of that. Too much could happen given another five minutes. The momentum would surely leave Wisconsin, and you just never knew how college kids would handle something this huge.

No, best to walk off the court a loser now, and not take any more risks. I mentally whispered this to DeShaun. He nodded and I blinked hard, thinking perhaps I'd said it out loud (and he'd miraculously heard me fifty rows below), but then I realized he'd been nodding to his coach, who was doing a "You've got this, just *keep it together" thing with his hands.*

The first shot was all net, as was the second. A few of the Wisconsinites in my section sat down, as if physically preparing for the certain eventuality of overtime, and needing to rest their bodies.

Sliding my finger into the neck of a couple of layers of clothing, I found my hidden horseshoe pendant and gave it three taps as I watched DeShaun dribble the ball and line up his final free throw.

And then he missed.

DeShaun missed the third shot.

There was a beat of stunned silence and then the red section—half the stadium—erupted in pandemonium. The blue side of the building moved in one motion as everybody dropped to their seats, stunned.

The Badgers ran to their bench, embracing their fellow players.

DeShaun crouched, still at the foul line, and held his head in his hands, just as I'd imagined it moments ago.

I knew his despair wasn't faked. I knew exactly how he felt.

No, I'd never personally thrown a national championship basketball game. But I'd let down my team. Lots of times. Even if they'd never known it.

I stayed in my seat, thinking, as the elated fans rejoiced around me.

I had thought it would never happen again. I would have sworn it was all over. I did swear it was all over. But I was wrong.

JoJo was back. And the bitch wasn't alone.

But this time it was much, much worse.

Two

❖

Five weeks earlier

"It's Ben," I said to Jack, who sat next to me on my bed. "Ben is your father." I held up the DNA results to him, the brown envelope discarded and on the bed between us.

Jack, a man I had recently reunited with, let out a sigh of relief that I realized I was also mentally feeling.

"It wouldn't have mattered, not really," Jack said, touchingly embarrassed at the relief he'd just shown me. Big, tough Vegas homicide detective Jack Schiller was quickly sliding back into place. His posture even started to change, straightening, his hands unclasping from where they were clenched together upon his lap.

I reached over and held them close, waiting until he met my eyes. "It mattered," I said to him when he did.

He nodded, a quick jerk of his chin. His body relaxed again, his shoulders—now heavier because they carried the burdens of my wayward behavior—easing downward.

"Yeah," he said through another sigh. We sat that way for a moment, until my reach became awkward from the way I sat, and I rested my elbow on the bed so that I could still hold his hands. But my elbow landed on the brown envelope, the one that had held the DNA report revealing Jack's paternity, making a rough crinkling sound, which seemed to break the spell we'd created in my bedroom.

The sound made Jack look away from me, and he leaned forward, moving his still-clasped hands from his lap to knees, his elbows on his thighs. I put my hands behind me, resting my weight on them, leaning back on my bed, watching Jack's head as he bent it forward over his hands, like he was in some sort of silent prayer.

What would Jack pray for, I wondered.

That he'd known Ben Lowenstein was his father sooner?

That he'd grown up with Ben and Rachael as his parents? (Though this would not have been possible, as Rachael had been married to Saul Greene at the time of Jack's conception.)

Would Jack pray for Saul's soul? Yes, probably. He was much more forgiving than I could ever hope to be. Just look at how he was with me. And the fact that he was here with me now, in my room, having just saved my bacon...again.

Perhaps if Jack was really in silent prayer (which I didn't believe), he was praying that he'd never met me.

He certainly had to wish for that often enough.

And I'd only known the man a couple of months.

Okay, yeah, let me get you up to speed.

My name is Anna Dawson and I'm a professional poker player. The big splash of tournament poker being on every channel may have passed, though you could still find it on TV plenty if you were looking for it, but I still played for a living. I'd even made a few televised final tables and within a small circle, was semi-famous.

There were plenty of big-time poker tournaments still out there, and in Vegas, pretty much every casino had a couple daily tournaments.

But they also had cash games twenty-four-seven, and that was where and how I played most days.

I didn't always win, but I won enough to live in a great

house in Summerlin, a nice area about thirty minutes northwest of the Strip.

I'm thirty-four and came to Vegas thirteen years ago just after turning twenty-one. The first three years were rough for me, bouncing from big wins to big losses.

About ten years ago I met Ben Lowenstein while I was rehabbing a broken foot. Ben was there doing physical therapy for his hip, which still caused him all kinds of pain, and had him using a walker to get around.

He knew right away that my injury had come from owing a debt to Vince Santini, and had been administered by Vince's strong-arm enforcer Paulie Gonads.

Anyway, Ben took me in, introduced me to his cronies, all now in their eighties, all retired oddsmakers for various sports books in town.

When we'd first met he'd misheard me when I told him my full name was Johanna but everyone called me Anna. I hadn't corrected him when he'd called me Hannah thinking I'd never see him again. He and Saul were the only people who called me Hannah, and I kind of liked it.

Lorelei Samuels joined us six years ago and runs the household. She's a forty-year-old, redhead—a former showgirl with a Jessica Rabbit killer body—who now spends more time taking care of Ben and me than actually dancing. She calls me Jo—short for Johanna, not JoJo. Only Jack and Raymond knew I used the name JoJo when doing less than scrupulous things. That it was JoJo's voice I heard in my head when shit was about to go down.

Ben's group, dubbed "the Corporation," had dwindled by two members over the past two months. First we lost Danny, our funny, sweet, beloved Danny. And then we lost Saul, Ben's best friend of over seventy years.

Jack and I met during Danny's murder investigation, and although we both had our demons to deal with—my sports gambling and his drinking—it had been natural and good between us.

Until it wasn't.

We broke up, and I became open to the advances of my loan shark, Vince. Talk about mixing business with pleasure!

It never went far with Vince, though. I think on some level I knew it wouldn't have been safe—for both my physical and emotional well-being—to sleep with Vince, to become more than we were.

Which was wise, because in the end, it was either Vince or me that was going to be flying over the balcony of his twenty-fifth-story condo in the high-rise Palms Place.

It was Vince. Obviously.

When I'd be into Vince for more money than I had, or would ask Lorelei for—even though it was my money, I couldn't bear the shame I'd feel to ask Lorelei for thirty thousand dollars to pay off a gambling debt because the idiot kicker for the Giants hooked one to the left—I would do a favor for Vince to wipe out my debt.

No, not that kind of favor.

I would don my alter ego, JoJo, and slip a roofie to some poor, unsuspecting college basketball player so he'd play like shit the next day, and his team wouldn't cover the point spread, thus making Vince a winner and my slate clean once more.

Until it wasn't.

That was how I met Raymond Joseph, who had become less unsuspecting and an outright co-conspirator with me until suspicion had been raised and he'd been forced to leave school.

He was now staying in the bedroom just down the hall from mine.

He was helping with Ben, too. And I hoped that whatever seed I'd planted in Raymond while getting him involved in my schemes would not make the trip to Vegas with him, but instead stay in Iowa, where they'd started, or even Chicago, where, hopefully, it had just ended.

I'd need to keep an eye on that, I thought as I continued to watch Jack think.

"Do we tell him?" he asked. My mind was still on Raymond and keeping him on the straight and narrow (ha! as if I was the one to help out with that), so I wasn't exactly understanding Jack until he added, "Ben. Do we tell him?"

Right. Ben was Jack's father. An odd coincidence, coupled with Saul's machinations, that Jack had come into the life of his father at the age of forty.

And, unbeknownst to either of them that they were father and son, they had grown to love each other over the past two months. With their feelings for me being the catalyst of their flourishing relationship.

Or maybe it was their concern for me that bonded them so tightly so quickly.

"Do you want to?" I asked. I wanted to reach out and put a hand on his back, feel the warmth through his familiar chambray shirt, but I didn't.

Jack and me back together was new, tentative, and I found my motions, my gestures, with him to be the same. I so badly wanted to wrap Jack up, crawl inside his skin, be a part of him. But I also knew what I was bringing to the relationship this time—a non-sports-gambling Anna—was newer and more tentative than Jack and me being together. And oh-so-much more precarious.

And so I kept my hands to myself, kept my pose of leaning back on the bed.

And then Jack came to me. He flopped his back onto the bed, then knocked one of my hands free so that I fell into him. Wrapping his arms around me—as only seconds ago I'd wished to do to him—he breathed me in.

I felt, then heard, my crutches slide off the foot of the bed. Jack held me tenderly, looking out for my bandaged arm, as he lifted my thigh up, swinging my leg—heavy boot protecting my injured foot—over his hip.

Oh yeah, forgot to mention that my last encounter with Vince—his last encounter of *any* kind—was only fourteen hours ago and had left me with a boot, crutches, and a really sore arm.

"I'm still furious with you, you know," Jack said.

Yeah, I knew. That was what had held me back from throwing myself against him moments ago.

But his fury had died down some since he'd found out that a man he greatly admired was his biological father.

"I know," I said, looking at him. The way his brown gaze bored into mine was better than even those lovely pain meds they'd given me at the hospital last night.

"If we're going to work…" He didn't finish his sentence.

And I certainly wasn't going to finish it for him. What? Make ultimatums up for him to dish out to me? Make promises I couldn't be sure I could keep?

I'd certainly *like* to keep them. As much for myself as for Jack. I'd even kept them for a few weeks now, not having placed a bet in seventeen days.

"I'll try, Jack," I said. "But…"

"Yeah," he said, then rubbed a hand across his face—a mannerism of his that at any given time both exasperated me and turned me on—before resting it on my hip. "I'll try too. You're not in this alone."

Honestly, Jack's drinking didn't bother me. Of course I knew it was detrimental to him, though he was highly functioning and was strict about not drinking while on duty and never getting behind the wheel when he was drinking.

But I knew it had affected his previous relationships, primarily with his ex-wife, his child, and his former partner on the force, all left behind in Portland when he'd moved to Vegas a year ago.

In a sick way, Jack having a drinking problem allowed

me to feel more secure in both my own bad habits, and in our relationship standing a chance.

Sort of a *Days of Wine and Roses* kind of thing. If we were both fucked up, we were better off together. One straight arrow and one broken? No, that couldn't work, could it?

We had agreed from the start that we wouldn't try to "cure" each other. That the cool thing about us was our ability to want to be together and not get into each other's faces about our shit.

But what we'd been through the last five days, with saving Raymond Joseph in Chicago, and then me nearly dying at Vince's hands—all of which had been born from my gambling—we didn't seem like such a cool couple after all.

I could tell he was thinking the same thing. "Let's leave it at that," I said. "That we'll both...try. See how it goes from there?"

Relief flashed across his face and he quickly agreed with a nod. "Yeah. Good."

I took a deep breath, let it out, and nodded, like the subject had been put to rest. It had, but I knew it wasn't buried very deep, and like a dog with a bone, just the barest scratching would dig it all up again.

"Ben," I said softly, getting back to where we'd started. Certainly where Jack had started...been conceived.

"Right," Jack said, his hand on my hip relaxing, his other hand starting to massage my upper arm, the one that had been injured.

"Do you want to tell him?" I asked.

"I want him to know, I think. Don't you think?"

"Yes," I said quickly. "I can't think of anything that would give him more joy than to know that he created a child with the only woman he ever loved." A soft smile played across Jack's tired face. "And to know that that child is you, someone he cares about so much," I added. "Major icing on the cake."

"I've never been called icing before. I'll take it."

"Rich, creamy, buttercream frosting. None of that pseudo-whipped-cream bullshit."

He chuckled, and the hand on my hip dug in a little bit, pulling me closer to him, my leg sliding over his hip more, so that my boot rested on the bed behind him.

"So, that's a yes. You think Ben should know?"

"Yes."

"But am I the one who should tell him?"

Damn, Jack Schiller was always one step ahead of me. I read people for a living. It was essential to win the poker games I played, for the stakes I wagered. But Jack read people too, and as a detective he thought about motivation much more than I did.

With the people I dealt with, the motivation was always the same: win the money.

I had come to the same conclusion—it might be better for Ben to hear the news from someone other than Jack himself.

Jack was thinking about Ben, but I was thinking about both of them.

I wasn't lying: Ben would be ecstatic that Jack was his son. But what his first gut reaction would be, I didn't know. There would be a great deal of pain, to know that Rachael had given away their child, had stayed married to Saul and never told Ben the truth.

If that was Ben's first reaction—the pain he would feel over Rachael—I didn't want Jack to misinterpret that in any way, turn it on himself.

"Maybe I should tell him," I said. "Give him some time to digest the news first, before you talk with him."

He was nodding. "Thank you."

"Anytime," I said, which caused him to bark out a small laugh.

"Christ, I can only handle this once. Hopefully I won't need another favor like this."

"It's not a favor. I love Ben. I wouldn't ever want to hurt him. And this news will hurt him—at first. But he's going to be so happy."

He nodded, his eyes leaving mine, looking up to the ceiling.

"Does this news make *you* happy?" I asked him. Like I said, I read people for a living, but Jack Schiller was always a tough nut to crack. Maybe that's why I was so willing to stick around… to eventually crack through. Although I think I secretly hoped that Jack would never crack. I needed to rely on that strength, that…unreadability.

I started to push away, to get up, but his hand tightened around me. "I'll go speak with Ben," I said, so he knew there was a good reason I was leaving a soft bed and his warm arms.

"Later," he said, and carefully rolled me, mindful of my leg and arm, so that he was on top of me. "I've been around forty years. I plan on sticking around if he—and you—will have me. I figure delivering the good news can wait a couple of hours." He started nuzzling his nose into my neck.

It felt like being dealt pocket aces. Better.

"A couple of hours?" I teased.

He licked my neck. "Okay. Twenty minutes. But they'll be a good twenty minutes."

It was thirty-seven minutes. And every one of them was good.

Excellent, in fact.

Three
❖

I LAY LOW FOR THE NEXT FEW DAYS. I told myself it was because of my foot and arm, but the truth was I wanted to be available to Ben in case he needed me.

It was a good thing Jack wasn't there when I told Ben he and Rachael had created a child during their affair forty years ago, and she had given it away.

That was devastating to Ben, so I quickly moved to the fact that the child she'd given away had led a good life, had been treated well, and was someone who was already in our lives and wanted to have a relationship with Ben.

And then dropped the bomb that it was Jack Schiller. My sometimes boyfriend, and a man Ben respected and liked. Loved, probably.

Jack texted me that night saying he was on a case and wouldn't be coming over. I texted back, telling him it was probably just as well and that I'd told Ben. We agreed that with Jack working it would give Ben the time he needed to come to terms with everything.

Ben ran the gamut of emotions too. One time I maneuvered my way on my crutches to the dining room to find Ben sitting at the big table with a box of photographs emptied out, its contents strewn about him.

I quietly asked if he'd like me to sit with him, but he shook his head, never taking his eyes from the photos, most of which were black and white, all faded with time.

Another day, he wouldn't come out of his room, not even to go out for breakfast as we did every morning, meeting Jimmy and the other surviving member of the Corporation, Gus Morgan.

In fact, since I'd come home from the hospital that morning, Ben and I hadn't gone out to breakfast once. I asked every morning, and when he'd decline I'd call Jimmy and let him know we wouldn't be meeting him and Gus.

"The guy learns he has a son, and suddenly he can't have breakfast? Man's still got to eat, am I right?"

"You're right, Jimmy," I said, knowing that hell or high water—not to mention the discovery of an unknown child—would never keep Jimmy from a good meal.

Ben had told me to let Jimmy and Gus know what was going on. "They knew Rachael," he said, I guess as some sort of explanation as to why he'd want his good friends to know about Jack.

I didn't question his reasoning; I was just happy that he wanted Jimmy and Gus (and Lorelei, for that matter) to know about Jack being his son. For Jack as much as for Ben.

On the fourth morning after I'd told Ben, I abandoned my crutches, making my way through my (and now Raymond's) wing of the house and over to Ben's room, my boot thumping noisily along the hardwood floors.

I knocked at his door and heard a muffled "Come in." When I entered I was surprised to see Ben still in bed. Even the past few days when we hadn't gone out for breakfast, Ben had still been up before seven and dressed and shaved when I'd come and seen if he wanted to meet Jimmy and Gus.

"Ben?" I asked, moving into his room, closing the door behind me. "Are you okay?" Sitting on the edge of his bed, I laid my hand on his back. His brown eyes were open, but were fixed on a point beyond me. If the blinds had been open, he would have been staring out the glass sliders to the pool area and the trees beyond. But the drapes were still closed (had been for a couple of days) and his eyes just seemed fuzzy and unfocused.

"I'm fine, Hannah darling," he finally said, and I exhaled slowly, not realizing I'd been holding my breath. "Just heartbroken," he added, and my heart broke for him.

"I know, Ben. It's very sad, the…what-could-have-beens."

A small nod from him, and he brought the blanket and sheet covering him up a bit higher, burrowing deeper into his nest.

This was kind of the behavior I would have expected the first or second day after I told Ben the news. Not the fourth.

"Ben, I'm worried about you. It's not like you to…be like this." I was going to use the word "wallow," but I wasn't sure how that would go over.

Yes, the man deserved a good wallow for what had been kept from him for forty years. For what had been taken from him. But Ben was old. Eighty-two years old. And though his mind was still sharp as a tack, his hip was crap, and his body had slowed considerably in the last few years.

One good wallow could send him down a road from which he might not so easily make a turnaround.

I knew Ben wouldn't live forever, just as I knew my parents back in Wisconsin wouldn't. That didn't mean I was in any way prepared emotionally for Ben to leave us. Thankfully my parents were only (only!) in their late sixties and in good health. (Sturdy, dairy-raised, Cheesehead stock, my parents.)

"I think I just want to stay here for a while," Ben said.

"Maybe I'll just stay with you. Is that okay?"

A small shrug—if the sheet hadn't rustled, I might have even missed it. "I'll let Jimmy and Gus know," I said, moving from the bed to the leather club chair across the room from Ben's bed.

I texted Gus, but called Jimmy. I told him quietly that Ben

and I would be absent—again—from breakfast this morning.

"Again? What the hell?" Jimmy said.

"I know," I said quietly, hoping not to wake Ben, if he was even sleeping. His eyes seemed almost closed, but I couldn't tell for sure from the angle I sat on the chair. "I think he just needs some more rest."

"Bullshit. What he needs is to get his ass back to his routine. That's what happens, you know. Old people get out of their routine and then it's all over," Jimmy said, and I was glad I had the volume down on my phone so that Ben couldn't possibly hear Jimmy's booming voice.

I agreed with Jimmy, and shared his fear, but I only said, "Hopefully we'll see you tomorrow."

"This is bullshit, Anna, and you know it."

Before I could answer, Jimmy hung up on me. Kind of harsh words, but then, Jimmy could be a harsh guy.

It was probably more than that, though, more than just Ben finding out he had a long-lost son. Ben's news probably unearthed a whole bunch of emotions in Jimmy that he would've been just as happy to keep buried.

Jimmy had a son. A boy born in Vegas to Jimmy and his wife Elaine nearly fifty years ago. This was well before I came onto the scene. Before I was born, actually.

Jimmy and his wife had divorced when the kid was little, and she took him back east with her. Jimmy never mentioned him; I found this all out from Ben.

So Ben having a son about the same age as Jimmy's—a son (Jack) who wanted to be a part of his father's life—might have stirred something up in Jimmy that he hadn't realized was there.

But it still wouldn't keep him from going to breakfast.

I slouched in the chair, taking a pillow from behind me and finding a good spot to rest my head. Halfheartedly I did my exercises for my arm that the doc had told me to do. Then moved onto my foot, doing the ones I could do while seated.

While rotating my ankle slowly, I thought about how long it had been since I'd placed a bet. Twenty-one days. I'd given it up shortly before going to Chicago to get Raymond. And then when the Vince stuff happened, there hadn't been much time for getting to a casino. Then the four days here, being available to Ben.

A record for sure. Twenty-One Days.

As I settled back in the chair, resting my head on the pillow, easing my tired foot and arm into comfortable positions, I tried to gauge how I felt about that. Twenty-One Days. Staying very still, closing my eyes, I pushed my thoughts of Ben and Jack, and Vince plunging to his death, and Raymond starting a new life here in my house, out of my brain. I waited, trying to identify the sense of panic I always felt when I hadn't placed a bet. My breathing became slower as I listened for "the voice" to make herself known. To tell me I was missing an opportunity. That there were games being played—*right now!*—that I could have money on. Money that would double when I won. (The voice never talked about possibly losing—it wasn't in her vocabulary.)

But I didn't hear her. That bitch, JoJo, was silent for once.

In fact, I had to stop and think about what games would even be playing now. The NBA and NHL were still in season. Baseball was six weeks away. College basketball. Of course. I was stunned—and a little proud of myself—that it had almost slipped my mind that we were entering the most exciting time in betting—college basketball tournaments. First would be the conference tournaments, then the field would be announced and brackets set, and then inevitably busted.

Even thinking of all those basketball games to be played didn't make JoJo come to life.

Was all the crap that I'd gone through in the past couple of months keeping her silent? For good, or just for now?

God, how I hoped it was for good.

I must have dozed (okay, fallen deeply asleep, based on the

drool on the pillow), but awoke when a dressed Ben patted my shoulder.

"I'm going to get something to eat. Can I bring you anything, dear?"

I was happy to see Ben out of bed and dressed. But he hadn't shaved (a first since I'd known him) and he was wearing sweatpants and a sweatshirt. Clothes Lor had bought him for around the house. Clothes that had stayed in his closet until this morning.

I wouldn't have been surprised if Ben asked for a pint of Ben & Jerry's for his breakfast, like some girl who'd just been dumped.

"I'll go with you," I said, rising from the chair, placing the pillow back on the chair, drool side down.

We walked down the long hallway that held Ben's and Lorelei's rooms as well as an empty guestroom. After the hallway, at the base of my large, U-shaped house, we went through the living room and were just about to turn to the kitchen when we saw Lorelei in the doorway of the dining room staring at us with her hands on her hips.

"Would you both please come in here?" she said, then took three paces back into the room, her eyes still on us.

"We were going to get some breakfast," I said, though it was well past breakfast time. Yeah, we had to get back to breakfast out with the boys. Ben's wallowing was starting to eat into my food time, and that wouldn't stand.

"I have food in here," Lor said. Ben and I looked at each other, shrugged, and shuffled our way—he with his walker, me on my unsteady boot without the aid of crutches—into the dining room, where we were greeted with the scents of coffee and freshly baked cinnamon rolls.

And also greeted by the sight of Jimmy, Gus, Raymond, and (a big surprise to me) Jack, all seated at the table with cups in front of them. All looking at Ben and me.

"This is an intervention," Lorelei said.

"Are you shitting me?" I said, outraged. "I've been *so* good. There is no way that—" I stopped when Jack shook his head at me and held up a hand.

I swung my head to Lorelei, ready to pick a fight, but she gave a shake to her head that mirrored Jack's.

"Ben," she clarified. "This is an intervention…for you."

Oh, well…yeah, I could get behind that. I walked to the table and took a seat.

Relief was clearly in my voice when I said, "Deal me in."

Four

❖

I SAT ACROSS FROM JACK, who gave me a smile. I hadn't seen him in four days, and I was surprised at how much I'd missed him.

I didn't usually miss guys.

"You should have seen your face a second ago," he said.

"I'm sure," I said. I reached for an empty mug at the center of the table and Gus handed me the carafe of coffee. "I gotta say, it sure is nice from this side of the table," I added, pouring myself a big mug full of strong, black coffee.

"I'll bet," Jimmy said as he slid the creamer and sugar bowl across the table to me.

To Raymond, sitting next to me and surely with a confused look, Jack explained, "Lorelei usually holds these for Anna. What, a few times a year?"

I nodded.

"As needed," Lor said firmly as she settled Ben into the chair at the head of the table.

Raymond looked to me. "For your gambling?"

My gambling, and where it had led me, was no longer a secret. It couldn't be when the evidence was sitting next to me, drinking a Gatorade.

We had Gatorade in the house? Lor must have already incorporated Raymond's preferred food and beverages into our kitchen. Which was good, because I hadn't paid Raymond much attention since the night Vince died.

"Yes, for my gambling," I answered him, then took a sip of coffee.

"Let's hope this one works out better than yours have," he said. Jimmy snorted, Gus tried to hide a smile, Lor looked as though she wondered if she'd been insulted, Ben's brow furrowed, as he no doubt thought of my not-so-distant deeds, and Jack had a small, sad smile on his face.

"Thank you for coming," Lor said once she had taken her seat at the foot of the table, where she had several sheets of paper in front of her. She was always prepared for her interventions, with statistics and signs of addiction or compulsion or whatever.

I was interested to see what she'd dug up on "being in a funk because you found out the love of your life had given away the child you'd created from your undeniable, but unattainable, deep and abiding love."

But if anyone could prepare for such an intervention, it was Lorelei Samuels.

I snuck a peek at Ben to see how he was reacting to being under Lorelei's spotlight. He seemed to be okay, a little confused, but certainly not out of it or anything.

I knew if it got too much for him, if he got upset, I'd shut this thing down. Fast.

I wondered how Ben had felt during all the interventions Lor had done for me. Most of the time I laughed off her interference, and most times Ben would defend me. Had it caused him the concern and watchfulness that I now felt for him? Would he have jumped in and shut it down if I'd truly gotten upset?

Or would he have felt that it needed to be done?

"I'm afraid I was a bit misleading in my reason for you all to attend," Lor continued, and my hand, with the coffee mug in it, froze halfway to my mouth.

"Shit," I said under my breath.

Apparently not under my breath enough. Jack shot me a glare from across the table and Lor quickly jumped in. "No, Jo, it's not for you. I wouldn't bait and switch you like that."

"You wouldn't?" I asked, my hand unfreezing, and I lowered the mug back to the table. There was just too much chance of doing a spit take, or choking on the stuff. I'd better just keep it on the table until I heard the rest from Lor.

She looked sheepish as she said, "Well, I'm not saying I'd *never* do that to you. I'm just saying I didn't today."

"She probably never thought to do that to you. Then you gotta go and give her the idea," Jimmy said, and I did a mental head slap. He was right.

Ignoring Jimmy—as she often did—Lor continued, "This intervention is for all of us. Our household is growing, changing. Ben's had some great—but startling—news. Both Ben and Jack have."

Ben was staring at Jack, a look of such pain on his face that I was ready to jump from my chair and rush him back to his room.

I glanced at Jack; he was looking at me, but I knew he was aware of Ben's gaze. He was letting Ben look his fill without meeting his eye. Jack gave me a small, subtle shake of his head, more of his eyes, really. I stayed in my seat.

"Well, if it's just for you guys, there's no reason why you had to pull Gus and me away from our breakfast," Jimmy said. He didn't make to leave the table—he still had half a huge cinnamon roll in front of him.

"You and Gus are members of this household. It doesn't matter that you don't live here. You too, Jack."

Jack nodded at her, and looked over at me. I suppose he was waiting for me to dispute that fact. But Jack and I, shaky as it might be, had a bond that wouldn't go away just because we weren't "dating" at any particular time. And now with Ben… Yes, Jack was a member of our household, though there were times I was sure he regretted ever meeting me.

Probably daily. But still, there he sat.

Lor even gave Gus a warm smile when she included him. They'd had a...flirtation?...fling?...something while Gus had been staying with us recuperating from being shot. I wasn't sure where they stood now—didn't *want* to know.

"Okay, okay, let's get on with it, then," Jimmy said, waving a big, meaty hand in a "hurry up" motion, but not showing any emotion over Lor's words of his inclusion in our lives.

She cleared her throat and picked up the top piece of paper from her small pile. The size of her pile was somewhat reassuring—I'd sat through these things where she'd had a stack of index cards three inches high.

"As I see it, there are two issues we really need to get out... on the table, as it were."

I took another look at Ben. Everyone else had turned their attention to Lor, but Ben continued to stare at Jack, though Ben's expression seemed a tad less pained than it had a moment ago, and more...curious, I guess.

"One, is the obvious one, because he's sitting at the table."

"Uh, maybe not so obvious," Jimmy said, pointing first at Jack and then Raymond.

Lor took that in, nodding in acknowledgement. "Right. I meant Raymond. But Jack—well, Jack and Ben are the second item on the agenda."

"Agenda?" Jimmy said. Looking to me, he added, "We have agendas at *your* interventions?"

"Oh, there's always an *agenda*," I said. "Most times it belongs solely to Lor."

"There's no reason to get the digs in this time, Jo. You're not the target. Keep your gun holstered."

"You're right," I said. I wiggled my finger. "Proceed."

"Should I maybe leave while you discuss me?" Raymond said beside me.

"No," Lor and I said at the same time.

He looked at me, seeming to want extra confirmation. I placed a hand on his arm, squeezed, then took it away. "I'm guessing Lor is thinking what I am—that we want to know *your* thoughts on next steps."

Lorelei confirmed her intentions. Raymond was staring at the hand that I'd just touched him with.

The truth was that I didn't really know how Raymond was feeling toward me right now. He could be looking at my hand as if he wanted to ram it in a meat grinder. (A not unknown punishment for those who got in over their head.)

Raymond had been one of those unsuspecting players whom I'd drugged so he'd play like crap. JoJo had met Raymond and been impressed. When I became deeper in debt, JoJo returned to Raymond, getting his buy-in, using his little sister who desperately needed money for drug rehab as leverage, to be complicit in point-shaving.

The whole thing went public, and though it couldn't be proven—my involvement hadn't been uncovered, and no charges came of it—Raymond was asked to leave school. He returned to his rough neighborhood in Chicago, where he was headed in a dangerous direction until Jack and I swooped in and won him in a poker game against a gang leader with his hooks in Raymond.

So there my winning pot sat, his dream of playing in a national championship game shattered. Hell, his whole life was shattered.

But it seemed that maybe Lor was leading the charge to give Raymond a new shot at a life worth building, albeit different than he'd thought.

"Raymond, of course it's your choice, and Jo will support you—both financially and whatever else you need. Isn't that right, Jo?"

"Yes," I said, not hesitating. It was the least I could do for the kid. We got his mom and sister in a good place in Atlanta; it was now time to make reparations to Raymond.

Making amends, they called it in the twelve-step programs. Not that I'd ever gotten through all twelve.

"So, Raymond," Lor continued. "I have some thoughts, just to get the ball rolling. Obviously it's your decision."

Raymond was blinking now, and it wasn't because he was trying to hold back tears. No, it was more of a defensive gesture, his eyes darting around the others at the table. He'd met Jimmy and Gus—they'd been to the house lots of times since I'd brought Raymond home with me from Chicago.

"You're amongst friends, kid," Gus said to him, correctly reading Raymond's expression. "Nothing goes past this table. Ben, Jimmy, and I knew college kids' secrets by the ton back in the day. We learned then to keep our mouths shut."

Raymond looked at Jack, who nodded his agreement with Gus's words. When he got that, Raymond turned back to Lor and motioned for her to go on. Then he sat back in his chair, clutching his Gatorade bottle. It was the blue flavor (whatever that is), and I absently wondered if Lor had asked him his favorite flavor, or had just bought a variety for him.

She would have asked—she was that thorough. Which was why she had several options for Raymond to think about.

He had been a sports medicine major at Central Iowa, and was on track to graduate. Lor had found a similar program at UNLV and procured the necessary paperwork for Raymond to apply for admission next fall. There was a chance he'd be in Atlanta by then, reunited with his mother and sister, but it was good to have a plan.

"It might be best to wait until then anyway," I softly said to him. "Things will be quieter, and this semester has already started."

"Yeah," he said, with no great emotion in his voice.

"Until then, or if that's not an option you want to pursue, Jo can pay you to help us out with Ben and the house."

"You girls are help enough," Ben said, but not in a way that meant he didn't want Raymond's help. More in a tone so that my feelings wouldn't be hurt thinking I wasn't pulling my weight with Ben's care and that we needed more help.

"We try to be a help to you, Ben, that's true. And we love doing it. But there will come a time when having a man around might be helpful. And with Jo's schedule…"

I wanted to bristle at this. I played poker most nights late. Really late. Usually getting home just in time to take Ben to breakfast, a pastime I never missed if I was in town. (And I basically only left town when JoJo had to pay a visit to some college campus.) True, I slept most days. But I was always up to play cards with the boys after dinner, before I went out to play poker.

But I didn't bristle. Because I knew it was for Raymond's benefit, and also because I had let everyone down the past couple of months. Though I was feeling that it was all behind me, I couldn't really assure them all of that.

I wasn't really assured myself.

Five

❖❖

WE TALKED OVER OPTIONS FOR RAYMOND, and made a tentative plan for him to look at the UNLV stuff Lor had acquired for him.

"Now," Lor said, setting a couple of sheets of paper aside, and pulling the second set in front of her. "Jack and Ben."

Jack cleared his throat. "Lorelei, it's great that you want to help. But this is probably something that Ben—"

"What did you have in mind, Lorelei dear?" Ben said, the first words he'd spoken since we'd sat down.

Jack looked to Ben, and as far as I could tell, it was the first time their eyes had met since…well, since they'd found out that they were father and son.

They had the same eyes, though I might have been the only one to notice that, as close up as I'd been to both sets of soft brown peepers.

When I'd be helping Ben, guiding him with my arm, assisting him with a stuck seatbelt, I'd look into his eyes and see…what was that old saying? The window to his soul. Yeah. Ben was an open book, but his eyes showed you every page—in large type.

Jack was anything *but* an open book, keeping every emotion in check, never letting you know what he was thinking or feeling. But in quiet moments—moments when he wasn't furious or exasperated with me—when he'd look at me, his eyes told me things that his words never would. Never *could*.

"Well," Lorelei continued, forging on and answering Ben. After all, she did have a few sheets of paper—surely great plans—that she wanted to share. She wasn't about to listen to Jack's suggestion of leaving it between the two men alone. And after the way Ben had been acting the past four days (not to mention Jack staying away so as to give Ben space), I was pretty open-minded about Lor playing matchmaker for Jack and Ben. "I have a few team-building things that we could all do together. That would give Jack and Ben a more structured togetherness, with no pressure for them to interact directly."

"Team building? Like that shit corporate bigwigs do so they can take a trip to the desert in the winter?" Jimmy said.

Lorelei shot Jimmy a "shut up" look. "Well, yes, these are exercises that different corporations have used in order to foster a safe environment so that new ideas have a place to be brought up and developed."

I knew she had memorized that last part from whatever brochure she'd printed out.

I started looking around the dining room, trying to find lengths of rope or several two-by-fours with which we would— as a team—make our way across the front lawn. I was spying something that looked suspiciously like lumber under the sideboard when Jack stood from the table.

The last intervention—at this very table—I'd stood so violently that my chair tumbled to the floor.

Jack, ever the master of understatement, slowly rose, moved from around the chair, and smoothly pushed it in to the table. "Ben, how about if I help you back to your room. Maybe we could have a word?"

My eyes shot to Ben, and I tried to assess if Jack's request would bring on panic, pain, or something else.

But he only nodded, and allowed Jack to help him out of

his chair, waving both Raymond and me to stay seated as we started to rise.

Jack guided Ben to his walker, then they both moved across the large foyer and to the wing of the house that held Ben's bedroom.

Just as they were about to turn the corner down the hallway, Jack turned back to our group, who hadn't moved since Ben had so quickly—almost eagerly, it seemed to me—risen from his seat.

"My case wrapped up last night," Jack said to all of us. "So, if you guys are playing cards tonight, I'd be able to join you."

With Jack and me being in Chicago, then the stuff with Vince, then the paternity news breaking and its aftermath on Ben (and Jack), we hadn't had a game of cards around the dining room table in over a week.

"I'll make dinner," Lor said, taking her intervention hostess up another notch. "So maybe come around six. I mean, come whenever, obviously, all of you. But dinner will be ready around six."

"Great," Gus said, smiling at Lor, causing a tiny blush on her face. Poor redheads; they could never hide a blush.

"I'll be here," Jimmy said, as if there was any doubt once Lor had mentioned she was cooking.

"That'd be great. Thanks, Lor," Jack said, then turned to help Ben to his room.

Gus and Jimmy finished their breakfasts, then took their leave. Jimmy loading his hands with Lorelei's cinnamon rolls, Gus loading his hands with Lorelei, as he gave her a hug goodbye.

Gus was pushing eighty, had four divorces behind him, and was a charmer with twinkly blue eyes and beautiful white hair. Still vital. Still chasing pretty women.

Another blush from Lorelei. I wanted to ask her about the status with Gus, but Raymond helped us clear the table and tidy up the kitchen, so I kept my questions to myself.

The three of us then went into the living room, and Lor brought Raymond the information she'd already picked up from UNLV about their sports medicine program.

The woman was miraculous.

It was about an hour and a half before Jack came from the back hallway.

"I've got to get going," he said when he saw our questioning faces. He came over to where Lor and I shared the couch. Leaning down, he kissed the top of Lorelei's head. "Thank you for today," he said. "Count your intervention as a raging success."

I wasn't sure what caused the very deep blush to creep up her neck—Jack's words of praise, or his kiss.

To me, the kiss was on the lips, not the top of my head. "See you for dinner," he said. As he straightened back up, he looked at me with those probing eyes. "And for dessert," he added, then walked to the front door.

Leaving more than just Lorelei fighting a blush.

Six

THE NEXT MORNING MY PHONE rang while I was still sleeping. With Jack nicely spooning me from behind.

Honestly, my phone going off, especially while I was at home, was kind of rare.

The only people I spoke with pretty much lived in this house, or I'd be meeting them in an hour or two for breakfast.

I reached for the phone on my nightstand, thinking maybe something was up with Jimmy, who wouldn't text, and certainly wouldn't care that he was waking me up.

Seeing the caller ID sent a chill down through me, and I very tentatively said hello when I connected, afraid that I might be hearing the voice of a dead man on the other end.

A dead man who wouldn't be very happy with me.

"Anna? It's Carla," the very feminine, and very alive, Carla said.

"Hi," I said, still a little tentatively. Like maybe Vince's ghost had come back to haunt his killer and was having her use his phone to give me a call.

I needed coffee.

"You happen to be in bed with the hot homicide dick wrapped around you?"

Jack's arm wrapped more tightly around my waist.

"Yes."

"Call me back when he leaves. I need to talk to you."

"And you can't with him wrapped around me?" I asked, fearful of her answer.

"Nope. Just give me a call. Soon, though, okay?"

"Yeah, okay," I said, and she disconnected.

"So, I'm the hot homicide dick to your friends?" Jack mumbled into my naked shoulder, his stubble more than just one day old for sure.

"Apparently," I said, setting the phone back on my nightstand, then setting my hand on top of Jack's, which was lazily drawing circles around my belly button.

"Dare I ask if that's dick short for detective, or something else entirely?"

I snorted. "Take it how you want to."

"Is that what you call me? How you think of me?" he asked, teasing more than fishing.

"Depends. Sometimes I think you're hot. Sometimes I just think you're a dick."

"A homicide dick."

I couldn't see it, but I knew he was smiling. A sight so infrequent I wanted to quickly roll over so I could catch a glimpse. I didn't; having him tight against my back was just too delicious to interrupt.

I shrugged, causing his mouth to move across my shoulder. "Whatever." I was rewarded for my joke—or my insolence—by a soft bite on the side of my neck.

"You tensed before you answered," he said, missing nothing. "You don't want to talk to Carla?"

"It wasn't that. She was using Vince's phone. His name came up."

His body stilled for a second, then he placed a soft kiss on the spot he'd just nipped. He obviously knew Vince would be a contact in my phone, but probably hadn't really thought about—hadn't processed—that brief moment when Vince and I were thinking about taking our relationship beyond that of loan shark and degenerate gambler. That was when Vince made his appearance on my "real" phone. Not the burner ones JoJo used to speak with Vince and his muscle, Paulie.

"Didn't want to talk to a ghost?" Jack asked when he got past whatever had made his body still.

"Not particularly."

"Why do you think Carla needed the cop gone before she could talk?" His voice was casual, but I knew his intention was anything but.

I stretched, liking where Jack's hand moved when I did. "I have no idea. It may have nothing to do with you being a cop, and more with allowing me to...get my groove on."

"Seriously?"

I laughed. "No. But she could have thought I might be distracted with your hot homicide dick body right beside me."

"I guess I'd be insulted if you weren't. Distracted, that is."

"See. So in a way, it was a compliment."

I didn't buy that for a minute, and neither did Jack. We both knew Carla didn't want to talk to me with a cop in the room. Any room, not just the bedroom.

He rolled me over so my side hit his hard chest, looming over me, head resting on his hand, elbow in the pillow. "I have just enough time for one more...distraction," he said.

I reached for him. "Distract me."

JACK HAD LEFT, I had showered, and I still had about fifteen minutes before I'd go collect Ben from his room to take him to meet Jimmy and Gus for breakfast.

For the first time in a long time.

Playing cards the night before, and Lorelei's magnificent chicken cacciatore, had been smooth and awkward-silence free.

Even Raymond seemed to enjoy the evening. Ben had insisted on Jack sitting next to him, which had Jack nodding quickly with approval.

When Gus and Jimmy had left—Gus being the big winner for the night—Ben had said he'd see them in the morning, like he hadn't just missed the past few days. They'd even decided to return to the Corporation's original home of the Sourdough Café in Arizona Charlie's, much to my stomach's delight.

I was hopeful that when I went to his room I'd find him fully dressed and ready to head to breakfast. But first, I returned Carla's call, using Vince's contact info, which again made me feel a little uneasy.

"He gone?" was her greeting.

"Yes."

"Is he as good as he looks like he'd be?"

I paused. "Yes," I admitted, and she laughed.

"Lucky you," she said.

"Yes," I again said.

"Was Vince as good as he looked like he'd be?"

"I wouldn't know," I said, not liking how the banter had turned.

"No? I thought you two—"

"Never got to that point. And we weren't going to." Definite edge in my voice now. I'd known Carla for years, had some good conversations with her at the card games Vince hosted, but we weren't exactly braid-each-other's-hair close. Not sex-secret-spilling close, for sure.

"Got it. Moving on," she said.

Carla Rossetti had been Vince Santini's bookkeeper and poker game runner for years. She was a pretty woman with what she would tell you—and often did—twenty extra pounds. She had dark hair that had just started showing streaks of gray, which she wore in a severe bob. In her late forties, she was originally from Brooklyn and had come out to Vegas with Vince. Carla had made herself invaluable to Vince, and I was sure it wasn't easy for her to have pushed him over the railing.

She was also shrewd as hell, and had learned a lot from Vince, so I was anxious to get on with why she'd called me.

"I'm taking over Vince's operation," she said. I shouldn't have been surprised, but I kind of was.

"The poker games, or the loan sharking?" I asked. Lord knew what else Vince was into. I wasn't about to ask.

A small pause on Carla's end before she said, "Both. Well, first the poker games, sharking only for those. When I build up my reputation, when people know they'll still get Vince's... customer service with me, then I'll be able to do both."

"Customer service? Would that be finding someone who knew how to break a foot without leaving a mark?" My foot, in a boot right now because of Vince, had had a much more severe injury ten years ago also courtesy of Vince, though it had been Paulie who'd done the dirty work.

"Yeah, mostly. I've got some collecting to do on Vince's outstanding debts. I'm going to see how that goes with my own powers of persuasion to see how much muscle I'm going to have to hire."

A chill went through me at the thought of what means of persuasion Carla could come up with. Men were simple: threaten with strength. Threaten with a broken foot. Women? Oh, I highly suspected a smart woman like Carla could come up with much more creative ways to convince someone to pay their debt than just the threat of physical pain, or even dismemberment.

"My money's on you," I said, which caused Carla to chuckle. It was an odd sound; I wasn't sure I'd ever heard her laugh before. But then, there wasn't a lot of joking going on when I was negotiating interest terms with her.

"Thanks for the vote of confidence," she said. "While I'm letting those deadbeats know that their debt didn't fly off that balcony with Vince, and are very much still on the books, I want to get the games started again. Any more time passes and everyone who played will find somewhere else to go."

That was probably true. "Good idea," I said, starting to see why she'd called me.

"That's where you come in," she said, confirming my thought.

"You want me there at the first game." It wasn't a question.

"Yes."

"Carla, I'm flattered, but really, there are much bigger fish out there to get for drawing power than me."

"Maybe. But you're a *name*, and that will be helpful."

"I'm a name in a very small circle."

"But that's the circle I'm after."

"You get a Mr. Chow or one of his cronies back and you're set."

"Mr. Chow has turned me down. So far. He did, however, ask if you were playing."

Shit. "And you said?"

"I said that you were always welcome at the table and I'd be happy to let him know the next time you planned on joining us."

Double shit.

She didn't say anything else. She certainly didn't say "You owe me one," though she had every right to. And, knowing that, I told her I'd play.

"On one condition," I said. "You are not, under any circumstances, allowed to loan me money. If I lose, I walk. No exceptions."

"Fine," she said.

"I'm serious, Carla. I'm cleaning up my act. I'm only playing in casino games. When I lose my stake I walk, not walk over to where you're sitting with your ledger and a fresh stack of chips."

"Okay, okay," she said. "Nobody *made* you get more chips, you know."

Yeah, someone did. JoJo. Her damn voice was always telling me I needed to stay in the game, had to win enough to have a stake to place a sports bet.

"I know," was all I said to Carla.

"There's one other thing."

"Yes?" I asked, never liking when people added that dreaded "one more thing" to anything.

"Am I correct in assuming that you currently have a new addition to your household? One formerly of Chicago, via Dubuque?"

She knew Raymond was here? Had Vince told her that I was in Chicago, and why I'd gone? Did she know *every* aspect of Vince's transactions? Even those with JoJo?

"And if you were correct in assuming that? Why would that be of interest to you?"

"Is he looking for something to do, or is playing canasta with a bunch of old farts enough for him?"

"Gin rummy. And so far he hasn't complained." Mostly because only about a week into his new existence, Raymond hadn't said much of anything.

"I'll pay him a thousand bucks for the night to be on the door." A job Paulie had always had. A menacing presence who made you feel both safe and scared at the same time.

"He's hardly a Paulie. He's not that big, and not very… Paulie-esque." I hoped that conveyed my general impression without insulting her former coworker.

"He's an angry young black man. He can play that up," she said.

I was about to argue with her stereotype, but if you took it literally, she had pretty much summed up Raymond. Angry only since he'd met JoJo, but the rest was true.

"He's more than that," I said, pretty sure that Carla knew that, too.

"That's all I need him to be. For the night. A thousand

bucks."

"I'll ask him," I said, "but if he says no, that's the end of it."

"Agreed."

"When do you want to play?"

"Friday night. That'll give me time to make some calls."

"Okay, I'm in as a player. A non-money-borrowing player. I'll get back to you on Ray—the other."

"That works. Thanks. I'll text you time and place."

"Are you going to be using this phone?"

"For a while, yeah, until I get all of Vince's stuff in order and switched over. Why?"

"I think I'll just change the name on the contact, then."

She snorted. "Yeah, I can see how that might be disconcerting."

"A little bit."

"Okay, gotta go. Thanks, Anna. Let me know if your guy wants to pick up some easy cash."

"I will. See you Friday."

"Bye," she said, then disconnected.

I walked to Ben's side of the house. He was just coming out of his room, dressed, shaved, and, though it was hard to tell with his walker, with a little more spring in his step than I'd seen in a while.

Apparently an evening with Jack Schiller had done wonders for the both of us.

Seven
❖

RAYMOND, SOMEWHAT SURPRISINGLY, was very interested in Carla's offer.

"You think this could be a regular thing?" he asked.

We were sitting in the kitchen at the breakfast nook having Lor's leftover cacciatore for lunch. Which I certainly didn't need after the breakfast I'd had with the boys.

I chewed and shrugged. When I was done swallowing, I took a drink of water, then said, "Could be. Vince used to run games almost nightly. At least every weekend. It depended on who was in town."

"And why are these people playing in a private game, when they can go to the high-roller poker room at any casino and be treated like a king?"

I explained to him that the casinos took a piece of each pot, called the rake, and that Vince didn't do that. Also that the people in Vince's game were in a way vetted. You knew you were going to be playing good poker in his games.

"Plus, sometimes the players are famous and don't want to be seen laying down big money in a poker game in the casinos. Those stories always tend to get out."

"Think there'll be anyone famous there on Friday?"

I picked at the chicken on my plate with my fork. "Probably not. Carla is trying to prove she can keep Vince's games going.

Pulling a big-name celebrity most likely won't happen the first time out. I mean, she'd love that, but she's probably more interested in some of Vince's regulars returning. That's why I'm playing—to help her out."

"Like getting the band back together?"

I smiled, and thought I saw a glimmer of a smile on his face, too. "Something like that."

"Are you that famous out here that you need to play in his games? Away from the public casino poker rooms?" There was no admiration in his voice, just curiosity.

"No. I mostly play in the casinos. It's how I make my living, so playing against tourists who play in a weekly game back home is always my best attack.

"But sometimes I want to play against the best. Like if there's a tournament coming up or something, I'll play more in Vince's game to practice against…"

"The varsity," he said, finishing my thought.

"Exactly." I didn't bother telling him about Vince's Bank and Loan, available at all of his games, and how I had needed those services.

He'd see on Friday night how Vince, and now Carla, made money on the games. And then he'd surely put together why I played there—Raymond was a smart kid. He would figure out where—and why—JoJo had been born.

"Any chance I'll be recognized?" he asked.

I shook my head. "I doubt it. These are mostly big-time CEOs and Wall Street types. I'm not saying they don't follow college basketball, but I don't think their imaginations would go to you being the strong arm at the door in a private poker game in Vegas. Plus, you look so different without your braids."

"Without hair," he said, rubbing the top of his head.

"Maybe you should keep the bald look, not let it grow back."

"Why, does that look more menacing?" he asked. "Isn't just

being young and black enough?"

"Ha ha," I said, careful not to mention that that was pretty much the reason Carla wanted him. "I just thought the bald look really changed the shape of your face. If you're worried about being recognized." I hoped he was. I wasn't going to set any parameters on Raymond Joseph—it wasn't my place. If he wanted to go on ESPN and say that yes, he did shave points, that was his right.

But I hoped he just wanted to live a quiet life and let everything slip away with the sports world's short memory.

Because if he was in fact exposed as a point shaver, it would inevitably lead back to me. And then who knew how many players would be yelling that I was the one who had shown up in their lives the night before they played their worst game ever?

"Bald head. Got it. I'll take it under advisement. Or maybe I'll just wear a hoodie pulled up—that'll scare the shit out of them."

I rolled my eyes at him, and he gifted me with a smile that was closest to the one he'd perpetually flashed on the court when he had a basketball in his hand.

"No hoodie," I said, and that made me think of something. I grabbed my phone and texted Carla, happy that I'd changed the contact name. (And somewhat surprised I did it on my own—Lor usually did that type of stuff for me; it was in my best interest to be as technically unversed as possible.)

"Do you own a suit?" I asked Raymond, when I got Carla's reply to my question of what she wanted Raymond to wear Friday night. I couldn't remember if Central Iowa was one of those teams that had their players wear a sports coat and tie when they were the visiting team, or if they just wore team warm-up suits.

"No. I had a jacket that I wore a couple of times—like a blazer thing. But I left that in Chicago."

Yes, we had left Chicago in rather a hurry.

I'd told him to only pack his personal things, stuff that couldn't be replaced. Clothes could easily be bought—Lor would love to do that, actually.

No suit. We'll get him one by Friday, I texted back to Carla.

A good one. I'll pay for it.

Like Vince good? Got it. I've got it covered, but thanks.

There was no way I wanted Raymond beholding to anybody, especially someone like Carla, who was breaking into a new level of business and might need to call in any favor at any time.

Yes, Vince good. I'll text you his tailor's info. His name is Lorenzo, and he's brilliant.

"Eat up," I said to Raymond. "Looks like we're going shopping."

I WAS SITTING ON A LOVELY LEATHER wingback chair waiting as Lorenzo draped some exquisite pieces of fabric over Raymond's shoulder.

"Definitely the pinstripes," I said. "Let's do the black and charcoal as well."

Raymond turned to look at me. "You think I need three?"

I shrugged. "I don't know. If you like the gig, yeah, you're going to need three, probably a few more. If you don't like it… Well, it's always good to have some good suits in your closet. In Vegas, you never know."

He pointedly looked at my cargo pants, baggy Henley, and denim jacket.

"I have some very nice pieces in my closet," I said. "I just don't have to wear them very often."

The tailor, an older, stooped man with an abundance of wild white hair who had introduced himself to us as Lorenzo, grunted. "You can tell by the way that you say 'have to' wear them rather than 'get to' wear them that you prefer…" He waved a hand at me, encompassing my less-than-stellar wardrobe.

"I do prefer"—I waved my hand over myself—"yes."

A small shake of Lorenzo's head and he returned his attention to Raymond, and I tried to cover up a laugh.

What was it with me and old men?

I was just about to defend my personal style—or lack thereof—to Lorenzo, when the door opened and Carla entered the private room, quickly closing the door behind her.

"I thought I'd find you here," she said. She looked around the room, taking everything—and everybody—in. She nodded to Lorenzo, who nodded back, then said quietly, to me only, words that never boded well.

"We need to talk."

Eight

❖❖

I CHECKED MY PHONE to see if maybe Carla had called or texted me and I'd missed it, but she hadn't.

"I was nearby running an errand, and I thought you might have already started on the suit. Then I saw your Porsche out front and knew for sure."

"I'll tell Jack if he ever needs another detective on the force to come see you," I said, admiration in my voice.

Although, much like a poker player, it was in a loan shark's best interest to be able to read people—whether someone was a good bet with their money, or whether that person was going to end up taking a drive with an enforcer and in a boot like the one I was still wearing.

An enforcer like Paulie Gonads. Whom Raymond would soon be replacing.

"We are still talking about Raymond for games only, right?" I asked as Carla made her way over to Raymond, still standing on the small pedestal. They shook hands, Carla taking him in. I figured she was sizing up his potential for scariness while still being professional.

Even with the expensive fabric only draped across his frame, it was obvious he was going to outclass Paulie at the door. Carla seemed to know it, too, as she slowly nodded in approval.

"Welcome to the team, kid," Carla said.

"Carla," I said, warning in my voice. "Just the poker games."

She waved my words away. "Right. Right. Just the games." Her voice made me think there was a "for now" that she'd swallowed, but I let it go. It wasn't something to discuss in public, even if we were in a private room at a very upscale men's store.

Carla greeted Lorenzo, who offered his condolences about Vince. I could only imagine the big chunk of business that this establishment was about to lose with Vince's passing.

"That was the errand I was running. The final arrangements for the funeral tomorrow."

"I plan on attending," the tailor said.

"That's very thoughtful," Carla said.

Taking the pieces of fabric from Raymond, the tailor looked at me. "I can have one ready by late Friday. Which one?"

"The black one," I said.

"Very good. Can you come back tomorrow afternoon for a fitting? My assistant will be here to take care of it." This he directed to Raymond, who looked over at me. I nodded. "You can take the Porsche, if I'm not available." With my boot, I couldn't drive my baby; the pedals were too small and close together, but I let Raymond drive us to the tailor. When I'd taken Ben to breakfast I'd driven our SUV, which had been a little awkward for my foot, but doable.

Raymond set up a time with Lorenzo, who then excused himself to go to a room off the one we were in. "Please, take your time, have more coffee. There is no rush for you to leave; we won't need this room for a bit," he said as he left.

Carla went over and helped herself to a cup of coffee and a biscotti that were both on an antique side table. She nodded to my cup and I put a hand over it, indicating that I'd had my fill.

"Raymond?" she asked, holding up a cup.

"No thank you," he said. He was off the pedestal and had grabbed his sweatshirt from the chair beside mine and pulled it on over his head.

Carla fixed her cup and took the chair opposite Raymond and me. They talked about what time Raymond should be at the suite in the Bellagio on Friday night, what all he'd be doing, that kind of stuff.

I stayed out of it, though I watched Raymond carefully to make sure he was comfortable with all that Carla was explaining to him, which he seemed to be.

Then Carla turned to me. "Is the reason you might not be available to come back here with Raymond tomorrow because you'll be at Vince's funeral?"

Her question startled me. "No," I said, quickly and definitively.

She nodded. "Yeah, I didn't think so. But you went to Paulie's funeral, so I thought that maybe…"

"That maybe I was someone who liked going to the funerals of men who did me bodily harm?"

She shrugged. "Hey, I don't judge."

I snorted. "I didn't want to go to Paulie's funeral. I did it as a favor to Vince." Carla opened her mouth to speak, but I held up my hand. "And before you ask, no, I won't go to Vince's as a favor to you. I'm playing in your game—and letting you tell people that I am—as a favor to you." Again with her wanting to speak and me holding the hand up—higher this time. "And yes, I know I owe you my life, and so there will be many favors to fulfill, but this won't be one of them."

She nodded as she chewed her biscotti. "Fair enough," she said after swallowing. "Besides, I have a different favor I'd like to throw at you. That's actually the reason I tracked you down."

Oh, oh. A favor that needed to be asked in person, not via phone or text. Because it was a big ask, or because she couldn't leave any kind of trail?

Or both?

"Lion LaGasse is going to be in town this weekend."

I waited. Of course I knew the name, even though I only

bet golf during the majors, not following it enough to wager every week. But I'd won my share of money off Lion LaGasse in the majors.

And lost my share, too.

"So?" I finally said, when Carla stared at me with an expectant look on her face.

"So? He needs to play in my game. Can you imagine the buzz that would create?"

Rumors had swirled around Lion for years that he had a gambling problem, which he denied, though he did admit he liked playing poker. I'd even sat a couple of tables over from him during an early round of the World Series of Poker a few years ago.

"He's not going to want word to get out that he's playing in a high-stakes backroom poker game run by a loan shark," I said, as tactfully as I could. "I mean, if you're looking to make your name off him."

She sat back in her chair, her black, straight bob swinging gently with the shake of her head, her bangs, almost aggressive in their severity, dipping as she raised an eyebrow at me. "Well, I'm not going to make it *public*. I just mean within the major players…the people who play in the high-roller rooms or private games."

"So, great. Lion plays in your game, and your reputation is set."

"Except…"

Yeah, I knew where this was going. I'd basically been waiting for the shoe to drop since she'd walked through the door.

"I don't know him," I said. "Never met the guy."

"But he follows poker. Don't you think he'd love to get an invitation to a private game from the Black Widow herself?"

I cringed at the name given to me by a poker broadcaster that had stuck. Yeah, it was a persona I'd play into for a televised event, or to intimidate a newbie (or as an entree into a heads-up match with a South Side Chicago gang leader, with Raymond's life as the buy-in), but I never used the name or reputation in my daily games.

Still, the idea had some merit.

"Maybe," I said, hesitancy in my voice. "But I have no idea how to get hold of him. We have no confirmation that he even knows who I am, let alone likes me as a player. He might think I'm interested in him or something."

"Would that be so bad?"

Taking Jack out of it completely—and I didn't want to take Jack out of it—for me to date a professional athlete, especially one who could throw a golf tournament with just the tiniest of missed putts? No. No way. "Yes. Yes, that would be very bad."

She studied me a minute, but I let her think what she wanted. Raymond too, for that matter, as he was just silently listening to Carla and me.

"You make it clear it's just an invitation to a game. Nothing personal. You know he likes poker; you have a game you think he might be interested in. Even drop in you have a boyfriend if you think he'll think you're coming on to him." She shrugged. Easy peasy.

"You're forgetting the main thing—I have no way to contact him."

Which was probably the wrong thing to say, because Carla now seemed to think that I was in if only we could find out how to privately contact Lion LaGasse.

Which I was, I guess. The woman had saved my life. And I had told the cops that I thought she had killed Paulie. So, there was debt, to be sure. But I was mentally reducing her tab as more of these "favor" requests came in.

"Surely someone we know has a way to get in touch with him."

Raymond turned to me at the same time the obvious choice popped into my head.

"Jimmy," we both said.

As if it were settled—and I guessed it probably was—Carla rose from her seat, putting her cup down on the little table. Raymond and I followed her out of the fitting room and into the main showroom. We had already discussed shirts with Lorenzo, but I steered Raymond toward the tasteful display of neckties. "Pick six or seven," I said to him, then turned to Carla. "I'm not making any promises, but I'll keep you posted on the Lion thing."

"That's all I ask," she said. She pointed to a tie in green silk. "That's a nice one," she said to Raymond, who put it aside with another one he'd picked. "See you both Friday," she said, waving to us as she left the shop.

Raymond picked out more ties, and I added one in purple with a paisley design to the small pile.

I paid with the credit card that Lor had given me before we left, and would no doubt demand back the minute we got home.

Just like I'd asked her to do six years ago when she'd come to live with us.

She wasn't only Ben's keeper.

"Well, isn't it just my *Pretty Woman* day," Raymond said as he got behind the wheel of my car and I adjusted my boot to fit in the passenger side.

"You don't sound like a happy Julia Roberts," I said, leaning back, hating sitting on this side of the car. Not that Raymond was a bad driver; it was just that I liked being in control.

Which was laughable when you think that I made my living (and lost it sometimes, too) by gambling.

Maybe I just liked controlling the little things in my life because the big things were so out of my control. Whatever. No need for psychoanalyzing now that Lor had already held her quarterly intervention. It could wait, for it would surely be there when I got around to it.

"It was a few suits, that's all. Work clothes," I said.

He grunted as he smoothly pulled into traffic. "Bullshit. You just dropped over ten grand in there. That's more than my whole family spends on clothes in a decade."

"You'll be traveling in a different circle now. You need to dress the part. Consider it part of your disguise. Or like your superhero costume."

"Mild-mannered Raymond Joseph by day, but when the suit comes on I turn into… What?" he asked. And the question was bigger than what his superhero name would be. No, his sights were set on something in a galaxy far, far away. Who was he about to turn into? College basketball player superpowers were no longer on the table.

"The thing is, Raymond, you get to decide that. It sucks what happened to you." He glanced quickly over to me, then back to the road. "What *I* did to you. But you have the luxury of time— and not needing money—to figure out who you get to be."

"I'm not a charity case," he said.

"Is that what it is? The money? Forget about the money. Consider it guilt money if it makes you feel better. Hell, milk me dry—I probably deserve it."

"But then Ben and Lorelei go down too."

A thought that haunted me. Daily.

"You need to look out for you, Raymond. But I'm glad you've taken to my friends."

He didn't acknowledge my statement. He didn't need to; I'd seen him with Ben and Lor—he fit well in to our little tribe.

He drove in silence for a while. When we were nearing my gated community, he said, "Muscle."

"What?"

"My superhero name. Muscle."

"Too literal," I said.

"That's the joke," he said.

"The Enforcer," I offered.

He shook his head. "I'll come up with something," he said. "I suppose you already have yours…Black Widow."

"I guess." But I couldn't help but think that there was another name that would better describe my superpowers.

The Destroyer.

Nine

❖❖

"YEAH, I CAN GET YOU A NUMBER," Jimmy said that night during our card game. I'd just explained the situation to him. It was Texas Hold 'Em tonight and Lorelei was our dealer, since she didn't play poker, but still wanted to hang with us.

Gus hadn't been able to make it, and I couldn't tell if Lorelei was bummed or relieved about that fact. She held her cards close to the vest on that one for sure, even though she wasn't much of a player.

I'd explained the situation as we started the card game, and, true to form, Jimmy knew a guy. We then discussed the other might-be players and that Carla was using my name for poker cred and Lion's for celebrity cred to get some new blood at her game.

"Umm, should you guys be talking about this when I'm sitting right here?" Jack said as he folded his hand.

"What? Just a private poker game. No more illegal than what we're doing right here," Jimmy said.

"Nobody here is going to be loan sharking money to anyone else at a thirty-point vig."

"You keep playing like you are, and you can be my first customer," Jimmy said to Jack.

Jack grunted, then laughed, as did the rest of the table.

"Besides, that's vice—you're homicide," I said.

"I'm still a cop," Jack said.

It seemed a little weird that Jack was pulling this stuff now, only days after I had confessed all my JoJo deeds to him on a flight to Chicago and he basically gave me a pass because it wasn't homicide, or carried out in Vegas. He could tell I was about to bring that up—not specifics, obviously—because he quickly added, "And this is before the fact."

I rolled my eyes at that, but before I could get in my comeback, Ben piped up.

"Hannah dear, maybe we should not talk about anything that would put Jack in an awkward position," Ben said, looking at his son with a compassion that he usually had for me.

I admit, petty as it was, it stung a tiny bit.

I placed my bet, a little higher than I normally would; Jimmy noticed and called right away. Damn, I was supposed to be unreadable. In "real" games I *was* unreadable, but at this wooden dining room table, I was sometimes an open book to those who knew me best. "Jack knows me, knows who I am"—I motioned toward Jack, who sat across from me—"knows the worst of me. If he thinks he's being compromised by being around me, then he's free to leave."

He quirked a brow at me, not of amusement, then looked at Ben, which caused me to look at Ben, and I was instantly ashamed at the look of pain that was on his wrinkled, beloved, face.

And then it hit me—Jack was in my life now for good. Even if we broke up (again) down the road—and of course I'd do something to make us blow up—Jack would be here all the time anyway to be with Ben.

He'd have to come here; Ben wouldn't be able to meet him out, unless I drove him. Or maybe Lor would. It'd be like some crazy custody situation, only it would be of an octogenarian instead of a child.

As I was trying to figure out if we'd meet at a McDonald's or a casino for pick-ups and drop-offs, Jack defused the situation.

"It's okay, Ben. Anna's right: it's a vice situation." He nodded at his father, gave him a smile, and Ben relaxed.

I should have given Jack a look of thanks, but I didn't. "That's right," I said, "Just stick to homicide, Jack, and we'll be fine. Nobody's going to be murdered playing poker Friday night."

He snorted, but had a smile on his face when he added, "With you, baby, you just never know."

THE NUMBER JIMMY CAME UP with was for an intermediary between Lion and myself, which I guess was to be expected. I didn't think it was his manager, but the woman I spoke with seemed a little more official than a low-level assistant. Though Lion LaGasse probably didn't have low-level anythings.

Surely his staff didn't include a seldom-dancing showgirl who took the occasional message and held interventions at various intervals.

Poor bastard.

Within five minutes of speaking with the woman, Lion called me back.

"I'm very interested in the game," he said after our initial, and somewhat awkward, introductions to each other.

Everyone in the world knew who Lion LaGasse was. He'd been at the top of the golf world for over fifteen years with no signs of giving up the title of Lion King, which the press had dubbed him years ago.

But I was shocked to know he'd heard of me, and apparently was a fan. Must have been, if he'd called me back so quickly.

"That's great. My friend who hosts the game will be delighted to have you."

"I have my foundation dinner and auction that night, but

that's usually done by nine. Then I make an appearance at the after-dinner party, but no one will notice if I slip away from that."

I was sure many, many people would notice if he slipped away from his own party. People noticed everything Lion did.

"Or, let's just say, I *will* slip away," he added. Yeah, that was more like it.

"Carla's games usually don't start until eleven anyway. I'm sure she'd be happy to push that an hour or more to accommodate you."

"Eleven should work."

"Great. I'll text you the suite number on Friday. Should I use this number? Or the one I used earlier?"

"Yeah, this one's fine. Or better yet…what are you doing Friday night?"

"Playing poker with you?"

"Before that."

"Taking a power nap, so I'm at the top of my game."

He laughed, a dark, hoarse sound that reminded me of Jack's a little bit. And made me wonder if perhaps Lion had a taste for bourbon as well as poker.

"*Or*…you could attend my foundation dinner."

"Oh, thank you. But I'm not really the charity dinner type. Though I'm happy to write a check to the cause." Which was true. Lor handled that checkbook, and would happily write a check to Lion's foundation, which, if I recalled correctly, helped underprivileged kids, or inner-city kids, or disabled kids… something with kids, anyway. My accountant would like it, too. He was always telling me to get more write-offs against my poker income.

"A check is good, but your attendance would be even better," he said.

"There are many more poker players who live here in Vegas with a much—much—higher profile than me. People who would make a bigger splash at your event. I can think of a few off the top of my head, and I'd be happy to call some of—"

"I want you," he said. There was an edge to his voice that hadn't been there before, and I wasn't sure if there was innuendo thrown in as well.

"Well, that's flattering, thanks. But like I said—"

"Listen," he said. "I'm assuming your friend wants me at her game to build her reputation, yes?"

Lion LaGasse did not become the marketing and endorsement god that he was by being dumb. "Yes," I said.

"And she will use that information, that I'm playing, or that I played, to secure other big fish for Friday, or the future, yes?"

"Yes."

"But she will do that very discreetly, within the small circle of poker players who play in high-stakes backroom games, yes?"

"Yes, of course. Very discreetly."

"Then what I want in return is your public attendance at my event—with me, at my table."

That was the back scratch I'd have to give him.

I tried to stay out of the public eye in any circles but poker. Even within my profession I didn't seek out or accept endorsement offers. I did not want my face on TMZ or elsewhere.

Too much of a chance that some player somewhere might make the connection between me and JoJo.

But, just this once, at an event that would get some coverage for the big names attending, and of course Lion himself, but probably not make a big splash otherwise, it was probably okay.

"Okay. I'd be happy to attend your function."

"Great," he said, his voice returning to the lightness of earlier, all signs of hard-bargain-driving Lion gone. "Lila—that's who you spoke with earlier—will send you the details. We can have a car come for you."

"Thank you, but that's not necessary. I'll drive myself."

"Whatever you want. I'm looking forward to meeting you

in person." There it was again, or was it? Was there just a trace of come-on in his words? That wasn't something I looked for, and didn't happen a lot, keeping to myself as I did, but I couldn't read Lion's voice. I hoped I'd be better able to read him across a poker table.

"And by the way," I added. I wanted to make clear my position, and that of Carla's, so there'd be no misunderstandings later. "This game isn't an appearance-fee type of thing. You play your own money, win or lose."

"Of course."

"And just because you're doing my friend a favor, doesn't mean I'm going to take that into account when the cards are dealt." I tried to keep my voice light, but not playful in any way. Kind of a fine line, but one I suspected Lion would understand.

"I would expect nothing less," he said. "Nobody's pulling any putts because I'm on the green. I got it."

I wasn't sure the golf metaphor was dead on, but I let it slide and we wrapped up our plans.

"THE BOOT CAN STAY OFF," the doctor said to me on Thursday. "But you'll still want to stay off the foot as much as possible. Keep it elevated when you're sitting. We'll get you started on physical therapy."

"I can do that at home," I said, causing Lorelei to lift her head from the notebook she was writing in.

She'd driven me to the doctor's office and had insisted on coming into the examination room with me, afraid I'd try to get away without following the doctor's orders.

Like I was trying to do now.

I said, to Lor more than the doctor, "I've had a similar injury before and have been through PT. It's all stuff I can do at home, on my own."

"That may be true," Doctor Galloway said. "But the idea of a scheduled therapy session is to make sure that you are doing the exercises, and so that a trained professional can observe to make sure you're making the proper progress."

"I live with a physical therapist. He can watch to make sure I'm okay," I said. Okay, so Raymond didn't have his degree in sports medicine yet. And I didn't even know if sports medicine and physical therapy had much to do with each other, though I suspected they did. So it wasn't that far of a leap. Besides, Raymond and I could bond while he spotted me doing my own brand of PT.

Lor let out a sigh, and lowered her head back to her notebook. She knew the battle had been lost.

The doctor looked at Lor, as if for some help, then back to me. His sigh sounded much like Lor's. He went to a cabinet and took out a sheet of paper, which he handed to me. "Okay, but at least take this. It's the recommended list of exercises for your foot."

I took the sheet of paper from him, folded it, and put it in my jacket pocket. I gingerly got down from his table, not really sure what to expect, but having had my foot mangled much more harshly ten years ago, this didn't seem so bad. Yes, the pain from ten years ago was so intense that I still remembered it, though it was probably the emotional pain—the shame—that weighed the most heavily.

But that injury had brought Ben, and the Corporation, into my world, which probably had saved my life, so maybe it had been a blessing in disguise.

Lor had brought a cane, because I'd be off my crutches, but I barely needed it. "Not bad," she said, walking behind me as we left the doctor's office.

"I was thinking the same thing myself." I hadn't known Lor ten years ago, so she hadn't seen me at my worst.

Okay, worst is relative. An argument could be made that a

couple of weeks ago, when the point-shaving news first broke, was me at my worst.

But that, like my broken foot of ten years ago, was behind me.

We had the Lexus SUV, and I let Lor drive us home, even though I was able to. It made her feel useful, I think. Her role in the house had altered somewhat since Raymond had arrived and Jack and Ben had learned the truth.

"Our little family is changing," she said as she drove up Town Center toward Summerlin, her words echoing my thoughts.

"Yeah, it is." I turned to her. "How do you feel about that?"

She wore her gorgeous red hair down today, and it slid down and behind her shoulder as she shrugged. "I'm not really sure, you know?"

"Yeah, I know."

She stopped at the red light at Sahara and turned to me. "Part of me likes the additions. I get a kick out of Raymond, though there's a sadness there that I'd like to help, but I'm not sure I can."

Knowing that sadness only too well, I said softly, "You can't. But it's nice you want to try."

She studied me for a moment, then looked ahead as the light changed and the traffic flowed once more. "And you know how much I adore Jack," she continued. "And after those first few days, Ben has been so excited. I think it's going to be really good for him—having Jack in his life."

Knowing the excitement of having Jack Schiller in one's life, I nodded in agreement.

"But it's a different dynamic now, isn't it?"

"Yes," I said, silently hoping that someone else shared my feelings, which seemed to me to be small and petty.

"I mean, I love having them both around. And I love the fact that Ben seems so…rejuvenated. But I loved it when it was just the three of us, too, you know?"

"I know," I said, relieved. "I feel the same way."

"And I feel shitty for even thinking that way."

"Me too," I said, my excitement growing, like I'd found a partner in crime. "I was even thinking last night during the card game that when Jack and I blow up, I'll still have to see him all the time because of Ben, and how shitty that will be."

"Why do you think you and Jack are going to blow up?" she said. I was pleased to detect the genuine curiosity in her tone. Perhaps I was the only one who continually questioned Jack's and my longevity?

"My history. My…issues. Jack's issues. Our history. Do I need to go on?"

"Pfft. That's all behind you now. Didn't you say you hadn't placed a bet in…how many days?"

"Twenty-three today," I answered without hesitation.

"See, you're cured." The simplicity of her answer, given the research she'd done on compulsive gambling for her interventions, gave me a little hope.

Maybe I *was* cured.

Maybe it didn't matter that I knew down to the second when I last made a bet, who it was on, what the point spread was, and every other detail that made my blood race. Maybe it was okay that even as Lor and I were talking there were sixteen college basketball games being played as the big tournament kicked off.

Maybe Jack and I had a real shot.

"Yeah, maybe," I said, as much to myself as to Lorelei.

As if the thought had just occurred to her, she sharply turned into the parking lot of a shopping center and parked right in front of a martini bar.

She looked pointedly at me, then nodded toward the drinking establishment.

I looked at the clock on the console. "It's not even two in the afternoon," I said. Which was ridiculous—we lived in Vegas, the land of no clocks.

"I've just come up with new roles for us, seeing as ours are being diminished with the arrival of two new men in our household. And you needing to fill the gap from betting."

"Drinking?" I asked.

"You know it," she said, turning on her high-wattage showgirl smile.

I was already unbuckling my seatbelt as I said, "Isn't that just trading one vice for another?"

"Pish posh. It'll give me something else to research for interventions."

I laughed as I got out of the car and slowly chose my footing into the dark—but sleek and well-designed—martini bar. And then I thought of Jack and his drinking.

"Maybe just this once," I said, taking my seat at the bar and letting Lor order for both of us.

After all, like all the interventions she'd staged, this was her show.

Ten

❖

IT FELT LIKE SEVENTEEN YEARS AGO and going to prom with Stevie Hocking, with my mom taking pictures and my father looking on with a look of both bemusement and concern.

"Jesus, Lor, get it over with already," I said as Lorelei motioned to Raymond and me to move where she wanted us for another picture.

"Indulge me. You both look like a million bucks. When will I ever get this chance again?"

Hopefully not very often, I thought, moving to stand near Raymond. Seriously, all that was missing was a corsage and boutonniere exchange.

It wasn't a flowy pastel-colored gown, but one of my Black Widow suits that I was wearing. With heels, which my still-weak foot was already protesting. Hair back in a chignon (thank you, Lorelei), subtle, but effective makeup (again, Lorelei), small silver hoop earrings, and my ever-present silver horseshoe pendant.

I cleaned up okay, but Raymond? Well, Lor was right: he looked like a million bucks. His black suit, of an Italian wool fabric that felt like a baby's bottom, fit his muscular, but small and tight, body perfectly.

I shouldn't have been surprised, I'd been impressed by Lorenzo's work on Vince for years.

The crisp white shirt was a stark contrast against the black of the suit and his dark skin at his neck. He'd chosen the purple paisley tie that I'd added to the pile, which gave him an air of quiet sophistication that would have been hard for any college kid to pull off.

"I've got to get going," he said to Lorelei, more patient than I'd been with her picture taking.

"You sure you don't need the Lexus tonight?" I asked her for the third time. She had her BMW, but I didn't like the idea of leaving Lor and Ben without the car Ben was most comfortable in. "I can drop Raymond off before I head to Lion's thing." I was going to suggest that Raymond take Lor's car, but didn't. I wouldn't want her offering up my Porsche.

"I'm sure. If there're any problems—"

"Hannah dear, don't worry about a thing. Jack is coming by and taking me out to dinner. My guess is he'll probably stay here for a while. So, we'll have a car if needed."

Lor and I just stared at each other, giving subtle shakes of our heads at our unspoken question to each other—did you know about this?

A sharp pain tweaked me, then was gone. Jack hadn't mentioned his plans to me. He knew I was playing tonight, that I wouldn't be home until the wee hours of the morning. We hadn't even seen or texted each other since yesterday morning when he'd left my bed.

He didn't even know I had the boot off and was walking on my own.

Going that long without connecting wasn't unusual at all— he would get caught up in a case, and/or I would be playing poker at odd hours, for long stretches of time.

But not mentioning him taking Ben to dinner—on a night I was busy—well, that had certainly never happened before.

"That's great, Ben," Raymond said, coming around from behind me and moving toward the foyer. "You guys have a great time." Picking up the keys to the Lexus SUV, he held them up and I nodded. I'd take the Porsche. Apparently Ben was taken care of.

"Thank you, Raymond," Ben said, looking at Lor and me. We hadn't quite pulled it together yet from our shock. "And you have a good night—your first day and all," he said.

"Thanks. I am a little nervous."

"Nothing to be nervous about," Ben said. "Just remember what we talked about." Raymond nodded, then gave us all a wave and exited the house.

What? They'd been having secret powwows about Raymond's new gig? Ben was giving tough-guy pointers? Sweet, tiny, bad-hip Ben?

Not that shocking when you considered the amount of advice Ben had given me when I'd first moved in with him. Still, none of that advice had been about being a…presence. Or maybe it had been, and I just hadn't realized it.

I got my cash for the game from Lorelei, not trusting myself to have twenty-five thousand just lying around at any given time. Because, let's face it, it wouldn't be lying around for long. And though I hadn't placed a bet in twenty-four days, I wasn't about to have ready cash around as a temptation.

Ben didn't even wait around to say goodbye or wish me luck, just started shuffling down the hallway toward his room.

Getting all gussied up for his big date, no doubt.

A pissy mood was creeping up on me, and I left the house already dreading the night to come.

ON MY DRIVE TO THE WYNN, I thought about poor Lorelei being home alone on a Friday night with Raymond and me gone and Ben out with Jack. She probably would have loved being my date to Lion's foundation event—Lor loved all things celebrity glitz and glamour.

But not knowing how involved (hopefully not too much) with Lion's night I might be, I didn't want Lor with me.

I reported to the suite at the Wynn, which Lila had told me about when she'd called with the arrangements. The room was full of people, and Lila, a beautiful Asian woman of about forty, dressed in a fashionable toga-style cream cocktail dress, brought me in and introduced me to everyone. They all were involved with Lion's foundation—the Mighty Jungle—in various roles. Except for a couple of really big, scary-looking guys—one white, one black, both bald and bulging—who I assumed were Lion's security guys.

Being at the top of the world in your profession was cool as hell. Having the kind of money and endorsements Lion LaGasse had was also very cool.

But living like this? With assistants, managers, and security people around you all the time? Not cool.

Of course, a case could be made that I had my own assistant (Lor), manager (Ben), and security (Raymond) around me at all times too.

But I didn't see Lion sitting down with these people around the dinner table and talking about nothing and everything, like I did with my posse.

Then Lion came in from one of the bedrooms, and the whole group looked up and started throwing out compliments on how good he looked, all vying to be the first—or loudest—to speak, so that their employer would hear them.

He did look good; his minions weren't lying to him, if possibly being a bit too effusive.

He was of average height, but Lion took care of his body, trained heavily in both cardio and weights. He'd set the bar on the PGA Tour years ago for physical fitness, and even now, at forty, he was in much better shape than the young hotshots on the tour.

A handsome man, he had on a black suit that fit him as well

as if it'd been tailored by Lorenzo himself. A light gray shirt, and in a weird twist, he wore the same paisley tie that Raymond did, only in a light blue instead of purple.

His hair was a tawny blond, in a shorter cut, with natural highlights, even in March. He lived in Florida, and the golf season had already started, making his face tanned, with some crinkling around the eyes, either from squinting while outdoors, or perhaps laugh lines, though he was more well known for his intensity on the course than his humor.

He made his way toward me, quieting the fawning from his staff with a wave of his hand.

"Anna Dawson, what a pleasure to meet you," he said as he shook my hand.

"You too," I said. His hand was cool (not cold), his shake firm, and when I tried to pull back my hand, he showed off the grip he was famous for, hanging on to me for a moment too long.

"Thanks for attending my event. You look amazing," he said.

I did not look amazing. I looked good—for me. Lion had gone through two divorces and had several high-profile girlfriends. All were knockouts with more legs, boobs, and hair than I would ever hope to have. Not that I hoped to have any of it.

"Thank you. And thank you as well for attending…*my* event." I wasn't sure how much he'd told the rest of his group, though of course Lila knew about him playing poker later.

He laughed, and I wondered if perhaps the lines around his eyes *were* laugh lines after all.

"Are we ready?" he asked to his group, who all nodded. Holding his arm out to me, he said, "Then let's get going."

I took his arm and he smiled at me as he said, "This has all the makings of an absolutely stellar night."

Eleven

❖❖

WE WERE ENSCONCED IN HIS ENTOURAGE as we made our way down from his suite and to the banquet center. Literally surrounded, like he was the president and the Secret Service were getting him out of Syria or something.

People in the casino were more likely to look up from their slot machines to see what the hell was going on with the bodyguards and people in suits than they ever would be with just Lion and me quietly walking past them.

But maybe that was the point.

When people would recognize him (through all those bodies…which wasn't easy), he'd wave to them and helplessly motion to the people surrounding him, as if were it not for the hulking bodies keeping him away, he would have loved nothing more than to sit down at a machine next to them and drop a few quarters.

"Jesus, move faster," he grumbled to the lead as he smiled to an older, tiny Asian woman who was sitting at the end of a bank of slots and pointing at Lion as we walked past.

They took us to the convention/banquet area through a series of back doors, where Lion then dispersed his group and had Lila do a check on him to see if the small walk among the masses had ruffled his very beautiful feathers in any way.

Assured by Lila that he was still picture perfect, he took my hand and said, "Time for the flashbulbs, baby."

How could I like when Jack sometimes called me baby in bed and my skin shivered in a non-good way when Lion called me the same thing? Delivery, I supposed. And the deliverer.

"What do you mean?" I said, standing put when he tried to pull me with him toward a different door than the one we'd entered.

"The red carpet. Well it's not an actual long red carpet." He looked to Lila, who shook her head. "It's a step and repeat."

"But we're here. Do we really need to go back out and pretend we're just arriving?" I mean, surely there were enough pictures of Lion LaGasse in the stratosphere already—did the world need more?

He looked at me like I was crazy. To him, I probably was. "This is my foundation—*my* event. I have to be seen arriving. There's a backdrop out there with all the logos of the sponsors of this event. I have to have a zillion photos of myself taken in front of it—greet some of the bigger names as they arrive. Pose with them and shit."

Well, yeah, that made sense. You had to keep your sponsors happy.

Which was why I'd never taken on sponsors. Unless you counted Ben when I first met him and owed money to Vince.

"Right. Of course. I'll wait for you back here," I said.

"That's not going to work. I could have had anyone be my date for this event. When you called, I knew it would be perfect."

I started to get nervous. It was one thing to be on television during a poker tournament—it was a small audience. It was quite another to be seen as Lion LaGasse's date at an event sure to get a lot of press.

My photo would surpass the poker circles and become part of mainstream entertainment. People would be Googling me left and right. Which some people would love, but not someone who didn't want to be recognized by the world. Or by a handful of college basketball players.

Although, if I was really "cured," as Lor said, and Vince would obviously never need to call upon JoJo again, what was the hold-up? With no JoJo in the picture, I was now free to pursue a more public persona that could possibly help my poker career. Get me invited to high-profile televised games, celebrity stuff.

My releasing myself from Lion's grip should have been my first red flag that somewhere—*somewhere deep*—I knew JoJo might resurface at any time.

Lion looked down at our broken handhold, then looked at me incredulously. "Are you kidding me?" The lines around his eyes were crinkling, and it was easy to see this was his more practiced expression.

"I'm happy to walk your carpet, if you think my minimal celebrity would add to your event." He relaxed and reached for my hand again, but I put it behind my back. "But I'd prefer to walk alone, that's all."

"You don't want to be seen with me? Are you shitting me? Do you know how much coverage that will get your little-known poker-playing ass?"

Yes, I knew exactly how much coverage it would get me.

"It's very generous of you, really, but—"

He leaned into me, his face close to mine, his voice low—so that the others couldn't hear him, or to intimidate me, I wasn't sure. "Listen, you are walking out there with me, pretending you're happier than shit to be on my arm, or I am not playing in your friend's rinky-dink game later. Got it?"

He had me there. I owed Carla, and she wanted Lion and me to play in her first solo game to set the stage for other high rollers.

I nodded once at him, offering him my hand, which he took and then led me to the door, his entourage staying behind.

"Would it have killed you to show some cleavage?" he asked

as we exited the room to a corridor.

Now that I knew what kind of guy I was dealing with, I was on sturdier ground. "You want tits, grab a cocktail waitress to be your date."

He snorted and looked down at me as he led me to a door at the end of the corridor, where a woman in a suit not unlike my own was standing with a clipboard crooked in her elbow, and a headset perched carefully around her expertly tousled curls. "Already did. She's back in my room. Didn't really think she was red-carpet material. Either of them."

"So I'm your beard? Because you want to bang cocktail waitresses, we have to go through some farce that's going to have both of us denying anything romantic between us for the next six months?"

My mood, not great since Ben told me about his private date with Jack, was now moving toward pissed for real. Yeah, he was doing me a favor by playing tonight, risking his own money at a game of chance. (I prefer to think a game of skill, but all pros do.)

"Oh, come on, you're going to *love* the attention you're going to get from one little walk into a charity dinner. It might even get you some endorsement deals—I noticed you didn't have any. Maybe you need a better manager. I could introduce—"

"I don't want any endorsement deals. I've turned them all down." He looked at me with skepticism. Yeah, in Lion's world, one didn't turn down endorsement deals—one just chose the best deals for the most prestigious products. I didn't bother trying to convince him.

"And my manager is just fine," I added, mentally defending Lorelei. Yeah, sure, Lila seemed crazy proficient—and she'd been introduced to me as an assistant, not a manager—but I didn't see her holding any interventions for Lion because she was concerned about him.

An *asshole* intervention was needed for sure.

"Whatever," he said, clearly not believing me. "Your career, not mine. But right now we are going to walk through that door, and you're going to look like you cannot believe that Lion LaGasse asked you to be his date."

"Yeah, not a stretch," I said, meaning a totally different take on "I *cannot* believe this" than Lion did. He smiled at me, and his half-sneer told me that he got my sarcasm.

He turned his body fully to me, his back to the closed door. He studied my face, like the way someone does when you know they want to kiss you. But I didn't fool myself about Lion LaGasse. He might have wanted me to up his *menage á trois* to *á quarte*, joining the cocktail waitresses back in his room, but he didn't particularly want to kiss me. He looked down past my face, to my neck, bare except for my horseshoe necklace, and quickly reached out with his free hand and flicked open the top button of my suit jacket. Nodding at the woman with the clipboard, Lion took a tighter grip on my hand and pulled me along with him through the door the woman opened as she said in her little microphone, "Lion is approaching. I repeat, Lion is approaching."

Yeah, Secret Service shit, for sure.

We were hit with a barrage of flashbulbs, which made me want to raise a hand to shade my eyes, but even the low-level celebrity that I was, I knew better than to actually do it. The same gene that had me so easily slip into JoJo's voice and mannerisms when needed allowed me to slap a smile on my face, first at the photographers, then up at Lion himself and—yes, exactly—act like I was happy as shit to be on Lion's arm.

The cacophony of voices all seemed to be saying the same thing in different ways—"Lion, who's your date? How long have you been together?"

Lion posed expertly in between the logos of his sponsors, almost as if he had eyes on the back of his head. Then I noticed the little "X" of red tape at his feet and realized that even something as simple as where to stand had been planned out for Lion LaGasse.

"Hang on, hang on," Lion said, holding his free hand up. With his other, he disengaged our entwined fingers and slid that arm behind my back, pulling me close to his side. "Let me answer you all at once." He looked down at me with what looked like deep affection in his eyes. "This is my good friend Anna Dawson. Most of you aren't from around here, but she's a legend in Vegas."

I looked up at him and smiled, seemingly absolutely delighted with Lion's completely inaccurate depiction of me. Yeah, JoJo training was paying off.

"She's not only beautiful, but is one of the best professional poker players in the world. She thrilled me to no end by agreeing to be my date this evening while I'm here on her turf. And she also graciously agreed to put up a private poker lesson with herself as an item in the auction later this evening."

I continued smiling while he promised something I had not even been consulted about, let alone agreed to. Looking away from the photographers—a motion surely completely foreign and anathematic to him—he looked back to me and smiled again, his arm pulling me even tighter. He dipped his head and pretended to whisper something in my ear that was probably supposed to make me giggle or some stupid shit. But instead of whispering, he swiped a quick lick of my neck just underneath my ear.

Asshole.

"You're going to pay later, at the table," I whispered back, looking like we were sharing a moment of intimacy.

"Come on," he said quietly, so that only I could hear. "Don't be so fucking stingy. You can give up one lousy poker lesson. It's for the goddammed kids." All with a smile on his face, and his hand sliding around my hip so it would be visible in the pictures taken from a side angle.

"I would happily have donated an auction item," I said truthfully. "But I would have appreciated being asked, that's all."

He laughed, his head tilting back with his movement. The photographers ate it up, their flashes and shouts to look in their direction intensifying. I slid my arm around his waist, even put my other hand on his chest, pressing into him. I felt him flinch in surprise, but nothing that would be noticed by anyone else.

If I was going to be hounded for the next few months about how close, exactly, Lion and I were, then I might as well make sure he got the same scrutiny.

Besides, Jack would actually get a kick out of it all when I told him. Some women might be afraid their guy would get jealous, but I knew Jack would only shake his head, chuckle, and give me that "the things you get yourself into look" that I both loved and hated.

"Anna, how long have you and Lion been together?" one of the photographers yelled loud enough for me to hear over the other inane chatter coming from them all. A bunch of them had their phones out, and I assumed they were Googling me and/or letting someone know they had photos of Lion and his "date."

I looked up at Lion with a question on my face, like I was thinking just how long we'd actually been together. He smiled down at me, a beautiful smile really, on a very handsome man. A handsomeness now marred for me by douchery.

He wouldn't be the first man I felt that way about.

I looked back at the photographers. "Um...would you believe we just met a few minutes ago?" I said it in a way that was playful, like I was trying to hide the truth.

"Come on," several of the photographers answered. They smelled a story now, with me being not only an unknown with at least some celebrity cred, such as it was, but also trying to evade their questions on Lion's and my "relationship."

"Isn't she great?" Lion asked the group, placing a kiss on the top of my head as the flashbulbs ratcheted up another notch.

The questions came fast and furious, but we only stared in each other's eyes.

You're not too bad at this, his eyes said to mine.

I eat assholes like you every day at the table, I conveyed back to him through a loving grin.

Again, he gave a big laugh, and it felt like the first sincere motion he'd made since we'd stepped onto the carpet—which, though small, was indeed red.

"Anna and I are just...friends. Very...very close friends. And I'm delighted she joined me tonight." He then launched into his spiel about his foundation and all the children it helped. I stood by his side until other guests started coming in and he turned to greet them.

He set me off to the side, but gave me a warning look when his back was to the cameras.

"Don't go anywhere. Just look at me adoringly, like you can't wait to get me alone later."

"Oh, I can't wait," I said, mentally calculating how I could destroy him—and embarrass him, *definitely* embarrass him—at the card table.

Huh. Maybe my superhero name should be the Destroyer after all.

Twelve
❖❖

THE DINNER WAS A FIRST-CLASS AFFAIR, and Lion and I were seated at a table with a couple of movie stars, a couple of sports stars, and a CEO of a hedge fund, as well as their spouses or dates.

I talked most of the night with the CEO and her husband, not wanting to get too close to the NFL and MLB players.

The auction was deemed a success, and there was actually a small bidding war on the private poker lesson that I'd so generously donated. The emcee for the auction was apparently a host on one of the late, late talk shows, and did a great job, really cracking up the crowd, and calling them out when needed. It almost made me wish I'd heard of him or watched his show, but I was usually playing poker when his show was on. If not, I was most definitely asleep.

Lion didn't balk at my wanting to drive my own car over to the Bellagio. In fact, he rode with me, choosing to let his staff stay on at the party and have the rest of the evening off.

"Should I change?" he asked as we walked the back halls of the Wynn.

"Up to you," I said. "I didn't bring a change of clothes, so I'll be wearing this."

"You don't wear your black suit every time you play a high-stakes game?"

I snorted and rolled my eyes. "Hardly. I'm a cargo pants and leather jacket kind of girl." I thought about how shocked anyone I regularly played with in one of Vince's games would be to see me walk in wearing a suit with my hair done and makeup on. Not to mention entering with Lion LaGasse.

Then I realized I had no idea who else Carla had invited to play—and who would have said yes.

"I'm not really sure who all will be there. A gentleman who I often play with, when he's in town, typically wears a suit," I offered to Lion.

"Fuck it, I'll keep it on. I don't get a chance to dress up all that often."

No, I supposed he didn't. His closet was most likely filled with golf shirts and slacks, with the occasional suit and tux tucked in the back.

All very expensive, but Lion got to wear comfy casual clothes to work like I did. And his "office" was in the sunshine and fresh air, whereas mine was in casinos and suites with a heavy cloud of cigarette smoke hanging nearby.

Lion had pretty much left me alone after our semi-pissing match on the red carpet, and after he decided not to detour back to his suite, I led him to the parking deck and to my Porsche.

The silence continued on the short drive to the Bellagio, where I once again parked in the self-parking deck.

"You know where you're going?" he asked as we entered the casino by the seasonal floral display and I quickly walked through to the front desk with its gorgeous blown glass flowered ceiling.

"Yep," I said, continuing at a clip, not wanting folks to recognize Lion. (Or myself, but that was less likely.)

It was late Friday night and the place was pretty crowded, so a man and a woman walking in the traffic flow didn't attract much attention.

When we got to the guest elevator banks, I flashed a Bellagio hotel room key to the security guard and he nodded to us. It seemed he might have recognized Lion, but the guy was too used to the rich and beautiful at his place of work to look twice.

In the elevator, Lion fidgeted with his cuffs and I watched the movement intently. Was something wrong with the heavy silver cuff links he wore, or was it something more? Was he nervous about playing? Was it a movement that would be a tell at the table?

"You said initial buy in is usually twenty-five K?"

I nodded. "That's typical, but you can do whatever you want. If you don't want to spend that much, ten would start you off. If you wanted to bully the table by having more chips in front of you—that's a way to go too."

He cut me a side-eye look, then stared straight ahead at our reflection in the elevator doors. "I don't need to bully anyone with a big stack of bought chips," he said. "I'm going to bully them with a big stack of *won* chips." The door slid open and he stepped out first, with me following and then checking the signs to see which way we needed to go.

Turning right, I said to him, "Are you going to be as much of a dick at the table as you were on the red carpet?"

He laughed, and it sounded much different than the laughs he'd bestowed on the people he'd talked to at the event. Probably because this one was real.

"You know it," he said, walking alongside me as I made my way down the long hallway. "You said this Carla was discreet, right?"

"Yep."

"Then I can assume the players will be as well?"

"Yes," I said without hesitation. Though I didn't know who exactly would be playing, I did know people played in these types of games instead of in the casinos for many reasons, but a big one was because they didn't want to be seen dropping huge sums of money in a public venue. Vince's players, and I could assume Carla's as well, didn't talk outside of the hotel suite.

There would be no requests for selfies with Lion.

"Then yeah," Lion said as we reached the door of the suite Carla had procured for the evening's game, "I'm going to be as big of a dick here as I was on the red carpet. That's the Lion, baby, and when he gets the chance, he lets it roar."

Seriously? Ugh. But I held it together, telling myself I'd have my sweet, sweet revenge by having most of whatever wad of money he had in his pocket placed in my purse in just a few hours.

"Whatever," I said to him, shrugged, and knocked on the door. "It's your funeral."

"Oh, no, baby," he said, the "baby" again making my skin crawl. "I'll be doing the killing tonight."

Thirteen

❖

"MS. DAWSON, MR. LAGASSE, welcome," Raymond said as he opened the door to Lion and me. He didn't show any signs of recognition when he looked at me, and I played along.

"Thank you," I said, entering the large suite.

Lion followed me in, barely nodding at Raymond, his eyes scanning the room. I knew Lion was a big poker player, but wasn't sure how many private games of this type he'd played in.

Carla had done a nice job with her first solo outing. The food spread was in one corner of the large room, with comfy chairs and small side tables set up around the table holding what looked like a far more superior fare than the normal subs and chips Carla arranged for Vince's games.

There was even a small bar near the entrance with a designated bartender who took our drink orders—scotch for Lion, Diet Coke for myself. The bartender's eyes bulged with the recognition of Lion, but he didn't say anything, just served us our beverages in heavy cut-crystal glasses.

I wondered if Vince had held the purse strings tight for his games (which he seldom attended) or if—and this was likelier, knowing how appearances mattered to Vince—Carla and Paulie went to the cheap side and pocketed the difference?

The setup tonight—from the bar, the food, the beautiful full-size casino-style poker table placed in a cleared area in the middle of the living room—was what I would bet Vince had envisioned was happening at all his games.

"Anna, Mr. LaGasse, so happy you could join us," Carla said, approaching us at the bar. She herself had upped her game now that her name was at the top of the bill, so to speak. The severe bob cut of her black hair had a swingy gloss to it, and the bangs had been shaped, giving her more of a darker Anna Wintour look than her usual Nancy from that old comic strip. Typically wearing a sweater and slacks to Vince's game, and showing a slight disinterest in the whole thing, she was now wearing a smart navy pantsuit that immensely flattered her, with an artfully arranged scarf at her throat. I was in no way an expert, but I would have guessed her heels were Louboutins. Yep, I caught a glance of the red sole as she turned and led us deeper into the room. Lor had bought me a pair for a final table appearance a couple of years ago. I'd thrown them in the back of the closet the minute I'd gotten home (having placed sixth—as good as losing!) and hadn't seen them since.

Looking down at my shoes, I noticed I was wearing Jimmy Choos, another Lor purchase for me.

Carla led us into the huge room, and I wondered who would need all this space when they came to Vegas. Apparently Lion LaGasse and his entourage, because this suite was about the size of his at the Wynn. Maybe Carla had two cocktail waitresses stashed in one of her suite's bedrooms? If she'd known that was what it would take to make Lion happy, she might have. Or at least had some kind of…pleasurable distraction available to him.

Yeah, she saved my life, but I didn't owe her *that* big.

I followed Carla and Lion to the table, looking over my shoulder at Raymond and giving him an "all right?" look, which he returned with a subtle chin nod.

It appeared we were the last to arrive, as there were six places set up for players at the semicircle-shaped table, with the dealer's spot facing all the players, as if someone had cut a doughnut in half and the dealer sat in the hole. The dealer himself was the only one sitting, and he was checking decks of cards and chips and basically readying himself. He was a man of about fifty, with his hair graying slightly. I didn't recognize him, but it wasn't like I knew every dealer in town.

Okay, I knew a lot, but not *all*.

He nodded to us as we came around the table, and I nodded back, looking for a nametag, but he wasn't wearing one.

Four men were standing near the table, drinks in their hands, making small talk. They were all wearing suits, and I was happy that I'd had to dress up for Lion's event, or I would be hopelessly underdressed. Not that I would care, but Carla would.

I also secretly hoped that the good food and top-shelf booze would be the only things from tonight's premiere that would be retained for Carla's future games, and not also the dress code.

The group opened their circle for us to join them, and I saw that Mr. Chow, my long-time adversary at Vince's games, had indeed accepted Carla's invitation. My ego had me thinking that I was the draw for his attending, but who knew? The last time I'd played with him I'd had to leave suddenly because Danny had been killed, making a hasty betting decision and basically handing over all my money (and plenty of Vince's) to Mr. Chow.

I was surprised to see I knew one of Carla's newbies. And not from around Vegas or the professional poker circuit. "Ralph?" I said, after I shook Mr. Chow's hand. "Ralph Stankowski?"

The man I addressed smiled at me and stuck his hand out for me to shake. "How are you, Anna?"

"Surprised," I admitted, quickly shaking his hand.

Ralph Stankowski was a man whose private poker game in Pittsburgh I'd crashed weeks ago. So had Jack, though I hadn't known he was going to until I had faced off against him in Ralph's gorgeous home. We'd both been investigating Danny's death and had reason to believe a heavy hitter from Pittsburgh might have been involved. Ralph's game included the heaviest of

Pittsburgh's hitters.

The last time I'd seen Ralph, he was putting Jack and me in a tram to take us to the bottom of Mount Washington, and had in no uncertain terms said that he would be very displeased to see Jack or myself again.

Apparently he'd only meant in Pittsburgh, because he was in no way surprised to see me, and seemed pleased.

"Lion, Ralph Stankowski," he said, sticking his hand out to Lion, who returned the firm handshake. "You won't remember this, but we played together in a pro-am in Akron about ten years ago. Was one of the great thrills of my life to play a round with you."

"I'm afraid I don't remember, Ralph, but it's a pleasure to see you again."

The other two men were introduced as Brandt Whitaker and Calvin Spencer. Both were white, well dressed, and had the polish and extra touches of the extremely wealthy.

Calvin would be in his sixties, I'd guess, from the lines on his face and the graying of his hair. Brandt I'd put in his mid-fifties from his face, but at first glance he appeared older due to a head full of beautiful silver hair that reminded me of Gus's. They both had an air of authority about them that pervaded the room. I was used to that. Get a bunch of whales from any profession in one room and you'd feel the underlying testosterone start to rise like the heat of a steam room, with almost as much visibility.

I'd never heard of either one of them, and they obviously hadn't come together, since all of the men were asking the usual "Where are you from?" types of questions.

I vaguely paid attention, taking a sip of my Diet Coke and watching their mannerisms. That would tell me more at the poker table once we started than the fact that Calvin would be marrying his third wife at Caesars on Sunday. Though I did store that intel away for later, as that could sometimes say something in and of itself. Would Calvin fold easily? Was he a runner? Or was he always looking for new and shiny? Would he stay in a hand thinking it could be "the one"?

Personality sometimes indicated how someone would play poker, but not always. Mannerisms, however, were harder to hide, though everybody tried, but the trying itself was sometimes a tell.

I looked at Mr. Chow, who was watching me watch the other men. He gave me a sly smile, or what passed as a smile from a man with a face of granite.

I had yet to crack Mr. Chow, and I'd been playing against him for years. Well before the movie *The Hangover* had come out with its own Mr. Chow, who was different in every conceivable way from mine.

After a few more moments of pleasantries, Carla announced that the game would begin, and if we would like to buy our chips she'd take care of us.

"The initial buy-in for this evening's game is twenty-five thousand dollars. This is a no-limit game. If you should have need of additional funds, I'd be happy to offer that to you, terms to be discussed on an as-needed basis."

One by one we went with Carla to a little table, where we gave her our twenty-five large and she in turn gave us our chips. I noticed a familiar blue with red edging ledger on her table, and nodded to it. "Same one?"

She shook her head. "I'm dealing with those accounts separately. New ledger, new accounts."

"Probably best," I said, handing over the envelope Lor had given me with my stake.

Once we all had our chips, Carla had the dealer show us six cards, an ace through six of hearts. The dealer then shuffled up the six cards and we drew for our seat assignments. After we took our seats, there were just a few more pleasantries and then we were off.

My eye was on Mr. Chow, as always when I played against

him, due to our longstanding rivalry. I'd played with Ralph before, and he was a good player, and seemed like a good guy. Brandt and Calvin I would size up quickly and be pretty much able to tell if they'd be any kind of threat. But oh, how I wanted to beat Lion. Badly.

I wanted to walk out of there with winnings that would pay for a car for Raymond. A nice car. And I wanted most of that money to come from Lion LaGasse.

TWO HOURS LATER I TOOK my second bad beat of the night. Both, infuriatingly, coming from the king of the jungle himself. Down to my last five hundred dollars, I should have said good night, wished them all well, made sure Lion could see himself home (just to be polite; the town crawled with cabs), and got the hell out of there.

But I didn't. I had played stupidly, letting my desire to kick Lion's ass make me more aggressive than normal, staying in pots—raising them, even—that I should have folded.

I played poker against assholes all the time, and I never let them dictate my strategy. Never let them get under my skin much, except that time I played against Jack at Ralph's home, though I would say that was driven more by sexual tension than the kind of animosity I felt toward Lion.

And it wasn't just me. Lion didn't keep the façade in place for very long before my fellow players realized that he might have been the world's best golfer, but he was also possibly the world's biggest dick.

I could almost physically feel Ralph's admiration for his favorite golfer shriveling up, dwindling like the pile of chips in front of me.

Brandt turned out to be either a better player than I'd guessed, or was incredibly lucky. I'd never know for sure, since several times he didn't need to show his hand to pull the pot to his pile of chips. But it was the pocket kings he showed that took me down to limping level.

For the next hand, I was the big blind and could just about cover that and have enough for a tiny bet. I could stay and play the one hand, having to go all in, and thus everyone would know I probably didn't have anything, but only bet because of my low chip count. Everyone would call and someone would knock me out.

Of course, it not being a tournament but a cash game, I could pull out more money—which I didn't have—and continue to play. Or borrow from Carla, like I used to do, to continue to play, so that I could win and have money to place a bet on a game.

But I didn't need money to place a bet, because I wasn't betting. Plus, Carla was under strict orders to not lend me any cash. I wasn't letting JoJo back out from the closet if I had any say about it.

And let's face it, I always had a say in the problems JoJo created.

So, I could stand up from the table, collect my meager chips, bid adieu to my fellow players, and get the hell out of Dodge.

It was so easy. I *could* walk away. I was able to. There was nothing hanging over my head except the sting of being beaten, which I felt all the time. You had to get used to it in my profession and not let it be the decision maker.

It never had been my decision maker—placing a sports bet was what led me around by the nose.

But not anymore.

I pushed my chair back smoothly, like it was a motion that was okay by me. And it was. Sort of. Until Lion looked at me. He glanced at my chips, then his eyes moved back to mine and the smallest flicker of a smile played at his mouth.

No worries. I frequently dealt with pompous asses who did a lot more than smile about knocking the Black Widow out of a poker game.

But instead of taking those remaining chips, or handing them to the dealer as a tip, I left them at my spot, like I was just rising to take a potty break or get some food. Like my giant stack would be sitting there waiting for me after I wet my beak at the bar.

All of those things I could do. I did kind of need to pee. I was a little hungry. And I almost felt like Jack needing a bourbon, my thirst was so great.

But it wasn't what I thirsted for. Booze couldn't quench the feelings that surged through me as I stepped away from the table.

My heart sped up, and I thought I could actually hear my swallowing when, instead of heading to the bar, the buffet, or the bathroom, I walked over to the little table Carla had set up for the chips and her ledger.

My palms weren't quite sweaty; it wasn't that bad because I knew that even though it seemed as though I was weaker than I thought, I had a safety net. Carla wouldn't lend me any money. She'd promised as part of our agreement for me to play and to contact Lion.

It was kind of like having Lor handle my cash and making sure the house and everything in it were not available for me to get my hands on. Because even though I still had no intention of placing a bet later, clearly I still had some work to do on walking away when I was losing.

At least walking away from a smirking Lion LaGasse.

I was happy to note that Raymond was away from the door at that time. In fact, I didn't see him at all in the large room. He was either in one of the bedrooms, or a bathroom or Carla had sent him somewhere for something. Either way, I was glad he wasn't there to watch and hear my next move.

"I need to borrow twenty K," I said to Carla as I entered

her space at the table. My body felt less tense, almost started to relax (though none of this would be visible to anyone else—I had trained myself better than that), with the thought that I was smart enough to protect myself from myself with good people.

"You got it," she said, pushing a pile of chips in front of me and turning her ledger around for me to sign for my debt.

I couldn't believe it. She was supposed to deny me. Tell me to go home. We had a deal. I stared at her, thinking maybe she'd forgotten that little detail, but the twitch of her brow as she nodded toward the chips was enough to realize Carla knew exactly what she was doing.

Oh, she would be a worthy successor to Vince Santini.

She slid it toward me, and I signed the fucking ledger.

Fourteen

◆◆

IT DIDN'T GET ANY BETTER.

And it got a whole lot worse.

I won a couple of hands with my fresh stake, but the trend of bad beats continued. And it wasn't just me. Mr. Chow became visibly frustrated at one point—a first. Not only was I not the only one losing, I was certainly not the only one to mention, either overtly or not, that Lion was not only an asshole, but a poor winner. Which, in my book, was worse.

"Is this man your friend?" Mr. Chow asked me during a break. Lion was in one of the bathrooms and I was standing at the buffet table nabbing some grapes from the fruit tray.

When I overcame my shock at Mr. Chow speaking with me, I quickly shook my head and said, "Absolutely not. And I apologize for bringing him. It was a favor to Carla."

He looked at me suspiciously, then gave a curt chin nod.

"A one-time deal," I reassured him.

"You talking about Lion?" Ralph asked, joining us. He started putting together a sandwich.

"Yes," I said.

Ralph was shaking his head as he piled the lean roast beef high. "He was like this a little bit when I played in that pro-am with him—talking trash. I figured it was a psych-out kind of thing."

"Maybe it is," I said. "He's got the majority of the chips."

Ralph shrugged and threw a few slices of cheese onto the whole thing. "Maybe. And maybe he's just an ass. But I've played in a lot of games, and I'm guessing both of you have. Trash talk you put up with."

He was right. I dealt with trash-talking players all the time and kept my cool. Was it just Lion getting to me because I had residual annoyance from being paraded on the red carpet at his event?

Suddenly a noise came from behind us that sounded like a dog trying to suppress a bark while his tail was being stepped on, then whimpering about it. Whipping around to see what animal had made its way into the room and who was torturing the poor thing, I saw that Calvin was recovering from a sneeze.

"God almighty," Ralph said to him, turning with me.

Calvin rolled his eyes and fished out a handkerchief from his back pocket. "I know. I know. I've been told." He sniffled into the cloth then put it away. "Had that sneeze my whole life. And the damn seasonal allergies aren't helping."

Brandt had joined us now, and nodded. "This desert-dry air is the killer for me." He proceeded to take a bottle of eye drops out of his jacket pocket and administer a drop to each eye, taking a napkin from the food table to dab with.

"It's supposed to be a bad year for allergies," Ralph added. "It's in the Vegas paper today. Record pollen counts or something. Has to do with the unusually wet winter out here. Or was it dry winter?" He shrugged and continued with his sandwich masterpiece. I wondered if he'd make me one if I asked.

"Ten minutes," Carla softly said as she came by the table. We all nodded that we'd heard her. Brandt went off to the restroom, passing Lion, who was exiting.

I braced myself for more of his insufferable humor as he joined us at the table.

"Monster sandwich, Ralph," he said. "Losing must make

you really hungry."

Ralph, a better man than I, only smiled weakly at Lion then took his plate and moved to one of the couches in the living room area of the suite.

Mr. Chow quickly left the food table as well, leaving Calvin, Lion, and me.

Lion and Calvin talked about a couple of hands that had been played in the last round. I sort of paid attention, but mostly tried to re-create Ralph's sandwich for myself. It didn't look nearly as good as his did, but I ate it standing while listening to Calvin and Lion.

"I mean, there have been some gutsy calls," Lion said. "But I'm guessing a bunch of those were half-bluffs."

"Maybe," Calvin said.

Lion turned in my direction. "Like the hand you lost on. I mean the one you most recently lost on—I know; there were too many to keep track. You had to be bluffing, right? My guess was bluffing. Otherwise, what? King/ten? King/jack?"

He had hit it right the first time, king/ten, but I just stared at him, not giving anything away. I may have had a tell with Jack Schiller, but I knew there was no way I'd given anything up to Lion LaGasse.

But he laughed anyway, like he could see right through me. The sound was a little too loud, and a little too long for this quiet room, and it made my nerves rattle. Of Calvin's sneeze or Lion's laugh, I wasn't sure which sound was more annoying. Definitely Lion's laugh.

Because I heard it way too many times over the next two hours.

Brandt, I noticed, made a trip to Carla's table. So at least I wasn't the only one who didn't—or couldn't—walk away after losing our money.

So, Carla would make six grand from the vig off me, and another six off Brandt. Others may have borrowed from her that

I didn't see, or even before I'd arrived, but at a minimum, Carla would have made twelve thousand for the night. Sure, there was overhead: the suite, the food and booze, paying Raymond, the dealer, and bartender. But still, not a bad take for one night.

It was more than I was going to take home.

Still, I hung around, losing the last of my money—the last of Carla's money—on the second to last hand.

I left the table, nodding at all the gentlemen, getting nods back, and a smirk from Lion. After using the restroom, I saw they were wrapping up.

Damn, I was hoping they'd go another couple of hours and I could ditch Lion.

Because he would be staying until the end, and was the night's big winner. Might have been the night's only winner, if my quick glance at the chips was accurate. (And my quick glances at chip stacks were always accurate.)

Unbelievable.

Why did the biggest assholes always seem to get lucky when they needed to the most?

I knew it was skill that had him winning all those golf tournaments, but from what I could tell tonight, he had no more skill at poker than Ralph did. Possibly about the same as Brandt and Calvin. Not nearly as much as Mr. Chow or me.

And yet eighty percent of the chips sat in front of him.

Brandt had busted out just before me and had already left. Calvin had maybe a thousand dollars in chips in front of him. Ralph around five thousand.

Lion was playing the last hand against Mr. Chow, the other players having already folded, and rising, gathering their things, but sticking around to see how it finished.

Mr. Chow was the only player with more than a few thousand in chips. Looked to be just under his original twenty-five thousand.

They went back and forth, raising and calling, then reraising.

Lion asked for a count of Mr. Chow's chips—so he could raise that exact amount—but Mr. Chow staved off the dealer from counting and just replied, "All in."

Apparently the jabs from Lion all night had gotten to Mr. Chow too, because he was usually a much more cautious player, seldom shoving his entire stack to the middle of the table.

Lion's bravado stumbled a little bit. He hadn't expected the trick of asking for a chip count to actually work; he just wanted to intimidate.

"The bet is to you," the dealer said to Lion, who blinked rapidly.

The first sign of a chink in the armor, and it would have to be on the last hand of the night, when I'd already busted out.

Lion looked at Mr. Chow, then at the others as we stood around the table watching. He seemed to be almost talking to himself as he considered his move. Finally, he said, "Call."

Mr. Chow turned over pocket aces and Lion came up with a pair of threes.

Interesting. Had I been beaten all night by low pairs? Was he a better bluffer than I'd thought?

No three on the board saved him, and Lion lost the last hand of the night, but it barely made a dent in his considerable chip stack.

"Mr. Chow had good hand. He berry happy. But no happy now," Lion said, in a horrifying fake Asian accent, trying to sound like the Mr. Chow from the *Hangover* movies.

I gasped a tiny bit, taken aback. Lion had been an asshat all night, but this went beyond that.

"Oh, lighten up," Lion said in my general direction. "Everybody has to be so fucking politically correct all the time." He rose from his seat and started stacking his chips in one of the racks Carla had provided for the remaining players. Most of us didn't need racks. "It's just in fun. Jesus, you lose your sense of humor with your money?"

The other players walked away from the table and I mouthed "I'm so sorry" to Mr. Chow, who nodded to me.

"I hope the next time we meet, you will come alone," he said softly as he passed me.

"You can count on that," I said.

I left Lion counting his piles of gold and made my way over to the bartender, who was stacking bottles in to boxes, cleaning up the bar. I took a fifty-dollar bill from my money clip in my jacket pocket. (At least I still had my walking-around cash.) "Thanks for keeping me refilled," I said, handing him the cash.

He nodded and thanked me, but his eyes didn't meet mine. Had I tipped too little? Did he think I was cheap? I'd bet some of the players hadn't even tipped him at all.

Still, his response seemed a little off.

A lot about this night seemed a little off.

I moved over to the foyer area, where Raymond was seeing the players out.

"Everything go okay?" I asked him when it was just the two of us.

He nodded. It seemed like he wanted to say more, but the dealer joined us then, saying his goodnights. I was kind of surprised he was leaving so soon, but I guess Carla had paid him in advance.

He probably hadn't made much in tips, most of us having been pretty cleaned out. And who knew if Lion, the big winner, was much of a tipper? Probably not.

"Hey," I said to the dealer, reaching into my jacket pocket. I had a couple of hundred-dollar bills, which I slid to him. "You did a good job tonight, dealing with all the chatter."

He thanked me and pocketed the money. "You have no idea," he muttered, and I guessed that Lion had been more obnoxious than even a professional dealer was used to.

He wasn't the worst I'd ever played with as far as that went, but he was definitely right up there.

And I'd brought him to the game.

I thought Mr. Chow had forgiven me, and Ralph I'd probably only see again if I played in Pittsburgh—which I had no intention of doing.

Brandt and Calvin? Who knew if I'd play with them again?

Who knew if I'd see any of these players again? That was how it worked in gambling circles.

You came in, spent hours together, made small talk. Won or lost a lot of money, and then went your separate ways.

Never to be heard from again.

Fifteen

❖

"SORRY YOU ASKED ME TO PLAY?" Lion said on the short drive from the Bellagio to the Wynn. Short in distance, but with the traffic lights on the Strip, it took longer than it should have.

"What do you mean?" I asked. I wasn't going to give him the satisfaction of knowing I was incredibly sorry I let Carla talk me into contacting him. Sorry that the whole damn night had even happened.

He snorted and looked out the side window while I stared straight ahead. "I get my ass kicked all the time," I said, like tonight was no big deal. "That's why it's called gambling."

What I said was true, but it had been a while since I'd played so badly, had misread the other players so completely.

And it had been weeks since I'd been in debt to Vince. Now Carla.

Lion prattled on about exactly how much money I lost, how much he won, how the other players really weren't up to his level, even though they played much more than Lion did. I just drove and escaped into my own thoughts.

Yes, it had been weeks since I'd owed money to a loan shark. A lot had happened since then. Lor and Ben basically knew about JoJo. Not every detail, and not the complete history, but bringing Raymond into our home had kind of let the cat out of my point-shaving bag. I could—and this thought, simple as it was, had never have been entertained by me before—simply tell Lor I had borrowed money to continue playing cards and needed some to pay Carla back.

My hands slid a little on the steering wheel, and I shifted down for the red light, my ankle feeling a tiny twinge as I did. Probably from wearing heels all night, I told myself. Not from how my body seemed to be reacting to the thought of paying back Carla right away, including the vig added onto the base loan, and not using any of that money to bet.

I should feel lighter, happier about it all. And yet my throat tightened and it was all I could manage not to strike out at Lion, who was now recalling a particular hand when he'd bluffed me out of a pot. (Or, at least, that was his story. I would never know for sure, which was its own kind of hell.)

The fact was, it was a foreign feeling. Well, not entirely. The physical feelings I was having on the ride were very similar to what I felt when I knew Vince would be calling with a proposition of JoJo making an appearance for my debt to disappear.

Apprehension. Dread. Deep foreboding. But I shouldn't be feeling this way about being able to get out of debt so quickly.

Maybe it was just some kind of twisted muscle memory, but with emotions. I leave a poker game after having borrowed money and the self-loathing and all the emotions that come with it kick in?

Yeah, I couldn't explain it, but somewhere in my head I heard JoJo laughing.

"I knew him, you know," Lion said, pulling me out of my thoughts.

"Knew who? Ralph? You remembered golfing with him years ago?" That would be just like him to pull some kind of power play and pretend to Ralph that he didn't remember a round that had been the highlight of Ralph's golfing life.

He snorted again, like I was crazy. "Uh…no. What, you think I can remember every rich prick who has the money to pay for a round of golf with me?"

"No, probably not," I said, silently feeling sorry for Ralph, who had also lost most of his money to Lion. And Lion's halo had definitely been dinged up in Ralph's estimation this evening. Not that Lion would have cared.

"That kid at the door. I didn't recognize him at first, but by the end of the night I knew it was him."

"I'm not sure who you mean," I said, the sense of dread that I'd had from the thought of paying off Carla so quickly—and not making a bet—ratcheting up a notch.

"No? That was Raymond James."

"Who?"

He turned to study me, and I conjured up my best poker face while I continued to look to the Strip in front of me. One more light and I'd be able to dump him at the Wynn.

"You know, that college basketball player that was accused of point shaving. I can't remember what school. Somewhere in the Midwest."

"I vaguely remember that. He was cleared, right?"

"Yeah. Well, sort of. The guy who made the claim was discredited or something like that. I forget the details. But it all kind of had a stink about it. And then he leaves school, or at least he's not on the team anymore."

"And you think that was him? Manning the door at a private poker game?"

"Oh yeah, that was him."

"Seems like a leap. Him being in Vegas, working a door."

"Not if he really was point shaving. Seems like Vegas would be the perfect spot for him."

Which was exactly why I hadn't wanted to bring Raymond to Vegas. And wouldn't have if we didn't need to get him out of Chicago so urgently.

"Whatever," I said, like the subject was boring me. Or I desperately wanted Lion to get off it.

"Kid was a good player. Nothin' but net for days every time he touched the ball." I said nothing to that. "You ever see him on a door before?"

I shrugged. "I don't know. Maybe. I told you this was Carla's first time flying solo, right? It looked like a new crew to me. Though I know I've seen the dealer around. I can't place where he normally works."

"Hope she hangs on to him. He was good." He laughed, and I knew his statement wasn't about how good the dealer was or wasn't, but the fact that Lion had been the winner.

"He was okay," I said, and Lion laughed some more.

Trash talk I could take. It was rampant among pros, but basically good-natured. Lion's laugh didn't really have the ribbing ring to it. No, his was more of a jabbing knife.

Thankfully, I pulled into the Wynn's long drive. "Wherever there's a door with the least amount of people," Lion said, and I veered toward the self-parking deck. I went to the lowest floor (where he'd have to ride the elevator the shortest amount of time) and pulled close to the elevator entrance.

I kept my foot on the clutch, already shifting into first. Lion looked at my hand on the gearshift, then to my face.

"Why don't you park? Come in for a while."

Was he serious? A tiny pull up at the corner of his mouth—his idea of charm, I was guessing—confirmed that he was.

"Thanks, but it was a long night, and I'd like to get home."

I could tell he was going to try and convince me, but I shot him a glare that said not to even bother.

He puts his hands up in surrender. "Okay, okay. I get it. Still, it was a good night. We made a good pair on the red carpet. We should think about hooking up for something like that again."

"Uh, yeah...no."

He laughed. "It's a win-win, baby. Think about it. No strings, just for show."

"I don't do things just for show," I said. Like I had the moral high ground on Lion LaGasse because he wanted to do high-profile things for his image.

When really I just wanted not to be high profile in case I was ever recognized, or needed to be JoJo again.

Which I wouldn't, because I wasn't betting.

"Darlin'," he said in a fake drawl that might have been sexy coming from someone else. Say, like Jack. "We *all* do things for show."

I was afraid he was right, so I didn't answer, just did a chin nod toward the door.

He took the not-so-subtle hint. "It was fun." He opened the door and unfolded himself out of my Porsche. I had my foot slowly descending on the gas pedal when he turned back into the car, resting his arm along the top of the door, his other on the roof. "You ever change your mind, whether it be for a public appearance"—he leaned deeper into the car—"a *private* one"—I revved the engine and he smiled—"or if you just want to relieve yourself of some money again, give me a call."

I squealed away from him, the door slamming shut, but not before I heard his laughter.

"Drop dead," I whispered as I drove away.

Sixteen
❖

I DIDN'T BOTHER TO GO TO BED once I got home. By the time I'd dropped Lion off—gleefully finally rid of him and his obnoxious gloating—and made it out to Summerlin, it was a little after six, so I decided to stay up and see if Ben wanted to do breakfast when he woke up.

Saturday was a day when we skipped breakfast out and ate light at home, depending on the time of year. But we were in basketball season and Jimmy and Gus would probably be betting the games, so they'd be out early. Ben loved looking at the line every day, but never placed a bet himself. And of course I was on the wagon—so to speak—so wouldn't be betting, but looking at the board was okay. Surely the bright lights of all the games being played that day were not such a siren's song that I couldn't resist it?

Jimmy would be up already, so I texted him that we'd meet him for breakfast, then I left a note on the coffee machine for Ben telling him that I was home and we'd be going out.

Making my way down the wing I shared with Raymond, I wondered if Jack would be sleeping in my bed. Maybe their dinner out had been such a success that they'd reveled well into the night and Jack had needed to stay here. But no, his car wasn't parked out front. Neither was the SUV, but I expected Raymond would have stayed behind longer in case Carla needed him.

Of course, either one of their cars could be in the garage, but I doubted it. The open doors and dark rooms of the bedrooms confirmed it.

I changed out of my suit and into my typical breakfast outfit of khaki cargo pants and a thermal Henley, then sat down on my bed to play the night over in my head.

And by the night, I meant the game—in particular losing so badly to Lion and borrowing money from Carla.

I couldn't believe I'd done either one.

Maybe it wouldn't be such a good idea hanging in a book room this morning.

I lay back on the bed, only now realizing that it was unmade. Placing my hand on one of the pillows, I felt the faintest trace of heat. Jack had been here after all, but must have been called away fairly recently. Somebody had died in Vegas tonight, or more accurately, this morning.

I almost wished it had been me.

I heard noises in the house, and footsteps coming down the hallway. "Hey," Raymond said from my doorway.

"Hey," I said, and motioned him in. He looked around my room, and I realized he'd probably never been in it. He moved to the cozy leather chair and ottoman Lor had placed in a little portion of the room. It was accompanied by a matching second chair, sans ottoman. A reading nook, she'd called it. The only things I read while sitting there were college media guides, sporting magazines, and odds sheets, but it was a comfy chair. And when the drapes were opened during the day (sometimes, most of the time, they were closed so I could sleep during the day), you could see the entire pool area from that chair, like a disinterested lifeguard.

Raymond pushed the ottoman away, then slumped down in the chair. He looked like I felt—tired and beaten. And he hadn't even lost forty-five thousand dollars. (And counting, as the vig kicked in.)

"You have the kind of money you can play like that every night?" Raymond said, not quite hiding both admiration and contempt in his voice.

"Not hardly," I replied. "I'm guessing Lion and Mr. Chow do, though. Possibly—probably—Ralph. The other two, I couldn't guess."

He nodded, slouching deeper into the chair. "But," I added, "I don't play like that every night. I usually play cash games in the casinos, at the regular tables. Sometimes in their high-roller areas, but not always."

"So tonight was unusual for you?"

I took a deep breath, then let it out. Raymond deserved to know the truth about me. Hell, he was the only person in my life who had actually come face-to-face with JoJo. He already knew the truth about me.

"Not completely unusual, no. When Vince ran the games, there was one nearly every night, but I usually only played in them when I'd lost my money in a cash game."

He sat up a little, studying me. "So, you'd play a cash game in the casino, lose, then go to one of these high-stakes games?"

"Yes," I said, trying not to squirm under his gaze. Carla was right: a good suit and a bald head and Raymond could seem quite intimidating if he wanted to.

"Why? I mean, if you were already losing, why not just go home?" he asked, and I suspected he knew the reason and just wanted to see if I'd admit it.

If I had admitted it to myself.

"Because I'd want cash to bet on games the next morning." The shame, such a familiar emotion in my life, but having been on the back burner for the most part for the past twenty-four days, came rolling back with full force.

Raymond continued to study me, but now spoke with less judgment, sincerely trying to figure it out.

Yeah, I knew how he felt.

"JoJo was in your ear, telling you there was a sure-thing bet?" he asked, but there really wasn't much questioning in his voice.

Raymond and I had talked about what I had called "the voice in your head" that told you about the sure things, the bets that absolutely *needed* to be made, the adrenaline from a big bet that had to be placed.

I'd warned him about listening to the voice, told him that I named mine JoJo. I suspected that Raymond had the propensity for the voice to take over his life, I just wasn't sure how it would manifest itself.

"And if you won the bet, if there were debts to Vince to be paid, you'd do that."

"Yes, right away. Then I'd play on my winnings for a while. When that was gone, enough time would have passed that I'd go to Lor for a new stake."

"And if your bet failed?"

I didn't answer him—he knew only too well what happened then.

"JoJo would make a little road trip," he said.

I nodded, not taking my eyes from him, though I really wanted to roll back on my bed, pull the covers over me, and stick my head under the pillow. A pillow that probably still carried Jack's scent.

I waited for a "Holy shit" or a "Jesus, you're a fucking mess" or something like that to come from Raymond, but instead he looked down at his beautifully polished shoes, then after a few silent seconds, lifted his head to look at me.

"You think you owe me?"

I gave a tiny nod, trying to catch up to his thought, but I couldn't. "Yes," I said.

"I'm not so sure you do. My mom and sis are in a better place. I'm going to get my degree. I... Whatever. Maybe you do, maybe you don't. But if you think you do, I'm going to ask for only one thing. If you still want to ease your conscience with the clothes, school, and housing, that's on you. I'll contribute around here for all of that."

"Okay," I said, mentally jumping ahead to what he really wanted from me, and what it would cost me. And I didn't suspect it would be in money.

"What I want from you is your watching my back. I don't want the voice in my head getting any louder. If you see me headed that way, you need to step in."

I didn't nod right away. I didn't want to promise him anything that I couldn't deliver. But I knew all the signs, knew what to watch for, because I'd lived them myself. I could keep an eye on Raymond. I nodded once. "Got it."

His body seemed to ease a bit, but there was urgency in his voice. "And I don't mean any bullshit interventions like Lor— even though she's hot as shit—does for you. I mean you gotta sit on me. Hard."

Shit. But again I nodded. "I've got you."

We stared at each other for a long time, then he finally nodded once and slouched back in the chair, resting his head on the back of it and closing his eyes.

I relaxed on the bed, thinking that if I was quiet he might fall asleep. I still had a few minutes before Ben would be up and about and I'd tell him we were doing breakfast out.

But Raymond didn't fall asleep. He must have been replaying the night in his head, as I had been before he came in. "That LaGasse," he said, still with head back and eyes closed, "what a complete motherfucker."

A small smile came across me, both outside and in. "Yeah, he's a douche," I said. "And my photo is going to be all over the Internet today looking like we're a couple and that I adore him."

"Sucks to be you," he said, then chuckled.

I closed my eyes, dreading the inquiries that were sure to come my way in the next few days. Maybe Lor could come up with some standard press release or something that we just sent anybody who asked for a comment.

Something about only knowing Lion a short time, that I was honored to be asked to be his guest for the evening for such a worthy cause, but I didn't expect to see him again.

I didn't bother telling Raymond that Lion had recognized him. I was pretty sure Lion wouldn't go public with that piece of information—there was nothing in it for him.

"You know that old saying—'Never meet your heroes'?" I said.

"Never heard that one. But it sure fit tonight," he said.

I heard Ben's walker coming down the hall. My first instinct was to jump up and help him, but he wouldn't like that, and probably didn't need it, so I stayed on my bed.

"There you two are," Ben said when he came into my room fully and saw Raymond. "How did last night go?"

We both groaned, and Ben laughed.

"How about breakfast out?" I said to Ben. "Jimmy's in. Gus isn't." I looked to Raymond. "Want to join us?"

He sat up straighter, looking at me with surprise. "Join the Corporation's breakfast? Seriously?"

"Well, they don't usually 'meet' on Saturdays, so this is a casual one. It's not up to me to get you an invite for the Monday through Friday ones. I had to work my way in," I said.

Raymond laughed. "I'm in," he said, hopping out of the chair with the enthusiasm and agility of a twenty-two-year-old athlete. "Five minutes to change," he said, and bounced past Ben, his bedroom door closing a few seconds later.

Ben moved deeper into the room. "I thought maybe Jack would be here," he said. "I told him last night that it would be okay to stay and wait for you."

Did Ben come over here expecting to see Jack? Was that the only reason?

A spark of irritation wafted through me, which was so

weird. I seldom became irritated in general with other people, and never with Ben.

Irritated with myself? All the time.

I shook the childish thought from my head. Petty.

"Looks like he stayed," I said, motioning the slept-in sheets around me. "He must have gotten a call or something."

Ben nodded. "Such a hard worker. So much evil out there, and he has to deal with the worst of them."

The spark rose again, and the insecure part of me wondered if Ben was speaking in a veiled reference about me. Yeah, petty. Petty and stupid.

"He's a hero, for sure," I said, keeping the sarcasm I wanted to convey out of my voice.

Raymond was back in casual jeans and sweatshirt, and the three of us left the house. I checked and Lor was still sleeping, so I didn't wake her.

As we made our way to the Lexus, Jack pulled up to the curb in his standard-issue cop Ford.

"Oh, good, he's back in time to join us," Ben said.

It would be nice to see Jack, and I'd be happy to have him join us, but did Ben have to sound like what had been a trip of duty had now become one of pleasure?

But Jack wasn't alone. Frank Botz, Jack's partner and wearer of cartoon-character ties, got out of the passenger side. Today Frank was sporting his Homer Simpson tie, one of my favorites.

There was an off chance that they'd just finished up whatever case they'd caught that had Jack leaving my bed and decided to both swing by for breakfast, but I knew that was highly doubtful.

This was not going to be good.

Instinctively, I took a step in front of Raymond, as if shielding him from the detectives' views.

"Jack! Frank! We're heading out to breakfast. Join us," Ben said, obviously not quite able yet to read Jack's cop face as I could.

There would be no breakfast out today.

"Can't do it, Ben. Sorry," Jack said to his father, then turned to me. "Anna, Raymond, we need to take you both into the station for questioning."

Raymond stepped out from behind me, even though I tried to stay him with my hand like he was a toddler.

"Why? What's happened?" I asked.

Frank looked at Jack. "At least it hasn't hit the news yet," he said.

Jack shook his head. "It may have. Anna isn't one to have her ear to the ground for this sort of thing."

"But it would have been on the sports channels," Frank said, and my skin started to prickle. Central Iowa had played last night. Had something come out about Raymond?

Jack shrugged. "Yeah, that's true. Maybe it hasn't broken yet."

I felt I'd been insulted in some way, but wasn't sure how. "What the hell, you guys. What's going on?"

Frank motioned to Jack in a "be my guest" kind of way.

"Lion LaGasse is dead. And you were the last person he was seen with."

Well, shit.

I guessed Lor would have a different kind of statement to prepare for the press.

Seventeen

❖

I TURNED TO RAYMOND. "Do not say a word. Not one word."

"Christ," Jack mumbled.

Frank took a step forward. "Anna, why don't you and your friend just come with Jack and me down to the station and we can get this all straightened out?"

"Hannah darling—"

"It's okay, Ben," I said. Even as I said it, I was thinking that the days of reassuring Ben that Jack wouldn't really arrest me were behind us.

Maybe not.

I slid a glance at Raymond to see his body tense up, and I knew he wasn't thinking about Lion LaGasse's death. He was thinking about taking a trip to a police station when he'd just barely been cleared in a point-shaving scandal in Iowa.

"We won't be going to the station with you and Jack, Frank. Sorry," I said to Jack's partner.

Both detectives gave me a look. Frank's full of surprise. Jack's was one of...resignation, I guess.

"The station is going to be crawling with press when word of his death gets out, if it isn't already."

"It's out," Jack said.

I nodded and continued, "And there is no way Raymond is walking into that station house. You want to talk to us both, you can come on in. But unless you have a warrant, we will not be accompanying you."

"Fuck," Jack said under his breath, turning away from Raymond and me.

"Hannah, maybe you should go with Jack. He's only doing his job," Ben said. I tried to school my features before I addressed him. I didn't want him to know how much his words hurt me, how small and childish they made me feel. Like my parent had sided with my sibling over me or something.

I cleared my throat. "I know he is, Ben. But I need to do my job too, and that is…protecting this family."

Raymond looked at me. "Family now?"

I shrugged. "I promised your mom I'd look after you. That you'd be safe with me, far from Bubba Kinsey or L'il Roy. And what, you're in a police station a week after you get here?"

"I got no problem talking to them," he said, doing a chin nod toward Jack and Frank.

"Me neither, but here. Not at the station. If we're not met at the door by press, it'll leak out that we were there." I looked at Jack as I finished, "This is going to be big news. Huge. Anybody who was within a mile of Lion last night will be swarmed. Right?"

"Yeah, but—" Raymond started.

"Raymond, Jack's not just a cop I sleep with." Jack raised a brow at that description, but I continued, "He's a homicide detective."

"Yeah? So?" Raymond said.

"When Jack comes knocking on your door, and there's a dead body, it's because…"

"Holy shit, he was murdered?" Raymond said.

I owned a large home in a pretty swanky gated community, with lots of space between homes, but I really didn't want to have this conversation in the driveway where neighbors could see, if not completely hear.

"Listen," I said, turning back to Jack and Frank. "Come

inside. Let's have some coffee. Raymond and I will tell you what happened last night. If, after that, you still need to bring someone in, I'll go to the station with you. Not Raymond. Just me. Deal?"

There was a shared look between the two cops, and it made me think that perhaps I'd given them more than they'd thought they'd get, though less than they'd wanted.

"Deal," Frank finally said, and started moving toward the house.

Raymond followed, and I turned to help with Ben, but Jack was already there, his hand on his father's hunching back. Standing out of their way as they passed I said, "Ben, I'll text Jimmy and let him know you're going to be late. Lorelei can probably take you."

His hand came off his walker to wave away my words. "No. Tell Jimmy I'm not going to make it. I want to be here."

He didn't tack a "for you" on the end of that sentence, and it flashed through my mind that it might not be my side of the table that Ben would be sitting at.

"You can't join us, though, Ben," Jack said. "We need to keep it official, even if it's not at the station. Just Anna, Raymond, Frank, and me. Are you sure you don't want to meet Jimmy?"

Ben patted Jack's hand that was still on Ben's shoulder. "No, no. That's fine. I want to be here, even if I can't be in the room. I'll help Lorelei make us all some breakfast."

Jack and I shared a glance over Ben's head, both of us slightly amused at the thought of Ben helping Lor in the kitchen.

But it felt wrong, the look being shared, when Jack and I would momentarily be squaring off against each other.

Again.

I woke Lor and told her what was going on, and she took over alerting Jimmy for me, then ushered Ben into the kitchen.

I led Frank and Jack into the dining room, Raymond trailing after us.

"Separately," Frank said, indicating with a finger that Raymond and I should be split up.

"Not going to happen," I said, grabbing Raymond's arm and walking him to a long side of the rectangular table. We sat down next to each other. I placed my elbows on the table, clasping my hands together, like a student waiting for the teacher to begin.

Raymond rested his forearms along the arms of the chair, his body not giving away any of the tension he had earlier.

Frank and Jack shared another look, then Frank shrugged and took a seat at the table across from Raymond and me. Jack continued to stand, but leaned against the sideboard behind Frank, crossing his legs at the ankles and his arms across his chest.

Bad-cop move.

Frank leaned toward Raymond and me, arms placed open on the table, encompassing, welcoming almost.

Good cop.

"Let me do the talking," I said to Raymond, who only nodded and waved his hand nearest me in an "it's all yours" motion, before letting it drop back to the chair.

"How was he killed?" I asked Frank before the detective could speak.

"We're not sure yet," he said, and I felt a tiny bit of relief trickle through me.

"So maybe not a homicide at all?" I asked.

"No cause of death yet," he said, not really answering my question.

"And you need us for, what, a timeline or something?"

"Something like that," Frank said. He was running this show, not Jack, which was probably for the best.

"We left the Bellagio around four in the morning. Lion and I were the last two players to leave. Carla, Raymond, the dealer, and bartender were still there, but the other players had left. I drove him to the Wynn. I used the parking deck at the Bellagio.

I always park on the second floor, in row B if I can, in case you want to get their security cameras."

As I talked, Frank took his ever-present notebook from his sport coat pocket and started scribbling notes. When he stopped and looked up, he said, "2B at the Bellagio. Got it. You always park in the same spot? They got it reserved for you or something?"

I shook my head. "No. Luck. Superstition. Habit. Call it what you want."

He studied me for a minute. "Plus," I added, "then I never have to remember where I parked. I do it all over town, every casino." His brow furrowed, but this explanation seemed to sit better with him than the gambler's superstition one.

"And why were you the last two players to leave?" Frank asked.

"I know the runner of the game. I was talking with her."

"Carla Rossetti," Frank said. It was not a question.

"Yes."

"What were you talking about?" Jack asked. Frank twitched, and he glanced over his shoulder at Jack.

"Is that relevant?" I asked, and it seemed like Frank wanted to ask Jack the same thing. But in true partnership, Frank only turned back to me and nodded at me.

I thought back. "We talked about the game. If I thought the new players would want to play again, stuff like that." I wasn't sure how much Jack had said to Frank about Carla taking over Vince's games—how much Jack had really absorbed by sitting around the table playing cards when I'd discussed it with Raymond.

Knowing Jack, he'd absorbed everything.

"Were you discussing any money borrowed?" Jack asked.

"I know that's not relevant to Lion LaGasse being dead this morning," I said, not looking at Jack but at Frank.

I spoke over his muttered curse. "Lion used the bathroom

while I spoke with Carla. I saw him tip the bartender and the dealer as he came to the front of the room where Carla and I were."

Frank turned to Raymond. "And where were you during this time?"

"He was helping clear things up. Putting the chips in their case, moving chairs, stuff like that," I said.

"But in the same, main room?" Frank asked, and I nodded. I noticed Raymond heeded my warning and not only didn't say anything, but his body never even shifted. Not giving the police anything. Probably something learned early on Chicago's South Side.

"I don't mean to interrupt," Lorelei said, interrupting us. "Just thought maybe you could all use some coffee."

She had four mugs in one hand and a carafe of coffee in the other, which she settled on the sideboard not far from Jack's hip.

"Thanks, Lor," Jack and I said at the same time.

"Sure thing. And not to worry: Ben's fine with me in the kitchen. Jimmy has been notified that Ben's not coming. Ben's in the kitchen now having some toast. He's worried about you, is all."

I started to tell her that there was nothing to worry about when I realized she was addressing Jack, not me. Jack was getting the Ben update. Ben was sitting in the kitchen worrying about how his son was dealing with having to question his girlfriend—again—in a homicide case.

It was almost a physical blow, and it took every poker-honed muscle I had not to let it show. But when my eyes moved from Lor back to Jack, I saw that he read me. Knew exactly the cards I was holding.

Jack was hard to read, but I swear—though I didn't want to even consider it—that a look of pity flashed across his tired-looking face before he caught it and blank cop came back.

Seriously? Pity? Because Ben...what?

Liked Jack better than me?

Sheesh. What was I? Eight years old?

"Let me know when you're wrapping up and I'll do some eggs or something," Lor said, still addressing Jack, though she had the good grace to turn at that and include Raymond and me.

"Thanks," Raymond said, breaking his silence. I nodded my thanks, not really trusting my voice.

Which was ridiculous, because there was no way I was done talking.

But the thing was, Ben would have sided with me before. He *had* sided with me, at least the last time Jack brought me in for questioning over a murder.

Yeah, such was my life—this wasn't the first time Jack had come for me.

Frank asked me to go on, and I explained the drive back to the Wynn with Lion and dropping him at the front of the registration entrance. I took a perverse delight in mentioning the fact that Lion asked me to join him in his room.

"That wouldn't have been the night he was suggesting," Jack said when I finished. "He made it to his room, but collapsed inside the door."

"He showed no signs of anything when he left the car," I said, then thought on it. "I guess he was a little warm, maybe a little sweaty, but I just attributed that to…"

"Passion?" Jack said, with a straight face.

I wasn't sure eye rolling was advised during a police questioning, but I let it rip nonetheless. It couldn't be helped.

"The high of winning," I said.

"And he thought he was going to win even more than everybody's money?" Jack asked, gaining another glance from Frank. Raymond shifted in his chair, like he was settling in to enjoy the show.

"He knew from minute one that the only winnings he'd be

collecting were chips. We had an...understanding early in the evening."

"And what understanding was that?" Frank asked before Jack could.

"That we didn't like each other very much."

A chime went off, and Jack looked down at his phone, his fingers swiping rapidly. "Fuck," he said, then took two steps forward, placing his phone on the table, and sliding it across the table to stop in front of me. It was open to a gossip website with a picture of Lion and me on the red carpet. It was snapped when I'd put on my fake adoring smile and was looking into Lion's face, he looking slightly down into my eyes.

I looked at the headline.

Lion spends his last night with Black Widow.

Shit.

"I think it's time to move this amateur show to the station," Jack said, and I knew there'd be no arguing with him this time.

Eighteen

❖❖

JACK AND FRANK CAME BACK to me after they'd talked with Carla. When we'd arrived, they'd set me up in the room where I currently sat, made sure I was comfortable, then excused themselves when they were told by a patrolman that Carla was in a different room.

I could see from the frustration on their faces that she'd been no help, which wasn't surprising.

"She corroborated what you told us at your house, confirmed the names of the players. She didn't want to, but she knew they'd be on camera going to the room in the Bellagio. We've got a warrant being typed up as we speak to get those tapes. And any at the Wynn for Lion before and after he went with you. After that, she gave us the contact numbers of all the players. We're checking on those now."

I nodded, wondering why they looked so pissed. They had the names of the people in the room. Not that Lion's death—if it even *was* a homicide—would be connected to one of us. I had seen him safely home. Though I supposed one of the players, knowing Lion was the big winner with all that cash, could have followed us to the Wynn and done something to Lion after that.

Jack and Frank were keeping mum on Lion's condition when he'd entered his hotel suite, so at this point, I guessed anything was possible.

"How much weight do you have with her?" Jack asked, setting a cup of coffee in front of me and then taking a sip from his own. Frank also had a cup, and he straddled a chair at the end of the small table.

Yes, I was technically in an interrogation room with two cops and a dead body hanging over my head, but I wasn't being treated as a suspect or anything. In fact, I think I was there as more of a...*consultant* of sorts.

But that might have been what they wanted me to think.

"No weight with Carla at all. She saved my life." I waved at the both of the men, including them because they'd been there. Frank nodded. Jack waited. "I played in the game as a favor to her. Let her spread the word I'd be playing. Took her job offer to Raymond for her. I'm paying her back *a lot*... But then, I did tell you guys I thought she was the one who killed Paulie, when she hadn't, and...like I said, she did save my life."

"When is the debt paid in full?" Jack said, asking what I'd been wondering about myself.

"I'd say now," I said, and he nodded once, then took another sip of coffee.

"Okay," Frank said. "You don't carry any weight with her, and your slate is now clean. But will she listen to you? Take advice about this from you?"

"What advice are you suggesting I give her?"

"That she cooperate. Answer some questions."

"About last night? I was there the whole time Lion was. I could probably tell you anything she could about the game."

Frank looked from me to Jack, a silent message passing between them.

"Can you tell us everyone that Carla contacted about playing in her game? To whom, of those people, did she mention that Lion would be playing?" Frank asked.

I sat back in the hard chair and took a sip of coffee. "No, I can't tell you any of that," I said, knowing why Carla had kept her mouth shut.

"Can you get her to tell us?" Jack asked.

I shook my head. "No. It'd be like asking a reporter to give up their source. That kind of stuff is privileged."

"Like a doctor," Frank said, with a hint of bemusement in his voice.

"Exactly," I said, then tried to elaborate. "Listen, this is not your first rodeo. You couldn't really expect she'd willingly give up those names. Having you know who was actually in the room will be bad enough for her."

"Why? If they're just people she invited to play poker? People who weren't even there. It's not like she's a low-level dealer giving up the kingpin of the cartel."

"Actually, it *is* kind of like that. Except we're not dealing with murderers and drug dealers." At least I didn't think we were—I was never really sure how Mr. Chow became…Mr. Chow. "But the essence remains the same. These are people who don't want anyone else to know what they're doing, even though it's just a high-stakes poker game."

"Where people die," Jack added. "High stakes indeed."

"Once," I said, then realized how ridiculous I sounded. We both sounded.

"Anna, in the short time I've know you, there have been five dead bodies that…surround you," Frank said.

I was about to argue with them, but then quickly did the math in my head. Danny, Saul, Paulie, Vince, and now Lion. Shit.

Bluffing, I waved a hand of dismissal. "But only one was because of a poker game."

The words sounded as stupid to me as I imagined they sounded to Jack and Frank. Their expressions proved it.

Jack leaned toward me, putting his elbows on the table. If it had been a different location—and a different man—I would have thought he wanted me to clasp his hands with mine. But no, he just wanted to get his point across to me. Strongly.

"Okay, here's the thing. Yes, it'll suck for her...*business* to give us those names. Nobody wants us calling them about a game they were invited to but didn't even attend. Doesn't make them too hot to take another one of Carla's calls. I get that."

I nodded, drank some coffee, and waited for Jack to go on. I suspected he knew exactly what he was going to say to me when he'd walked in the door.

"And she may take a hit on the games for it. They may go away entirely." He waited to see how I'd react to that.

Not good, but I didn't let it show. The truth was, Vince had run a good game, and Carla showed that she was going to continue in his path, but if it folded I'd be merely inconvenienced. I played in casinos all the time, and could easily make a call to one of my fellow pros and be invited to any and all private games that I could handle.

Granted, none of those options had the one thing that kept me going back to Vince's games—that I could pay off my debt as JoJo.

But now that JoJo was gone, that didn't need to be a consideration anymore. Right?

"But let's face it," Jack continued when he didn't get a rise out of me. "Those games are not where Vince made the big chunk. There were...by-products of the games that were lucrative, that's true." He might as well have added "Isn't that right, *JoJo*?" to the end of that sentence.

"The bottom line is Carla's a survivor; she'll regroup if the games go under—which might not even happen. The loan sharking alone will make her a very rich woman, if she keeps even half of Vince's business."

"But why would she want to give up any of it?" I said. "I mean, she's not heartless, and I'm sure Lion being at her game in his last hours has shaken her, but you're basically asking her to take a dive on her livelihood to give you a few names that may or may not even pan out to anything. The people she called who weren't even at the game? It feels like a crazy long shot even to me. I mean, I'm sure she's all for social justice and all that, but—"

"Long shot or no, we need the names of everybody who would have known where Lion was going to be after his charity event."

I leaned forward, elbows on the table, looking first at Frank, then at Jack. "Tell you what, I'll make you a deal." They looked at each other, then Frank nodded for me to go on. "I'll talk to Carla, try to get her to give up those names and numbers. I won't guarantee that she'll go for it, but I'll give it a good try."

"In exchange for?" Jack asked.

"You keep Raymond's name out of it. No press, no reports, nothing that could be leaked anywhere."

Again they exchanged a look, one that I took as not encouraging. Thinking I'd sweeten the pot, I said, "Look, you've already got the sacrificial lamb to throw to the press. Me. People saw me with Lion at his event last night; those photos are going to be all over today. You can say you know I was at the game and you would be speaking with the others. Give out no other names, especially not Raymond's."

"Deal," Frank said. Maybe too quickly, and I wondered if perhaps they'd had no intention of releasing any names at all.

"I don't mean just today, or the next few days. I mean ever," I added.

"We can't promise where this investigation will take us," Jack said.

"I get that. I'm just asking that you don't put his name on anything official unless you absolutely have to. Use 'Player A' or 'Doorman' or whatever. Like you would for a confidential informant."

Jack let out a sigh, one I knew well. It meant he didn't like it, but he was going to agree. Frank must have known it too, because he gave a short nod.

"Deal."

Nineteen

❖❖

CARLA LOOKED A LOT LESS freaked out than I probably did, though I tried to hide it.

Frank had led me to a small room exactly like the one we'd just left, and let me in to join Carla. He'd closed the door as he left, saying we'd have privacy. There was no mirror or anything that could have been a two-way, but I did notice a camera mounted in the corner, which I had to assume was on.

I would also assume we were being bugged.

Not that Carla and I needed to discuss how we'd conspired to kill Lion, but I kind of felt like I should be talking in code, or writing instead of talking or something cryptic like that.

Cops, man—they can make you paranoid.

"Jesus Christ, can you believe my luck?" Carla said to me by way of greeting.

Personally, I was thinking Carla and I were having a little better luck than Lion LaGasse, but I kept that to myself, pushing the thought aside.

Which I'd pretty much done since being informed of his death. I didn't particularly like the man—okay, he was a complete ass—and had only spent an evening in his company, but I didn't want to think about him lying in the morgue or, more likely, on the coroner's table while they figured out a cause of death.

Yeah, no. I *really* didn't want to think about that.

But the fact was he was a man in the prime of his life, at the top of his profession, with the world at his feet. I should be mourning this loss a little more than I was.

"What did you tell them?" Carla asked. There was a slight accusatory tone, and I had to remind myself that we had nothing to hide.

"Basically the timeline, so they could start working backward. When we left the Wynn, when we left the suite at the Bellagio, that kind of stuff."

She looked at me closely, then seemed to relax. "Yeah, I guess they'd need that," she said. "Did they tell you how he died?"

I shook my head. "I don't think they know yet. Or at least they're saying they don't."

She snorted at that. I was guessing Carla had more experience with police holding on to information than I did. Although, given the past two months and my involvement with the Las Vegas Metro Police Department—and one of its homicide detectives—maybe not.

"Did they send you in here to get me to spill?"

I nodded once. "But you do what you need to do."

"Yeah? You're not going to go to bat for your boyfriend?"

I shrugged. "I understand you not wanting to give out names of people you contacted to play. But Carla, I think you have to cooperate with them. Show them that you're not stonewalling them. I mean, they could make this very unpleasant for you as the organizer of that game."

She looked at me closely again, her head tilting. Summing up if this was my tactic all along. Of course it was.

"And maybe it pisses off a small bunch of players, and you don't get them back. But I'm telling you, if you don't cooperate, show you're willing to help, they are going to lean on you. Hard. There is no sense worrying about pissed-off potential players if you can't run a game in this town. They can make that happen."

"Yeah, maybe," she said. "My lawyer should be here any minute. I'll see what he says about giving them the names. And hope that it doesn't kill any future business."

"You called your lawyer?" I asked. I was somewhat surprised, but I guessed I shouldn't have been. Carla was probably a lot smarter about this than I was.

Although I could only imagine how pissed Ben would have been at me if I'd told Jack I was lawyering up.

"Of course. You didn't?"

"No," I said, feeling stupider by the second.

"Well, Marvin can do you too, if you want. Unless you've got someone you usually work with?"

I shook my head. "No, I don't have anyone." I didn't add that I didn't feel I needed one, and given Carla's look of almost pity, I kept my mouth shut.

"They knew about your guy being there, of course," she said.

"Yeah," I said, knowing they had that information early. Like days before the game.

"Might not be too smart sleeping with a cop," she said.

"Yeah, might not be."

She sat back in her chair and glanced at the camera. "But I've seen him in action, so I get it."

Carla had worked with Frank and Jack recently to help catch Paulie Gonads' killer.

"Yeah," I said again. Really, it was about all I could say.

I could tell she wanted to ask me more—probably about how much of JoJo's work Jack knew about—but she had the good sense not to bring it up.

"I gave them names and contact info for the bartender and dealer," she said.

We spent the next ten minutes comparing the night and timeline, not coming up with anything different than I'd told Jack and Frank.

A hard knock came at the door and Jack opened it, looking unhappy. "Lawyer's here," he said to Carla. Nodding at me, he said, "Let's go."

"Marvin's going to help Anna out too," Carla said, earning a thunderous look from Jack to me.

"That has yet to be decided," I said as Carla's lawyer, Marvin, made his way into the room, setting a briefcase on the table and looking from Carla to me.

"Would you be Anna Dawson?" he asked me. I nodded. "Then I have business to discuss with you, whether you choose to have me join you when you speak to the police regarding Mr. LaGasse's death or not."

I sat up in my seat, surprised. "Umm, okay."

"Thank you, detective," he said to Jack, clearly dismissing him.

Jack shot me a look, then left the room.

"Marvin Harrison," he said to me, shaking my hand. "Harrison and Associates."

Marvin was a man in his late fifties with salt-and-pepper hair worn in an expensive cut, and wearing an even more expensive suit. He had a deep tan and a worldly polish. He kind of reminded me of Vince, which made sense. I was guessing he had been Vince's lawyer too. And by the way he was dressed, he and Vince probably had Lorenzo in common, too.

He asked Carla and me a few questions to get caught up. Obviously surprised that the cops let me sit and talk with Carla, Marvin looked at me with something between admiration and suspicion when Carla clued him in on my relationship with Jack.

"I'm happy to sit in with you while you speak with the police," he said to me. "Whether you end up retaining my services or not."

"Thank you. I've spoken with them already, and I'm guessing when I'm done here, I'll be leaving." Yeah, it was a guess, but I didn't think Frank and Jack would spend too much more time on me. There would be other stuff coming down, not the least of which would be a cause of death.

"Whatever you choose," he said. "The reason I'm glad you're here is my office was going to contact you today."

I leaned toward him. "For?" My mind spun with things an expensive (guessing from his suit and that he worked for Vince and Carla) lawyer could want with me.

"You are named in Vince Santini's will. We'll be doing a small gathering to read the will on Monday at my offices." He pulled out a business card from his briefcase, wrote down a time on the back, and handed it to me.

Dumbfounded, I took the card, staring at it like a speechless idiot. Which is exactly what I was.

He turned to Carla. "You should be there, too, of course." Carla only nodded, as if she was expecting it.

That made one of us.

"And I have reason to believe," Marvin said, his attention turning back to me, "that you may know the whereabouts of a Raymond Joseph?"

My protection instincts came out, as they had when Frank and Jack wanted to question Raymond.

"And if I do?" I said.

"He should also be in attendance on Monday, but my office was having a hard time locating him. There was a note that perhaps you would be aware of his location."

What the hell?

"What the fuck?" Carla said. "What do you mean he should be there? Is he in Vince's will?"

"I can't really answer that," Marvin said, although he pretty much had. Why else would Raymond's attendance be requested at a will reading?

"When..." My head was spinning with dates and events. "When would Vince have created this will?"

"That will become clear on Monday," Marvin said.

"Shit. Just how many people are invited to this thing?" Carla asked. It then occurred to me that Carla probably thought, depending on the timing, she would be a—if not the only, or at least main—beneficiary in Vince's will. He didn't have any family, and Carla and Paulie had been his right and left hands for nearly twenty years.

She was probably assuming the will was quite old, when she was still in Vince's good graces. But if Raymond was mentioned then that surely wasn't the case.

"Would you be able to give my office Mr. Joseph's contact information?" Marvin asked, ignoring Carla's gaping mouth.

"How about if I just have him accompany me?"

Marvin didn't seem really happy with that option, but I didn't budge.

Finally he relented, and I promised to have myself, and Raymond, at his office on Monday at three.

"Now," he said, turning to Carla, "your first foray into Vince's territory hasn't ended so well, has it?"

Carla's body language said "fuck you" to Marvin, but she only nodded.

I said my goodbyes to them both and left the room, hoping I was going to be able to go home and not take Marvin up on his offer of representation.

Twenty

❖❖

I DIDN'T NEED MARVIN. Or at least not yet.

Frank and Jack were too busy to deal with me, or take me home, so they assigned a uniformed police officer to bring me home in a squad car.

At first I was grateful, not wanting to be subjected to Frank and Jack pumping me for any info I may have gleaned from Carla on the ride home. Info I didn't have.

But as we neared the gatehouse to my subdivision, and saw the crowds of media vans and reporters, I cursed out loud. Just how I wanted to be plastered on the news—riding in the back of a squad car.

I didn't want to think it, but couldn't help but wonder if Jack and Frank had thought about that and wanted me to feel some pressure?

I thought Jack would get a kick out of the Lion-and-me photos when I told him what a jackass the guy turned out to be.

Now that Lion was in the coroner's office, and I was being questioned, we probably wouldn't get around to laughing about it.

But Jack wouldn't want me to be thrown to the media wolves. Would he?

"Shit," the police officer who was driving said, echoing my words. "Is there a back entrance?"

"No," I said.

"Would you like us to go around the block?" the other officer asked, turning to speak to me through the grate divider. The grate to keep prisoners from getting unruly.

I toyed with the idea of having them bring me to Jimmy's house, but I'd eventually have to go home. Besides, I wouldn't be surprised if Jimmy and Gus weren't already at my place, hanging out to get the scoop.

"No, that's okay. I really want to get home," I said to the officer.

They both seemed so young to me. Probably mid to late twenties, so they were likely only seven or eight years younger than me, but I felt older than my thirty-four years. And today I felt *way* older.

"You could slide down," the driver suggested. But I didn't want to do that. For one thing, the windows weren't tinted and the gate was a slow opener, so there would be plenty of chances for a photographer to get a photo of me sitting on the floor of a police cruiser. Secondly, it just screamed "guilty."

"I'm good," I said, holding my head up, looking straight ahead, ignoring the cameras that got close to the car as we went through the gate.

Eddie, the guard on duty, waved to me, then held up his hands in an "I tried" way about the reporters. I gave him the tiniest of nods so he'd know I saw him.

Good guy, Eddie. We'd chat every now and then when I'd be getting home in the early morning from playing poker and he'd be bored out of his mind.

I could hear the reporters' questions, ranging from "When did you last see Lion LaGasse?" all the way to "Are you pregnant with his child?"

"Bloodsuckers," the passenger-side officer said as we made our way through.

I was about to agree and then thought about the fact that

it may have been many of the same people who I posed in front of last night, with Lion happy to soak up the spotlight for his foundation.

A useful tool then. Bloodsuckers now.

Jimmy's and Gus's cars were indeed in my large circular drive, and the police car pulled as close to my front door as possible, navigating around them. I thanked them for the ride, then exited the car.

When I got inside, I moved into the dining room, where everyone was sitting around the table, cups of coffee in front of them. Ben looked behind me, and didn't even try to hide his look of disappointment when he saw I was alone.

"He had to stay at the station," I said to Ben.

He nodded. "Of course."

Stung as I was, my voice was gentle when I said, "He might not be over for a few days. I think this is going to keep him pretty busy."

"It's important work, what he does," Ben said. He didn't mean anything by it. I knew he didn't. So why did I take it as a personal jab?

"It's a zoo out there," I said to the group. To Raymond, I added, "You might want to stay in the house for a few days until this blows over."

He nodded. "It's not like I'll have to shift around my busy social calendar. And I'm doubting I'll have a job with Carla again."

I moved to sit beside him, shaking my head at Gus's offer of the coffee carafe. "Maybe. Maybe not. I think it's going to be a bit before she gets a game together again, but I don't think she has any knock on the job you did."

"How exposed am I?" he asked.

"So far, not at all. The police aren't giving out the names of anyone at the game…except mine."

All eyes turned to me. "Why you?" Lorelei asked.

I shrugged. "Lion's camp knew he was playing cards with me. We were together earlier in the evening. It's a jump everybody was bound to make anyway. By releasing my name, and that they're aware of the other players and speaking with them, the police are giving the press something."

"And not giving them me," Raymond said.

"Not if they don't have to," I said. "It's not in their best interest, anyway. The more they can keep to themselves, the less they muddy the waters."

"So, what, you're taking all the media heat? No other player? Or anybody else who was in the room?" Jimmy asked.

"Yeah, she is. For me," Raymond said, then rose from the table and left the room.

I started to stop him, but Jimmy put a meaty hand on my arm. "Let him digest it."

I stayed in my seat.

Lorelei, who had her phone next to her, her finger on it, said, "Do you want to say something? I can open a Twitter account for you if you want."

Twitter? I had avoided all that crap, though lots of professional poker players worked the social media game well.

Because of JoJo I turned down endorsements, so really, there was no reason to promote myself. I was happy to stay away from all that.

"No," I answered her. "But I think I'll write up some kind of statement, have you read it, then send it…um, somewhere, I guess."

"I can take care of that for you," she said, and I thanked her.

"I'd kind of like to wait until we know what actually happened," I said. At their questioning looks, I added, "When I left the station, they still weren't sure how he died."

"I think they know now," Raymond said from the doorway. "You better come into the book room."

The book room was what we called the room with all the

televisions. Several of them, just like a book room at a casino, with comfy recliners and even a little concession stand area that Lor kept stocked with snacks and beverages.

We all left the dining room and made our way into the book room, me bringing up the rear with Ben. He went to the recliner that he always used in the front row, and every one else grabbed a seat. I was about to find a chair until Jack's face splashed on several of the screens.

It wasn't just Jack. It was him and Frank standing behind someone who was at a podium. The chyron read *Dr. Alexander Prescott, Clark County Coroner's Office.*

The man was speaking and there was a dash in the room for a remote, which Lor found, then turned the volume up.

"...levels of toxicity in Mr. LaGasse's system. Though the final toxicology report is yet to come, it is the belief of our office that Mr. LaGasse's death was caused by heart failure brought on by unnatural causes. We have informed the Las Vegas Metro Police Department that we believe foul play may have been a factor."

There was an audible gasp in the room where the press conference was being held.

And dead silence in my book room.

Twenty-One
❖❖

"JUST FACEBOOK, THEN," Lorelei said. She sat across from me at the desk we shared in the office. "And we'll do a page and set up everything so people can't just randomly comment or anything."

"Just Facebook," I said. "Nothing else. No Twitter. No... whatever."

She nodded, her head bent, reading. "Just Facebook." She handed back the piece of paper after she finished. "I like this. It sounds good."

I reread the statement I'd prepared. It was simple, stating that I'd met Lion yesterday, had enjoyed the evening as his guest at his foundation event, he had joined me and several others for a poker game after the event, and that we had parted after the game. I was stunned and saddened to hear of his death and I was cooperating with Metro to help piece together a timeline of events. That I was, to my knowledge, not a person of interest.

That last part Lor wanted me to add, saying it would just head off any follow-up questions asking the same thing.

I wasn't sold on adding it—not convinced it was the truth, but as long as I had the "to my knowledge" part, I felt I was covered.

There were a few more lines about praying for his friends and family, and what a great guy he was, and how the golf world would miss him.

Stretching it a bit, but no reason to speak ill of the dead.

"Okay, you now have a page, and I'll have the statement up in a second. Email it to me so I don't have to retype it."

I did that and waited for a few minutes while Lor tapped away at her side of the desk.

I resisted the temptation to go online and look at news coverage of Lion's death. Instead I pulled out my phone and scrolled through the contacts until I found the one I wanted. One I'd never used before and was hoping I'd have no need to ever use.

"Yes?" the woman on the other end answered. She would know who was calling, but was being cautious.

Halia Joseph was a smart woman who had raised a smart son.

"Halia, it's Anna Dawson. Are you free to talk?"

I heard the sound of a door closing. "I am now," she said.

"I'm not sure if you've seen the news, or made the connection, or spoken with Raymond today, but—"

"Dear God in heaven, Raymond wasn't with you and Lion LaGasse last night, was he?"

So she knew some of it, but not all. "Yes, he was. For part of the evening, anyway."

"Sweet Jesus," she said, and I heard some rustling, like maybe she was sitting down.

"He's not involved," I said quickly, then thought perhaps I shouldn't have.

"Are you?" she asked, no sound of relief coming at my statement.

"Not really. I was the last person that spoke with him before he collapsed, so the police have—"

"Did they talk to Raymond? Do they know...who he is? About what happened in Iowa?"

Yes, intimately, because of Jack. "Remember Jack Schiller,

who was with me in Chicago?"

"Yes?"

"He's actually the detective on the case, so he was already aware that Raymond was at the poker game where Lion was last...um, active."

"Why was Raymond there? He doesn't play poker." A pause, but before I could answer, she plowed on. "You don't have my boy playing poker for a living out there, do you? You swore to me—"

It was my turn to cut her off. "Raymond wasn't playing, no. He was working the game, sort of a host. The woman who runs the game needed an extra set of hands, and hired Raymond."

"A...*host?*"

"That's right. A small, private game, where people keep their business to themselves. Even if somebody had recognized him, they wouldn't have said anything."

To my knowledge, the only person who had recognized Raymond had been Lion.

And he sure wasn't talking.

I shook the thought away. It sounded too much like motive.

"So, he's okay?"

"Yes, he's fine. He's here in the house with me somewhere, probably watching basketball."

A long pause, then, "Okay."

I relaxed a little bit. "I just wanted to give you a heads-up, seeing as my face has been all over the news. Let you know that Raymond's not involved—other than the police know he was there—and is fine."

"You told me you'd take care of my boy," she said.

I thought back to my deal with Jack and Frank. "I am, Halia."

"Looking like he might have been better off staying in Chicago, taking his chances with L'il Roy."

She didn't mean that, I knew, but I let it go. "Well, I won't keep you, Halia," I said. "I just wanted to keep you posted. So far, Raymond's settling in fine. He's looking at finishing his degree out here at UNLV next fall."

More rustling. "That's all I wanted for my boy—that he get that degree."

"I know," I said. "I think that's what he wants too. He'll get it."

A large sigh from her, then, "I didn't mean that about him being better off in Chicago."

"I know," I said.

"I know you're trying to do right by him."

Lor was typing away on her laptop, and probably wasn't even paying attention to me, and knew pretty much the whole story anyway, but still I swiveled my chair around and replied softly, "Well, I did wrong by him, too. I'm just trying to...make amends."

Make amends. Twelve-step speak to be sure. And yet true.

"I appreciate the call," she said.

"No problem. If anything changes, you'll be the first to know, but I'm pretty sure his name won't come out."

"Some advantages to having a detective in your bed, I guess."

It was the most...familiar Halia had been to me, but I wasn't stupid enough to think she wanted to be girlfriends and talk about the men in our beds.

"Some advantages, yes," I said. "Some drawbacks, too."

A small chuckle on her end—a sound I hadn't heard from Halia in my limited time with her. "I'll bet."

We said our goodbyes, and I disconnected as I swiveled back to face Lor, whose eyes were glued to the screen in front of her.

"All set?" I asked.

Her red hair swung as her head came up, a look of surprise on her face. "It's already been shared twenty thousand times."

"Are you shitting me?" I said, standing and moving from

my chair around the desk to look over her shoulder.

She hit refresh and the number went up by another three thousand.

"You're going to break the Internet," she said. "You're like a Kardashian."

"Good God," I whispered. It was what I wanted, in a way, to have the statement out there, to try and quell the calls and reporters at the gate. And to also throw the scent—hopefully nonexistent at this point—off Raymond's attendance at last night's game.

As the main picture, Lor had used a photo of me at a final table. I was the only player seated—the only player left—with a pile of cash in front of me. I was wearing the same black suit I'd worn last night, my hair done similarly. In the smaller pic, Lor had chosen a candid of me at a poker table, looking more like I did day to day. I recognized the poker room at the Aria, but wasn't sure when—or how—the picture was taken. My hair was in a ponytail and I was looking down at my cards, wearing a jean jacket and a black tee underneath.

It was indeed a good thing my JoJo days were over, because between me having a Facebook presence that was being shared over twenty—now thirty—thousand times, and the pictures from Lion's foundation red carpet, I was out of the poker circle and now firmly entrenched in celebrity gossip land.

Maybe I *was* a Kardashian.

I moved away from behind Lor, back to my side of the desk.

"Stop refreshing," I said.

"I don't think I can," she said, looking up at me. "This is amazing."

"Not in a good way," I said. "If you need to keep looking, just don't tell me."

She nodded, but her eyes immediately went back to her screen.

"I think I'll go watch some games with Raymond," I said,

getting back out of my chair. No longer wanting to be in the same room as…Facebook. (And yes, I knew *it* was everywhere, but not for me…computer or nothing. I purposely had Lor put no social media apps on my phone when she set it up.)

Then I remembered one little detail about last night's fiasco. One that had nothing to do with Lion LaGasse being dead.

"Oh, yeah," I said, getting Lor's attention away from my ever-growing numbers. "I borrowed money last night to stay in the game. I'll need to repay it within the week."

She looked at me, somewhat confused, but I just continued. "Can you get me twenty thousand by Friday? Actually, it'll be twenty-six thousand with the vig."

"Vig?" she said.

"Interest."

More confusion, and my heart started to race. Lor had recently told me I was very well off, but I knew a lot of it was in investments. Could she not get her hands on money that quickly? Would the vig go into week two and cost me another six thousand? Or longer?

Thoughts rushed through my mind of a suitcase at the back of my closet filled with wigs and clothes I would never wear in a million years.

JoJo hair and clothes.

"What? Do we not have it?"

"We have it," she said.

"But it's not liquid?"

"It's liquid. Or that much is, anyway."

My shoulders slumped in relief. I didn't feel it as much as watch Lorelei notice it. "I'm just…surprised, that's all," she said.

"Why? I lose all the time," I said. I won a lot too—that was why we lived the way we did, but Lor knew this.

"But you don't borrow money to keep playing. When you lose, you come home. Is this because of Lion LaGasse?"

Yes, but not the way she meant. I did want to keep playing

to beat him, but I also borrowed money to stay in games frequently. Most times staying in meant a comeback win.

Sometimes it meant JoJo.

I saw the moment Lor got it, watched as her mind raced back, trying to put other pieces together. I could have imagined it, but I also saw the moment her estimation of me as a person went down a couple of notches.

And this was a woman who routinely held interventions in my honor.

Shame. A feeling I hated and felt all too often. One that I tried to avoid by letting JoJo do her thing.

It seldom worked.

"So, you've...borrowed before," she said.

"Yes," I said. I knew she wanted to get into it. Had sensed that something had changed, that things were different.

They were, and at some point I'd be able to talk about it all, tell her everything. But today was not that day.

"So, you can have the money by Friday?"

"I'll have it," she said. Sensing my reluctance to talk further, she turned back to the screen.

I squeezed her shoulder, said, "Thanks, Lor," and left the room.

Twenty-Two

❖

I FELT HEAT AT MY BACK and a hand on my hip.

"What time is it?" I whispered, trying not to come fully awake. I didn't dislodge his hand, but I didn't turn into him either.

"Four," Jack said, sounding tired. Which was basically twenty-four-seven Jack.

He had crawled into my bed in the wee hours of the morning other times. And I'd crawled in with him after playing poker late. Sometimes we both went to sleep quickly, exhausted.

Sometimes we didn't get to sleep at all.

Not really sure where I stood with Jack at the moment, I kept my body facing away from him and my voice neutral when I said, "Late. Break in the case?"

"Not really. And yeah, late."

That was all he said. No "go back to sleep," but no other movement, either.

After a few minutes I could tell he was still awake, but I didn't say another word. I certainly didn't pump him for details on the case. Finally his hand on my hip moved. I was waiting for it to leave my body, for him to turn his back to me and settle into some much-needed sleep. But instead of leaving, his hand slipped under the tee I wore to sleep in and up to my bare waist.

"You tired?" he said, obviously asking a different question.

I rolled over to face him. I'd left the nightlight in the attached bathroom on for him, and its dim glow allowed me to just shake my head instead of speaking.

The corners of his mouth turned up, but I wouldn't go as far as saying he smiled. There was pain behind his eyes, and I knew another dead body wasn't the only cause.

I brought my hand up out of the covers and placed my palm on his cheek, trying to take some of the pain, but knowing he wouldn't let me.

Just like he couldn't take mine, though he gladly would if I'd let him.

But our pain was our own. Self-inflicted, mostly, at least for me.

I slid my leg up his, hitching my calf over his hip, his hand moving from my waist down my hip and along my leg, raising it higher.

Our eyes stayed on each other, and we didn't say a word as he moved my panties aside and pushed inside me.

It was slow and tender, our bodies moving in a smooth motion. No urgency, no hard pounding against each other. In fact, other than where we were joined, we barely touched.

His hips rocked to me and I met him, my hand still on his cheek, the bristle of his two-day-old beard tickling my palm.

"Johanna," he whispered, and my throat got tight at the exquisiteness of being with Jack. Tears threatened my eyes at the pain of being with Jack.

"Jack," I whispered back, trying to convey more, but failing. But I think he got it. His cheek moved under my hand and he kissed my palm.

I felt a tear finally forming and sliding down my cheek as Jack rolled me to my back and moved inside me.

He brought a hand between us. Not needing much, I gasped and clenched around him, and he took another few thrusts before he joined me.

We lay like that for a while—Jack on top of me, elbows and forearms holding him up, his hands framing my face.

With his thumb he swiped away the residue of the single tear I'd shed.

He didn't ask why I'd cried, probably because he knew I wouldn't tell him.

Couldn't tell him something I didn't understand myself. I was guessing he knew that, too.

After a while—and yet still too soon—he moved off me, pulled his boxers up, and settled back where he'd been on his side, facing me.

I turned to him, not wanting to lose sight of him—almost fearing it would be the last time.

I felt like that with Jack a lot. Too much, but I knew that was on me.

"Want to talk about it?" I said.

He shook his head. "Not now. I'll tell you what I can in the morning."

I didn't point out it was the morning, just nodded.

"It's weird, though, hey?" I said.

An actual, real smile from him. "There's a whole hell of a lot that's weird with us, babe, but what in particular?"

I nudged his bicep playfully, then tucked my hand with my other one under my cheek, like a little kid going to sleep. "That you keep pulling cases that somehow involve me."

"Involve you?" he said, but his voice was soft.

"Not *involve* me, not as, you know, an actual suspect or anything." Before he could add his two cents to that, I went on. "I mean involve me peripherally. Friends, acquaintances, being at the scene, stuff like that."

"And you think it's weird that those cases keep ending up on my desk?"

I shrugged. "Well, yeah, don't you?"

He moved his hand under his cheek too, mirroring me.

Though there was no way Jack looked like an innocent child heading off to dreamland.

He probably didn't look like that even when he *was* an innocent child.

"I think the better question is, why are you *involved* in so many homicide cases? Peripherally or otherwise."

"Coincidence," I said without hesitating.

"Coincidence? Seriously? That's what you're going with?"

It was easy to nod—I believed it. Wasn't it coincidence?

"I know things have changed, Anna." Oh, he was back to Anna. I liked it better when he called me Johanna. "And you've really turned a corner…"

"Twenty-six days without placing a bet," I said quietly. More to myself than to him.

"Right. And I'm happy for you." He didn't say he was proud of me, and I was glad for that. "But the fact that you're around illegal activity—murder included—is less of a coincidence when you are involved in *any* kind of illegal activity."

"But I haven't—"

"Unlicensed backroom poker games are illegal."

If my hands hadn't been so comfy tucked under my head I would have waved his words away as inconsequential.

"It's not nothing, these games. You know that," he said.

I didn't want to admit it, but I knew Jack was right.

"Time to take a look at your life," Jack said. "And I say that knowing full well that I need to do the same."

He wasn't wrong. I *had* taken a hard look at my life recently, at Paulie Gonads' funeral. When I saw a bunch of degenerate gamblers and knew that if I didn't pull it together, that that would be my future.

"Twenty-six days," I repeated, still softly, and not with the same conviction I had a couple of seconds ago.

"Keep it going, babe," he said. He pulled the covers up over both of us and closed his eyes.

I watched him fall asleep, then continued to watch his face, about as at peace as he got, for a long time before I followed into dreamland.

Myself a long way from an innocent child, too.

Twenty-Three
❖❖

IF JACK MENTIONING that I needed to take a look at my life hadn't resonated then (and it had), sitting with Raymond in our book room watching his team play later that day sure did.

He was cool, not showing how much it was killing him to be sacked out on one of the cushy black leather recliners instead of being on the floor with his teammates, but I knew.

I felt like shit all over again for being the beginning of his downfall.

True, he got caught when he went rogue, but he only went rogue because I cut him off from JoJo.

The Wild Hogs played tough, but without Raymond they were no match for Duke, who took them out of the tournament.

A weird kind of stillness permeated the room when the announcers mentioned that perhaps it would have been a different outcome if Raymond Joseph had still been with the team.

Raymond didn't move, didn't respond, but it was like in cartoons where you could visibly see emotion pouring off him, like the dust cloud that always followed Pig-Pen. Only it wasn't dust coming off Raymond, but something much deeper.

And more dangerous.

Jimmy, who had joined us for brunch earlier and then the games, broke the tension. "Sorry, kid, but that guy's full of shit.

Duke would have still kicked your asses even if you was playing. They're just too deep."

It was my turn to stay still, waiting to see how Raymond responded.

He was sitting in a recliner a row down from mine—yes, we had stadium seating; Lor and I designed this room *right*. I could see the rise and fall of his shoulders, then they loosened. He glanced over his shoulder to Jimmy, who was sitting next to me. "Yeah, you're probably right," he said.

Jimmy shrugged, though Raymond had already turned back to the screen.

"The good thing is, kid, they didn't mention where you are now. Seems like if anything had leaked on where you were Friday night, now's the time to mention it."

That was true, and I nodded, reaching for the remote for the TV that had the audio pumping into the room. The other screens had other basketball games on, and a couple of NHL games at Jimmy's request. He must have had money on them.

I felt a tiny tingle in my fingers as I wondered who he'd bet, for how much, and all those other particulars that were no longer a part of my life.

Twenty-six days. Yeah, it felt like a lifetime. Probably longer than I'd ever gone without betting a sporting event.

I used my tingling fingers to turn to the golf tournament. It was a few weeks before the Masters, and the PGA Tour was in the Florida swing.

They were just starting their coverage of the final round and I kept it on for a few minutes, waiting to see if Lion was mentioned.

He most definitely was. The first fifteen minutes of coverage was a tribute to Lion, showing clips of amazing shots and Lion lifting trophies over his head, smiling and happy.

Several big-name players talked about looking up to Lion, emulating his swing, being in awe of his focus on the game.

I noticed not one talked about what a great guy he was. No mention of deep, abiding friendships; no funny anecdotes of shared jokes.

They showed pictures of him with his children when they were younger. I knew from all the news coverage that they were late teens now and didn't have a lot to do with Lion, living with their mom in New York. Besides that wife, there had been another, but neither of them were interviewed.

They showed a still of Lion and me on the red carpet Friday night, and a screenshot of my Facebook post.

No mention of any other players at the game, and especially none of Raymond.

"For once, no leaks," Jimmy said. "Sounds like no one knows you're in Vegas, kid."

"Thank God for that," I said.

"Well, we did have a deal," Jack said from the doorway, having just arrived. His eyes were glued on me.

I nodded and soaked in the sight of him, looking just as tired—more so—than he had yesterday.

When I'd woken up that morning he'd already been gone, so I'd never gotten the "I'll tell you later" part that he'd talked about when he'd joined me in bed.

And I'd been distracted from it very nicely.

I put the volume on mute and rose a little in my seat, taking my legs from beside me to the floor, making room for him.

"How's it going?" I asked.

"Slowly," he said, peeling off his leather jacket, which he tossed on one of the empty front-row seats. "Very fucking slowly."

He walked over to the concession stand area. "Anybody want anything?" he asked, and Jimmy, Raymond, and I shook our heads. He opened the little bar fridge and grabbed some cubes from the freezer area of it, plunking them into a highball glass.

Guess he was officially off duty for the day. Confirming my thought, he reached behind the bar and poured himself a healthy shot of Maker's Mark. "Ben?" he asked.

"Taking a nap," I said, and he nodded, pouring a splash more into his glass. He made his way to me and settled in, taking my legs from the floor and putting them across his lap so they were right back where they'd been.

It had a weird feeling to it—my guy home from work, fixing himself a drink, and getting comfy with me to tell me about his day.

Except we were in a family room converted to resemble a casino sports book, and instead of our kids surrounding us we had a twenty-two-year-old college dropout who had just been cleared by the FBI on point shaving and an eighty-year-old retired oddsmaker who probably had more money wagered on the games playing in front of us than Jack made in a year.

It wasn't just in March that my life was madness.

"So what's the scoop?" Jimmy said, asking Jack what I was dying to. Raymond twisted in his seat to look at Jack, his eyes cutting to me first.

"Still don't have a definite cause of death, but it's looking more and more like he was slipped something."

"So it was murder?" I said. That just seemed so fantastical to me. Random violence I could see, but the forethought to slip something to Lion that would kill him later—that was definitely some premeditated shit.

And I knew all about slipping things to people.

Jack was staring at me so intently that I physically moved away from him. His hands tightened on my legs, and I wondered if his using the words "slipped him something" had been intentional and for my benefit.

"Like he was poisoned?" Jimmy asked.

"Not officially classified as a murder case yet, but they think so. And yeah, poisoned. He had some other substances in his system, so we're unsure if it was just a bad mix or if it was meant to kill him."

"Jesus," I whispered. Not that it hadn't been real before—hell, thirty thousand shares on Facebook in a few minutes made it all crystal clear—but I guessed I held out some hope that it was just going to end up being a heart attack or something like that.

No such luck.

I'd played the game over in my head throughout the day, and more in-depth than I did after every losing game. But now my thoughts turned to the charity event.

"Man, so many people stopped by our table while we were eating. To say hello to him, shake his hand, whatever," I said. "And it was a crowded table anyway; it would have been easy for someone to put something on his food or in his drink."

"Pretty easy to do that, hey?" he said, staring at me.

I knew he didn't actually think I did anything to Lion LaGasse, but the way he held my legs on his lap, it was obvious that he wasn't happy about this turn of events. That Lion's death happened in a way that JoJo had done in the past. Although she used a basic Ambien or roofie cocktail, not something that could do actual harm to anyone.

"Coincidence." I repeated the word I'd said to him only hours ago in bed.

"One hell of a coincidence," he said. We had a staring contest for a few seconds, then I took my legs from his lap, which he let me do a little too easily. "We don't have a time estimate yet. Could have been at the charity thing, could have been at the game, might have been something fast acting."

"How fast acting? Because it would have to have been from leaving my car to getting to his suite."

"Yeah, well, there's a bit of a snag there too."

Great. Snags always seemed to be something to do with me.

"There's footage of you leaving the parking deck right about when you said you did, from the floor you said you'd dropped him off."

"Yeah," I said, sitting up in my chair now, feet planted firmly on the floor. Raymond slung his arm along the back of his chair as he turned even more toward Jack and me.

"Footage of him in the elevator. On his phone, texting. He leans against the wall, like he's shaky or something."

I thought back. "I don't think I watched him walk to the elevator. As soon as he got out of the car, I drove away."

"No tender goodnight kiss?" Jack asked, and I rolled my eyes at him. He quirked an eyebrow at me, and my heart did a tiny off beat. If Jack was raising a brow at me, I could believe that we were okay.

What was another murder in the course of true love, right?

"He gets off the elevator and hits a blind spot in camera footage."

"In a casino? I thought those places had cameras everywhere," Raymond said, echoing my thoughts.

"On the floor, yeah," Jimmy said. "But in the other common areas, not complete coverage. The hotel area is just like any other. Some have complete hallway coverage, some just at the elevator areas."

Jack studied Jimmy a bit, obviously wondering why Jimmy would know so much about casino security when he'd been retired for so many years. I'd given up guessing about Jimmy's extensive—and varied—knowledge a long time ago.

Jimmy just returned Jack's stare, giving a shrug. Jack turned back to Raymond and me. "Jimmy's right. There are blind spots. And no footage of LaGasse for twenty-six minutes." Twenty-six minutes? Weird that it was the same amount of days I'd gone without making a bet. Or weird that I was thinking about making a bet while Jack was talking about someone's last minutes of life.

"The cameras pick him up at a different elevator bank in the main casino and he heads up to his suite. He makes it down the hallway, now heavily leaning on the wall to keep his balance. Looks like he's really drunk, if you didn't know he was sober."

I nodded. After that first scotch during introductions, Lion had drunk a cola all night—as had most of the other players. Too much at stake to be heavily downing booze. Jack took a sip of his drink, and I could tell he was savoring the taste. I didn't know how long it'd been since he'd had any of the stuff.

Not twenty-six days, I was sure, but surely not since Friday night, when Lion died.

"He gets to the room, knocks, and is let in by someone. We can't see who on the footage, but were told it was his assistant Lila."

I nodded. "I met her," I said.

Jack took another sip, studying me over the top of the glass as he did. "Lila said he collapsed as soon as he was in the room. 911 calls prove that was true based on the time called and the time on the security footage."

I was kind of surprised Jack was telling this all to us. He and I had talked about a case before, but privately. And not one where I'd dropped the victim off thirty minutes before he dropped dead. And not with other people in the room.

"The video will be released in the next few hours," he said, clearing up why he was so willing to tell us. We were just getting a sneak preview, not top-secret information.

"Shit," Jimmy said, looking at me.

"Why?" I said, not getting it.

He turned to Jack. "All the footage? Him getting out of her Porsche?"

Jack nodded to Jimmy, but was watching me. I still wasn't getting it.

"So," Jimmy went on, "there is going to be footage all over the news with him getting out of her car, then needing to balance himself in the elevator, then it's going to cut to him walking down the hallway to his room barely able to keep upright."

"That's right," Jack said. "They sure aren't going to show twenty-six minutes of dead air."

"It's going to look like I dropped him off like that—stinking drunk. Or that I did whatever to him to make him act that way. Or that I let a man, obviously too drunk to walk or in some kind of distress, just leave my car without helping him. Actually tearing out of the parking lot away from him."

Silence and stares from all three men. I said a silent prayer that Ben was taking a nap and not privy to this.

"So much for the Facebook post putting an end to the public wondering about my involvement," I said.

"Yeah," Jack said, not unkindly. "Best if you lie low for a while. Maybe hang here where nobody can get to you. No casinos."

I motioned to Raymond. "We have to be somewhere tomorrow."

"Where?" Jack asked. I'd already clued Raymond in about his presence being requested at Vince's will reading. He was as much in the dark as I was about the reason why. I explained this all to Jack.

"Law firm should be okay. Go in Lor's car or the Lexus. Stay away from your Porsche for a while. We'll have the media around the gate dispersed before then. But no casinos, no poker games, nothing visible to a bunch of people. Yeah?"

"Yeah," I said.

"Looks like we're going to the mattresses," Jimmy said.

"Yeah," I repeated, mentally going through my schedule, shuffling things around. It was doable, after the will reading tomorrow.

"Think Lor has a cannoli recipe?" Jimmy said. "I'm suddenly hungry for cannoli."

"Yeah," I said for the third time in a row.

Twenty-Four
❖❖

IT PLAYED OUT THE WAY JACK said it would. The security footage was released—by the Wynn, not the police—and the missing twenty-six minutes were edited out so it looked like I was an uncaring asshole who left a sick man on his own.

Lor asked me Monday morning if I wanted to know what was going on in social media, and I told her absolutely not, to which she only nodded and left me alone at the large dining room table to have my coffee and nurse my reputation hangover.

I didn't think it would hurt me in poker circles. If I'd had any endorsements, maybe. But just as a player? My buy-in cash would be accepted at any casino or private game. Maybe even more so at some places.

I may even be considered a badass. Black Widow to the nth power.

Lor took Ben to breakfast in the Lexus. No need to draw attention to myself, even if it was only the Sourdough Café at Arizona Charlie's. The Porsche stayed in the garage.

Jack had left yesterday after dinner and hadn't crawled into bed with me in the wee hours.

Which was not surprising, but I was hoping it was Lion's death keeping him away and not the fact that I was "not coincidentally" involved in one of his cases, and it looked like somebody may have slipped Lion something—a JoJo trick.

I halfheartedly did the exercises for my foot. It was coming along nicely, and my arm only had a twinge of pain if I moved it wrong.

When Ben got back from breakfast I asked if he wanted to play cards or do something, but he just said he felt like a nap.

Ben napped, but usually in the afternoon. I wasn't sure whether to worry about him or assume he was just keeping his distance until Jack and I figured out what was going on with us.

Again.

It was intense being with Jack, and I had deep feelings for him. Yeah, I loved him, but it had never been easy for us. Even when things were good it always felt…transitional.

Visions of drop-offs and pick-ups of Ben at a McDonald's once again traveled through my brain.

At the appointed hour Raymond and I took the Lexus and—as Jack had promised—drove through a media-free gate and made our way to Marvin's offices.

They were in Summerlin, so it wasn't a long drive, and we were mostly silent during it. Until Raymond said, "That deal you made with Jack. And Frank, probably. It about me?"

He was too damn sharp—always had been; that was part of the reason I went to Raymond when I needed a player's involvement in a game.

"Nothing you need to worry about," I said, pulling into the parking lot of an upscale office building. I parked the SUV and cut the engine. As I tried to pull the key out, Raymond put his hand on mine.

"I'm thinking it's my business if some deal you cut involves me."

"It doesn't really, and it might not hold anyway."

I wasn't sure if Frank and Jack would be able to keep their end of the bargain and keep Raymond's name out of anything that could potentially be picked up by the media. Or the FBI.

"Then no reason not to tell me."

I shrugged. "I just said they could throw my name out there as being with Lion and driving him back to his hotel. Essentially being the last person to be with him. If they'd try to keep your name out of it."

"And they agreed to that? You were photographed with him earlier; his staff knew he was playing poker with you. That wasn't stuff the cops could *choose* to disclose." He took his hand away, but leaned back in his seat to stare at me. "There's more to it than that. What else did you give them?"

"I told them I'd talk with Carla," I said. "They wanted the names of the people she contacted to play in the game that didn't accept. People who would know that Lion was going to be there. She wasn't willing to give those up."

"So you snitched on her?" There was no tone in his voice, no accusation. Just genuine surprise. Which, I guess, I should have taken as a compliment.

I shook my head. "No." Then so he didn't think I was anti-snitching (I wasn't above it if it would protect someone from my tribe), I added, "I didn't have them to give. But I did talk with Carla and try to convince her to throw the cops a bone and give up those names."

"For me," he said quietly.

I shrugged. "For you. For Jack and Frank. On some level, even for Lion."

"Did she talk?"

"I don't know. Jack didn't say, and I didn't pry. As far as I know, they're holding up their end."

"Seeing as *I* don't have people calling me a killer on Facebook this morning, I'll assume they're still keeping up their end."

I groaned. "You're not supposed to tell me those things," I said. "Lor is so much better at this than you."

He laughed. "She's had more practice."

"True that," I said, and we both moved to get out of the car and head into Marvin Harrison's offices, still having no idea why either one of us had been asked to attend the reading of Vince's will.

WE WERE LED INTO A LARGE CONFERENCE room on the second floor with a spectacular view of the Red Rock Canyon and its surrounding mountains.

I thought for a second how that seemed to be fitting, as I had not too long ago driven through the canyon with Vince.

It had either been a date or a strong-arm tactic. I still wasn't quite sure.

Which basically summed up my relationship with Vince Santini—part attraction, part extortion. And all dangerous.

And all over before it really began.

Carla was sitting at the table, as were three other people, two men and a woman. The two men were in their sixties or seventies, if I had to guess. The woman would be around mid-forties, very pretty, dressed in a navy blazer, white silk tee, and khaki slacks. Very Ann Taylor. Blonde, with her hair cut in a sleek bob that was angled more in the front than the back. She had the look of money about her, and I couldn't help wondering who she'd been to Vince.

The men looked vaguely familiar, and nodded to me, but I couldn't place them for sure. Perhaps casino guys? But I knew most of the long-timers at the casinos through my own thirteen years of playing and my association with the Corporation.

Raymond and I took seats next to Carla, across the large table from the two men and woman.

Before I could say much to Carla other than hello, and a quick nod to the people across from me, Marvin came in and joined us with a female assistant, who sat to his left. Sitting at the head of the table, Marvin looked at all of us, then nodded and opened the thick file folder he'd brought in with him.

No introductions to the others were given. Maybe that wasn't done at will readings? Maybe it was assumed that everyone knew each other if we'd all been close enough to Vince to be included in his will?

Who knew—this was my first will reading.

"Thank you all for coming," Marvin said. "Just a few preliminary remarks and then I'll get to it. This shouldn't take long." Carla twitched a little where she sat next to me, but I wasn't sure what that meant. Did a short reading bode something to her? For her?

"First of all, Mr. Santini amended his will two days before he died, and—"

"Fuck," Carla said. It was quiet, and though Marvin probably heard, he didn't let on. I was thinking the same thing Carla was—two days before he died, Vince knew Carla and Paulie had been stealing from him. He had already killed Paulie and was in the process of framing Carla for it.

So, Carla probably wouldn't be receiving the family china or something like that.

"Besides amending his will, he wrote two letters and asked that they be disbursed at the time of his death." He took one regular number ten envelope out of the folder, got out of his seat, and walked to my side, where he offered it up. "For you, Ms. Dawson."

I took the envelope.

"As there is no monetary value, and as a personal letter not specified in the will, you do not have to sign anything saying you are accepting the gift," Marvin said, and I nodded my understanding. The front of the envelope said only "Anna" in what I assumed was Vince's handwriting. I tried to remember if I'd ever seen his writing before and couldn't come up with any time that I might have.

Marvin returned to the front of the table and this time his assistant handed him a larger envelope. As he brought it back to our side of the table, both Raymond and Carla tensed. I assumed for different reasons. Raymond didn't want anything from Vince—especially nothing that could tie Raymond to Vince-sponsored point-shaving schemes.

Carla wanted everything from Vince. She thought she deserved it, and she knew it wouldn't fit in that envelope.

But she still had hope, because Marvin handed the envelope to Raymond. Again Marvin returned to the head of the table, and this time he sat back in the black leather chair.

"Do I open this now?" Raymond asked, and I shrugged, not sure on the etiquette.

"Okay then, let's get on with the reading," Marvin said. He had to go through the preliminary legal stuff, which went on longer than the actual disbursement of property. That was because there were only four line items of actual…gifts.

"To Carla Rossetti I leave one set of ledgers used in my… financial planning business. These ledgers were falsified by Carla and Paul Coscarelli and are of no monetary value. They should be considered null and void."

"Fuck," Carla said again. Marvin's assistant pulled a box from under the table and brought it over to Carla, who tipped the lid on it to see it was full of ledgers. All black leather with gold piping. All ones Carla and Paulie had cooked and passed on to Vince, keeping the originals for themselves. Lowering the amounts Vince thought he was owed and skimming the difference.

Yeah, Carla was fucked if she thought Vince had left her the capital to keep the loan sharking going. Of course, who knew how much outstanding debt there was—maybe Carla could use that as her jumping-off point.

Or maybe Carla needed to look into other lines of work.

Marvin continued, "All outstanding debts owed to me are absolved."

"Fuck," again from Carla. This time not quite so quietly.

Yeah, looked like it was time for an encore career for her.

Nodding to the two men across from me, Marvin continued reading: "Harvey Schneider and Patrick Monaghan are here as witnesses to that fact and to spread the word to debtors that they no longer owe anyone in my employ, including Carla Rossetti."

"Fucking Vince," Carla said.

Maybe something in food service for Carla? Like a hostess at a restaurant?

Marvin continued, "For their help with this matter, Mr. Schneider and Mr. Monaghan are to receive ten thousand dollars each."

Well, that made their days. Smiles for both of them. Carla, not so much. One of them—I wasn't sure if it was Harvey or Patrick—said, "Oh, we're going to get the word out, that's for sure. You wouldn't even have to pay me." He then leaned across the table, pointing at Carla. "What you did wasn't right. Vince was good to you. He kept you and Paulie on even though you were an embarrassment to him as he grew. And how did you repay him? Skimming the books. Oldest con there is. Shame on you."

"Shut up, Harvey," Carla said. Apparently she knew who they were, cementing to me the fact that there were a lot of other facets to Vince Santini of which I had no knowledge.

And I was okay with that.

Harvey sneered at her and sat back in his chair. As an afterthought, he said to Marvin, "But I'll still take the ten grand. Since Vince wanted me to have it."

"Of course," Marvin said, trying to hide a smile behind his polished veneer.

Obviously Vince's "financial planning business" wasn't legal, and just having two guys tell people they didn't have debt anymore was even less legal.

But it was the way this world worked. And my guess was that by dinnertime tonight, there were going to be a lot of people smiling because they wouldn't have Vince Santini's debt hanging over their heads.

"One last item," Marvin said. "All my real estate holdings, investments, cash, furniture, and other items…" Marvin looked up from the paper and motioned. "There is an itemized list here, which I won't take the time to read because"—his head went back to the paper—"I leave to Cassandra Hall."

Nothing from Carla this time, just defeat. Elbows on the table, hands clasped, she bowed her head like she was in prayer.

Looking across the table, I had no doubt who Cassandra Hall was. And at this moment, she was speechless. Obviously very surprised, a hand had gone to her chest and her eyes—a clear, striking blue—were huge.

And she was staring at me.

Twenty-Five

❖

I WAS A LITTLE DAZED when Marvin finished up, so I remained seated as Harvey and Patrick left together. It looked like maybe Cassandra Hall would have liked to talk to me, but with Raymond on one side and Carla on the other, Cassandra instead nodded in my direction and quietly left, Marvin walking her out. The assistant also left, leaving the three of us alone at the large table.

Not completely alone. Carla had a box of useless ledgers and Raymond and I had our unopened envelopes.

"I didn't see that coming," Carla said. Uh, yeah, I'd figured that. "Jesus Christ, what am I going to do now?" she added, but she wasn't really asking either of us.

Carla motioned to the envelope in my hand. "What do you think is in there?"

I shrugged and opened it. I pulled out a one-page handwritten letter. Unfolding just the top third, I saw:

Dear Anna,

You're not going to want to hear this, but—

I scanned the rest and folded the letter back up. It wasn't anything I needed to deal with now. It was too soon for Vince's words to really sink in. And I instinctively knew he was right in his opening line—I wouldn't want to hear what he said.

If he'd written the letter the same time he had amended his

will, it was when I would have been in Chicago trying to get Raymond to safety.

"It's just a personal letter," I said, putting it back in the envelope.

Carla nodded, then did a chin jerk to Raymond's larger envelope. He looked at me with a question in his eye, and I shrugged. He sighed and slid a finger across the top, tearing it open.

Pulling out the contents, he put them on the table in front us and spread them out. They looked like reports of some kind, and photos. On the top was a handwritten note, which said, *In case things go south. Use this information if you need something to barter with. Have Anna help you.*

"These are the feds who were investigating me at Central Iowa," Raymond said, pointing to one of the photos.

"He's investigating something entirely different in this shot," Carla said, unearthing a different photo, this one of the same man, but with a woman—a very young woman—riding him like an exuberant cowgirl. Chaps and all.

We looked through it all, putting it into piles. It was dirt—both financial and personal—on the two feds who had been after Raymond. Guys who had to give up the chase when their witness's credibility was shattered—thanks to Jimmy's help.

Huh. Vince must have been compiling this while I was in Chicago. He had said he wouldn't go with me to help, that I needed to handle it, but apparently he'd been trying to help in his own way.

I wondered if he'd lived, if his plan had worked and Carla had taken the fall for Paulie's death—would he have given this information to Raymond?

We'd never know.

We sat there for a few seconds, all staring straight ahead, as if we were enjoying the view of the mountains, when I knew none of us were even registering the majestic sight.

"I'm gonna need that money," Carla said, more to herself than to me. But seeing as I owed her over twenty thousand, it was safe to assume it was me she was addressing.

"We said by Friday," I said, coming out of my stupor a little bit and turning toward her. "I told my...assistant I needed it by Friday."

She shrugged. "We did say Friday, but after this shit show..." She waved her hand around the conference table, now devoid of anyone but us, though the coffee cups, napkins, paper, and pens of those departed still remained.

Those departed. Like Vince had left bodies in his wake. Carla's hands clenched into tight fists on the table. Yeah, maybe Vince had scorched the earth a little.

"Well, if you can get it to me any sooner..." Carla added, and I nodded, knowing I wasn't going to rush Lor.

It had been weird enough asking her for money to repay a loan, and it had been obvious how confusing it was for her. I wasn't going to make it worse by pushing up her timetable. If she had it to me early, so be it, but if not...so be that. Besides...

"You weren't supposed to lend me that money in the first place," I reminded Carla.

A snort from her direction, then she sat back in her chair, as did I. I swiveled mine in her direction.

"Brandt already paid me back," she said in a voice that insinuated if he could, I should be able to.

"We said Friday," I said more firmly. "You can't start changing rules on...customers. Especially when you're trying to get your feet on the ground."

"I know that," she said. Her shoulders sagged and she sank back deeper into Marvin's luxurious leather chair. "I know," she said in a regular voice. "Friday, then."

I nodded. I knew the past hour hadn't gone the way anybody thought it would, but I guessed I didn't realize how much Carla was counting on the hope that she had been Vince's only beneficiary.

"Two fucking days," she said, looking at me, but not really seeing me. She shook her head, and looked down at her hands clutched together in her lap. "Two days before he dies he changes his will."

"Almost as if he'd known," I said.

I didn't add that the two of us were the reason Vince was dead. No doubt if things had gone as planned for Vince, and Carla had taken the fall for Paulie's murder, he would have had the chance to change his will again. Perhaps he hoped that he and I would make it work.

Then maybe I'd be walking out with a fortune today instead of Cassandra Hall.

I shivered in my seat, even though the air conditioning wasn't even on. March was usually the time that switch was flipped, but it had been a little cooler this year. Still, it felt like… what was that saying? Walked over someone's grave? They walked over my grave?

Whatever it was, I tried to shake it off, even running my hands up and down my arms. The truth was, I couldn't have taken Vince's fortune, even if he'd left it to me.

It was dirty money, part of it won off the back of unsuspecting college basketball players. Another chunk off the vig from desperate gamblers.

I'd had enough of that in my life, and didn't want any of those spoils.

I was happy for Raymond, though. He deserved to have the safety net Vince had left him—his life had been turned upside down. And though there was some good that had come out of it all—his sister getting the help she needed, and she and Halia moving out of their neighborhood— it couldn't make up for the fact that Raymond had had to watch the Fighting Hogs play in the tournament from my couch, not the court.

"He paid you back already?" Raymond said to Carla, leaning

forward on the table to see around me. "That Brandt guy?"

Carla nodded, looking at Raymond. "Yeah, why?"

"Is that normal?" he asked, looking more at me than Carla.

I shrugged, as did Carla. "Not unheard of," she said. "But usually they'll take the whole week." She looked at me pointedly. "Usually they take every freakin' second."

"Is that what you do?" he asked, looking at me. "Normally?"

I sat back in my seat, reclining it a little with the weight of my body. The weight of my life. "There is no normal in this life," I said, my voice sounding wearier than usual, and I thought of Jack, who always sounded like that.

"Okay. So if *usually* people wait until the deadline—because it takes that long to get it, or as a fuck you to the loan shark— why would this Brandt guy, or anyone, pay off so quickly?"

"Lots of reasons," I said. I ticked off my fingers as I continued, "He had the money all along, just hadn't taken it to the game with him, thinking he wouldn't need it. He could easily get more money and wanted it off his books. He would be leaving town before the due date." My hand dropped to my lap. There were other reasons, but those would be the main ones. "Brandt was probably a combination of all three." Raymond nodded. "Why?" I asked.

He shrugged. "I don't know. Just seemed weird to me." He leaned around me. "When did he pay you back?" he asked Carla.

"Saturday morning. Early."

"Before the news of Lion dying broke?" Raymond asked. Carla nodded, as did Raymond, seeming to file away that information. So did I.

The conversation Raymond and I had had on the way to Marvin's offices replayed in my brain. "Did you tell the detectives who else you called?" I asked Carla. "At the station on Saturday," I reminded her, as if she'd already forgotten being questioned by the police.

Hell, it seemed to happen to me enough lately. Maybe Carla

needed the reminder.

"Yeah, I did. You were right—throw them a bone to keep the players' names quiet. Marvin said it would be okay."

"That's good," I said, thinking at least I was able to do that for Jack and Frank.

And Raymond.

"Yeah, we'll see. It'll probably fuck me over for future games. But who knows if there will even *be* any more games with this whole Lion thing."

I nodded, thinking that I'd probably be playing a lot more in casinos in the future. Which, given my new notoriety, was not a pleasant thought.

Marvin came back in, and at first I thought he was going to politely tell us to get the hell out of his conference room already, but instead of saying a word he went to the control panel at the center of the table and pressed a button. One of the walls moved, revealing a large screen behind the rich oak paneling. Marvin took a remote and turned on the television.

"They have a cause of death," was all he said. Instantly, Carla and I straightened in our seats, hands on the table.

It was one of the news channels, and they were showing clips of Lion winning the Masters from a couple of years ago, then cutting to a shot of him on the red carpet Friday night, thankfully alone. The writing beneath the video loop read *LaGasse Poisoned: Case Labeled Homicide.*

"Holy shit," Raymond said.

"Fuck," Carla said.

"Nobody says a word," Marvin said, turning and pointing to us all, going into lawyer mode. "Not even here to each other."

I pulled my phone out and looked to see when Jack had called, since I'd put my phone on silent for the meeting.

No missed calls. None.

Carla was looking over my arm at my phone, correctly guessing why I was looking at it.

"You didn't know? He didn't even give you a heads-up?"

I shook my head, wondering why I didn't hear about Lion's case definitely being classified as murder from Jack before I heard it on the news.

Twenty-Six

❖❖

"BECAUSE I WAS TAKEN OFF THE CASE, that's why," Jack said later that evening when I posed the same question to him.

Oh shit.

"In fact," he continued as he poured himself a healthy bourbon from the bar area on the sideboard behind the dining room table, "it has been...*strongly* suggested that I take some time off while this case is investigated."

"What?" Ben and I both said.

Jack nodded, took a gulp of his drink, and joined Ben and me at the table, sitting at the head, with Ben at his left and me at his right.

Everybody else had gone to bed, or at least to their rooms after our evening card game had broken up. Lor had been the winner, as she often was when we played gin rummy. Ben and I had stayed up talking, both hoping Jack would come home before it would be too late.

Jack had, but given his mood—and his news—I was wishing I'd just gone to bed and let Ben deal with it.

I had other ways to help Jack out of a bad mood.

And by the way he was glaring at me now, I guessed that whatever wiles I had to offer weren't going to sooth Jack's wild beast.

"You're looking at me like this is my fault," I said.

I could look at Jack's face all day long and never get tired of it, but right then I wanted to smack that damn raised eyebrow he was giving. No words. Just the look and another sip from his glass. My eyes stayed with the tumbler as he set it on the table, keeping it firmly in his grasp. When I looked back into his face, it was clear he knew which way my thoughts were headed.

"Icebergs, Johanna," he said in a quiet voice.

It had become our code of sorts to not go there. He had his *issues* (bourbon) and I had mine (betting), and we had agreed early on that we wouldn't try to fix each other.

I sat back in my chair, holding my hands up in an "I'm not touching that" way.

"But Jack, I'm sure if you talked to them…" Ben started, but didn't complete his sentence. He knew if there was a chance in hell Jack could have talked his way into staying on the case that he'd have done it.

"I'm sorry," I said, quickly adding, "that you're off the case," lest he think I was apologizing. I wasn't.

The look he gave me confirmed that he knew I wasn't.

I didn't push it. I didn't think bringing up the word *coincidence* would do any good after our pillow talk the other night.

We sat in silence, Ben looking at Jack worriedly, then across the table to me.

"Surely Frank will keep you involved, right? Off the books or however you say it?" Ben asked.

Jack looked at his father, his face holding a softness that he hadn't had for me. After taking another drink, he shook his head. "Botz is rattled. Our lieutenant read us the riot act. This case is getting so much attention that the Feds are trying to figure out a way in. Everything is going to be under intense scrutiny. Frank's not going to mess that up by keeping me in the loop." I sighed, and Jack shook his head. "No. It's the right call. I'd do the same thing in his position."

I doubted that, but didn't say anything. I liked Frank, and he and Jack seemed tight, but Jack had only been in Vegas a year, so it wasn't like they had been partners for decades.

I had no idea what Frank thought of Jack's involvement with me, though he'd always been cordial to me.

Even when pointing out that five deaths had happened in my periphery.

"Well, Hannah will keep you informed with anything she finds out, won't you, dear?"

Wrong thing to say. Jack swallowed the last of his drink and immediately got up and went back to the sideboard for a refill.

"I don't need her to keep me informed. And she shouldn't be involved either," he said once he sat back down at the table, his glass a little fuller than the first time. "I'm off the case," he said in a mock toast. After a healthy swig, he put the glass on the table. "I'm thinking a few days off would be a good thing. Especially since we just…found each other." I was thinking that was an odd way to put he and I getting back together, though I certainly agreed that a few days with some heavy Jack time would be wonderful. But when I looked at him, I realized he'd been speaking to Ben.

My face burned with embarrassment, but neither of them saw it. Ben placed his hand on Jack's arm, the one that held the glass.

"It would be nice to spend some time together," Ben said.

It was a weird combination of feelings that rolled over me. I was touched and elated for the two men I adored to have *found each other*. And yet I felt like my side of the table was drifting away from theirs, as if leaf after leaf of table extender was being put in between them and me.

It was a big dining room table, but it had never felt wider than it did right then.

I rose from the table, slid my hand across Jack's shoulders as I passed him, kissed Ben's cheek, and said good night.

"I'll be in soon," Jack said, Ben's hand still on his arm.

I nodded, but didn't wait up for him.

And he didn't wake me when he joined me.

"I'M TAKING BEN to Portland for a few days," Jack said in the morning.

We were in my bed, in a light spoon, Jack's arm loosely thrown over my waist, and I tried not to let my body tense when he told me his news.

I had a thousand questions, the first and foremost being "You're taking him, not *we're* taking him?" but on some level I already knew the answer to that one.

"When?" I asked.

"Tomorrow. I need to call Lisa and make sure we can see Casey."

Casey. Jack's son. Six years old and due here in a few weeks for his spring break. It would be the first time Casey came here. Jack had been going to Portland to see his son in the year since he'd moved to Vegas.

"I don't think she'll have a problem with it. I've told her about Ben. She was really happy for me about that."

Again I held very still, keeping my breath even, not willing to let Jack see how it hurt to know he had this whole other life. That he spoke with the mother of his child was no surprise, but it still hurt to think about him discussing finding his biological father with her.

"Anyway, it will be good for us to get out of here for a while," Jack said. What he didn't add was "while you deal with the fallout from Lion's death." It felt implied.

"Hey," he whispered, pulling me back toward him, pushing at my waist until I rolled over and faced him. When I did, I looked into his brown eyes. I saw that whatever anger he might have had last night had gone. "You know why you can't go, right?"

I nodded, but my mind screamed "no." At the most basic level, I didn't want my family to go on vacation without me. Like some seven-year-old who would miss Disney World because of the mumps. (Which actually happened to my brother when we'd been kids—totally sucked for him, but we had a great time.)

"But Casey's coming here soon, isn't he?" I said, and hated that there was a touch of whine in my voice that I couldn't quite squelch.

"Not for a few weeks. And I can't stay around here—around you—right now. Ben seems excited to meet Casey."

"Of course he is," I said, and knew it was true. A grandson for Ben.

"I'm sorry I can't be a part of the case for you, Johanna," he said, his voice smooth and silky as he said my name.

I ran a hand up the arm that held me and wrapped my fingers in his hair. "I never asked you to protect me," I said.

"I know," he said, dipping his head to gently kiss me. "But I still want to."

"Icebergs, Jack."

He nodded, then kissed me again, less gently this time. Rolling me to my back, he then said a proper goodbye.

Twenty-Seven
❖❖

WEDNESDAY MORNING I DROVE them to the airport. Jack didn't want me to, saying it was easier for him to just leave his car, even though they weren't sure what day they were coming back. Jack wanted to wait and see how the situation with Casey, and Ben traveling, went.

It was also probably a bad idea for me to go to a place as public as McCarran, but it was something I felt I had to do.

Part of me couldn't believe they were actually leaving. Leaving me. Then I would remember Jack's words of regret at not being able to protect me. It wasn't his job, his responsibility, to look out for me. Part of me had begun to rely on Jack, and that just wasn't my style.

Yeah, I knew independent people who found themselves in committed relationships adjusted, but for us it was more than that.

Anytime someone was bringing their significant other into police headquarters for questioning on yet another murder case, the regular adjustments of couplehood went out the window.

I pulled to the curb and told the sky porter we needed a wheelchair. He nodded, told us to have Ben wait in the car, then got on the phone.

We would check Ben's walker with their luggage and use the wheelchair service for the airports. I'd gone over this with Jack while packing Ben's suitcase for him. Lor had stayed behind at the house, but I could tell she was just as nervous about having Ben out of our sights as I was.

Not that Jack wouldn't take good care of him, but still.

We checked the luggage and got Ben situated in his wheelchair. I leaned over to kiss his soft, wrinkled cheek. "Take care of our boy," I whispered to him. His brown eyes smiled at me when I pulled away and straightened.

"Don't worry about us, Hannah darling. You just take care of yourself."

"I will," I said, hoping it was true.

It had been twenty-nine days since I'd last placed a bet. Almost a month. And never had the urge been greater to drive straight to a casino after leaving my boys and plunking down some cash on a game.

My thoughts were torn from me as Jack yanked and pulled me to him. I wrapped my arms around him, my palms sliding against the leather of his jacket. Feeling Jack's freshly shaved cheek as he buried his face in my neck, I briefly thought about how strange it felt. Normally there was at the least a five o'clock shadow—at most, a two- or three-day beard.

"Take care of our boy," I said to Jack this time as he reluctantly let me leave our embrace. The truth was I would have been happy to spend the entire day in Jack's arms, but I was leery of being recognized, and didn't want them to miss their flight.

That would be another thing for which Jack could blame me.

Which might not be fair. Jack hadn't come out and said he blamed me for getting him thrown off Lion's case, but I couldn't help but feel that this trip of theirs was some form of punishment.

"I will," Jack said. His brown eyes—*Ben's eyes*—were also warm, and I pushed my thoughts of punishment aside.

We'd never told each other "I love you," and though this

would have been the perfect time, something held me back. Some shred of pride, I suppose, beyond being the first one to say it. I didn't want the words to feel like an apology in any way.

We both looked at each other, waiting, though I wasn't sure we could say for what exactly.

"Johanna," he whispered, then leaned forward and gave me a very soft, and very sweet kiss on my lips. I pressed my hand to his cheek like I had in bed the other night, then let him go.

He made sure Ben was settled, slung his backpack over his shoulder, then led the way, the porter staying to his side with Ben.

I gambled with myself on whether Jack would look back at me at the door. I bet myself that he would, but like when placing bets for fifty large on an NFL underdog, half of me knew it was a losing proposition even as I was making it.

Still, I told myself he would turn around and look at me once more. I lost.

I sat at the curb in the Lexus breathing heavily, my hands on the wheel. My plan had been to just drop off the boys and head home, it being too late by now to meet Jimmy and Gus for breakfast. But as I pulled away, my mind raced with which casino was closest, and would anybody recognize the Black Widow on a Wednesday morning if I just slipped into the book room? Not even to place a bet, just to take a look at the board.

I mean, I hadn't placed a bet in twenty-nine days; I wasn't going to tumble off that wagon before a month was up.

The MGM would probably be closest if I took Koval.

No. No.

My phone rang, and although I would typically let it go to voicemail while driving, I lunged for it, thankful for the diversion.

I told myself that maybe it was Jack calling and something had happened to their flight and he needed me to come back for them. The relief that coursed through my body at that thought was a bit alarming.

But it wasn't Jack. It was a Vegas number, so I took the call.

"Anna, it's Frank Botz," he said when I picked up.

"Hi, Frank," I said, "I'm in the car right now, can I call you back?"

"Are you on your way back from the airport?"

"Yes." I guess I wasn't surprised that Frank knew Jack's plans. Partners and all.

"Any chance you could swing by the station?"

"Um, yeah. Should I call Marvin to have him meet me?"

"If you want, but I don't think it's necessary."

I got through the construction area near the airport and onto 215. "Yeah, but wouldn't you always say that?"

He chuckled, and so did I, but I wasn't really kidding.

Had Jack known Frank was going to call me to come in moments after he left town? Was this what Jack meant about not protecting me?

It didn't matter. Ultimately I was in this thing—which encompassed all things gambling—alone.

Well, me and JoJo.

"Okay, I can be there in about twenty," I said.

"Great. Park around back. I'll wait for you there."

"Reporters?" I asked. They had been gone from the gates of my subdivision since last night, but seeing me go into the police station would probably have them back in no time.

"Yeah, a couple are still around."

"Okay. See you soon."

"Thanks, Anna. See you soon."

As I drove, I tried to gauge my feelings on how I felt about going to the police station to talk with Frank instead of heading to the book room at the MGM.

Relief, for sure. And yet a feeling of dread, of inevitability, gnawed around the edges.

I tried to block it out and drive.

Twenty-Eigtht
❖❖

CARLA HAD BEEN CALLED in too, and we compared notes later that night. She'd called and said she knew I'd been there and wanted to talk. Knowing it was a bad idea to meet in public, I had her come to me, giving her name and car to Eddie at the front gate.

"Say it again," she said to me.

We were at the dining room table, Raymond joining us. Lor was at a dance class, and of course Ben was in Portland with Jack.

Safely, according to Jack's three-word text earlier. *Landed in Portland.*

"They said it was a combination of steroids, beta blockers, cocaine, and a foreign element. They couldn't pinpoint that element yet—or more likely wouldn't say—but the time frame it entered Lion's system matches when we were playing cards."

She was nodding. "Yeah, that's it. Exactly what they said to me. And that they were doing more tests."

"Who knew Lion was on steroids?" Raymond said. "Not like he was ripped or anything."

I shrugged. I of all people wouldn't speculate on people's private vices.

"Or cocaine," Carla said. "You were with him earlier—did he partake in front of you?"

I shook my head, then took a sip of my Diet Coke. "No, and we were in public pretty much from the time we left his suite until we got to the Bellagio."

All stuff I'd told Frank and the detective working with him, Peter Faxon.

Faxon was younger than Jack, probably closer to my age, mid-thirties. And he definitely took more care with his wardrobe than Jack or Frank. In fact, I thought I recognized Lorenzo's handiwork in Faxon's suit.

His elegant appearance couldn't hide his disdain for me, though. While Frank was hoping for some information confirming timelines, it started to turn into something else entirely at Faxon's hand. After about an hour I told them I was leaving, and if they wanted me for anything else to contact me through Marvin.

Frank walked me to my car and apologized for Faxon's behavior. His tie had Velma, Shaggy, and Scooby on it.

"He thinks this is his big break, with Jack being bounced," Frank said, holding open the Lexus door for me. "He's a little overzealous."

"A little," I agreed.

"Kid'll be a good detective, but he likes the flash of it a little too much. Whether you like it or not, Anna, you're the flash right now."

"I don't like it."

"I know. I'll be in touch. You too if you think of anything else, yeah?"

"Yeah." I started to shut the door, but stopped. "Frank, how much does Faxon know about Raymond?"

"Nothing yet. We have Raymond listed as a pseudonym in the file for now. His interview we did at your house is in there. We'll probably need to talk to him again, but we're concentrating more on finding the other players first."

So they hadn't found everyone yet—which was information

I didn't share with Carla now. I tried to remember everything Frank had told me, and, just as importantly, what I'd told him and Faxon.

"I mean, Lion did go to the bathroom before we left the Wynn, and I think a couple of times during the game, right?" I asked Carla. "So he could have hit a quick line then."

Carla nodded. "Yeah, I think a couple of times. But it was during breaks, so I wasn't really paying attention, you know?"

"Right. Me either."

"He went twice," Raymond said. "You went once, Calvin twice, Brandt once, Ralph three times, and Mr. Chow not at all."

I always suspected Mr. Chow might not be all human, and now I was really starting to think so.

"Damn, boy, you have a good memory," Carla said to Raymond, who just shrugged.

"What else?" I asked Carla, figuring she had more information from her visit with the cops than I did. Usually because of Jack, I was the scoop master of police information. I pushed away the weird feeling that Carla knew more than me.

"They can't find Brandt or Calvin. Apparently their stories don't check out."

"Calvin wasn't getting married the next day?" I asked, surprised. I shouldn't be—if you were going to lie and give a fake identity, a detail like that would make it more believable. In a weird way I was kind of hurt that he'd made it up, that I was secretly hoping Calvin was going to find happiness this time.

Yeah, a sucker born every minute for sure.

Next I'd find out Mr. Chow's name was really Myron Finkelbaum.

Was there really no honor amongst thieves?

Carla took a sip from her drink—oddly enough, bourbon and ice, like Jack preferred. It made me miss him, even though it'd only been hours since I'd seen him. "Who knows? The married part might be true, but the name Calvin Spencer wasn't.

The cops are looking at all the weddings from Saturday, seeing if they can identify him that way."

"And Brandt? They haven't tracked him down?"

She shook her head. "I guess not, because they were very interested in how those two players came to play in that game. So I'm guessing everyone else checked out. I mean, as far as who they really are and where they can be found."

Raymond and I shared a look across the table, and I made a tiny nod with my chin. I was trying to reassure him that even though the cops knew who and where he was, that it would stay out of the media.

For now.

But who knew what would happen now that a time frame had been established, a cause of death was confirmed, and—probably most important of all to Raymond and me—Jack was off the case.

He'd said he was sorry he couldn't protect me, but what was even more important was he wouldn't be able to protect Raymond.

And with Peter Faxon on the case, would Raymond be outed?

"Oh, and the bartender," Carla said, then took another sip of her drink.

"What about the bartender?"

"They can't find him either."

"But you hired him—wouldn't it be easy to find him?"

She gave me a look that said she couldn't believe how naive I was. Given my history, I guess I *was* being naive.

"Should I have been giving false names all these years playing in Vince's games?" I asked.

Carla chuckled at that. "You'd have been recognized. These are poker people, remember, and you're a pro." Yeah, there was that. "I don't think it happens a lot. I can remember a couple of people over the years who used aliases. That it happened with two players on the same night—three, if you count the bartender—and on a night where someone died, is a major red flag."

"Ya think?" Raymond said, and Carla gave him a snort.

"Back to you not knowing the bartender," I said.

She waved that away. "You get numbers and names all the time for these kinds of things." She pointed to Raymond. "Like Raymond for the door—he kind of fell into my lap. Same with the bartender's number; I had it around somewhere in some of Vince's things. That kind of talent isn't as important as the dealer. You gotta have a dealer who knows their shit. I make sure of that."

I nodded. "So the dealer checked out," I said, and she nodded.

"And has been questioned like we all have. So was Ralph, in Pittsburgh."

"How do you know?" Raymond asked.

Carla pushed her glass away, still half full (okay, so that part didn't remind me of Jack), and sat back in her chair. "I called them all. Wanted to apologize for the inconvenience, assure them that the police had agreed to be as discreet as possible, that kind of shit."

"Damage control," Raymond said, and she nodded.

"Yeah, but I don't know if it was enough. I may be up shit creek. I kinda thought I'd have a bit more cushion until I got up and running, but after Monday..."

She meant Vince's will and Cassandra Hall walking away with what Carla had probably assumed would be her inheritance.

Lots of capital would be needed for Carla to make a go of Vince's businesses.

"I might be royally fucked," Carla added.

She was right. But live by the sword, die by it, as I well knew.

She'd have twenty-six thousand from me on Friday, but I

knew that wouldn't give her the padding she needed either.

"Maybe it's time…" I didn't finish the thought. Who was I to tell Carla it was time to take a look at her life, to make some changes?

I could barely stand it when Jack said it to me—and I was sleeping with him.

She looked at me, not needing me to finish to know what I was going to say. And also knowing exactly why I didn't go on.

Wanting to get away from where we were headed, I said, "So they've talked to everybody there that they have identified, and are trying to track down the three they haven't."

"Right. I suppose at some point they could release the tapes of the hotel hallway at the Bellagio and ask for assistance in identifying them." She looked pointedly at first me, then Raymond, who had raised his head and stiffened his shoulders. "But I'm guessing that's their ace in the hole and they'd rather not release it. Or they're not helpful in any way." Still looking at Raymond, she added, "Or make public the names of the people in the room. It doesn't do them any good."

She waved a hand in my direction. "Besides, they have a poster child for this now—they're happy to have her field all the shit."

Yeah, just like Frank said, I was the *flash*.

Which was worth it if Raymond's name stayed out of it.

"Plus there's the cocaine and tracking that down. That could have been in his system for longer. The steroids, and I guess beta blockers too. Not to mention whatever this foreign element turns out to be." She slumped in her seat. "There's a lot of shit for them to look at, and I say the murkier the water, the better."

Yeah, for Carla, maybe—less scrutiny on her poker game. But I was thinking the sooner they had someone in custody, the sooner people would start to forget the Black Widow.

And I knew they would. A new celebrity death would come up, or some other scandal, and I'd be—happily, gratefully—

yesterday's news. A footnote in the life of Lion LaGasse.

Carla studied me for a moment, then said, "So, let's say somebody at my game did give him something, the something that killed him. And let's say it's not any of the people we *know*." I nodded, keeping up with her. "You're the gambler; you live with an oddsmaker. Put the odds on the three guys we know nothing about. Which one did it?"

I laughed, and the sound felt foreign and harsh. "You forget, I'm a shitty gambler. Poker, yeah, but betting? You of all people know I should stay away from that."

"Come on," she said, leaning forward, arms on the table. "What's the over/under on it being one of those three?"

I laughed again, shaking my head. "Nope. Not touching it." Then I thought back to the past few months. "And I'll tell you why. Of the two murders that have happened recently, I have had it wrong from the start."

"But figured it out eventually," she said, which was true in some cases, not in others.

"Yeah, but it was always the last person I originally thought. And ended up being someone I was close to, and I couldn't believe it was them."

She nodded, knowing that at first I'd thought she'd killed Paulie.

I waved my hand at the two of them. "Given my record, it would be one of the two of you who did it."

She snorted again, but glared at me.

"Kidding," I said, my hands up in surrender.

Raymond leaned forward, matching Carla's pose. "Well, you're the one at the table with experience drugging people. Let's not forget that."

Carla cracked up at that, which caused me to join in.

A famous man—douchebag or not—was dead. The three of us were on the police's radar. We all had a lot to lose if our... extracurricular activities were made known to the authorities.

And yet we were sitting at my dining room table totally cracking up.

Yeah, this was my life.

Maybe it was a good thing Jack and Ben were in Portland.

Twenty-Nine

❖❖

JIMMY TEXTED ME LATE THAT NIGHT, after Carla had left, and said that even though Ben was in Portland, I should meet him and Gus for breakfast the next morning.

Bring the kid if you want.

You sure? It was a hard table to crash. Lorelei hadn't made it yet, and she'd been taking Ben to breakfast when I couldn't for the past six years. When she did, she sat at a separate table or played the penny slots while the boys ate.

On Saturday Raymond was going to go with Ben and me before Jack and Frank had pulled up with the news about Lion, but that wasn't the same, being a weekend thing hastily thrown together.

Not a regular thing, Jimmy texted. *But he can have Ben's seat tomorrow. If you think it's safe.*

We ate at a back table in the Sourdough Café at Arizona Charlie's. Off the Strip, out of the way. It was safe.

I'll ask him.

Jimmy sent back a thumbs-up emoji, which cracked me up. I was pretty sure Lor had shown him the world of emoji. God help us all.

Before we left in the morning, Lor gave me a fat envelope. "I know you said Friday, but I didn't think a day early would hurt, and I got it while I was running errands yesterday."

"Thanks, Lor," I said, thinking how happy Carla would be to get it even a day early.

"Of course," she said. Something in her voice made me look from the envelope into her eyes.

It wasn't judgment. She was too good of a person for that. Concern, sure, but something else too.

I placed a hand on her arm. "It's cool, Lor, really."

She nodded, but the look didn't lessen. "I mean, at least this isn't because of betting, right?" she asked.

"Right. Exactly. Thirty days today. No bets."

The look eased from her eyes. "Like I said before, you're cured!"

My hand tightened a little on her arm, and I pulled it away. "Yeah," I said. "Must have been all those interventions," I teased.

She swatted at me. "Joke all you want. It probably *was*."

It was part of it, for sure. But I didn't need to rattle off my list of reasons to Lor, starting with Paulie's funeral, wrecking Raymond's life, and losing Jack, just to name a few.

"Well, given you hardly lose at poker, I'm guessing it'll be a while before we have to do this again," she added as I turned and headed to the closet to get my jacket. As I put it on, sliding the envelope into the inside pocket, I forced a little laugh.

"Yeah, let's hope not," I said.

Raymond, to his credit, seemed to know what an honor Jimmy had bestowed upon him, if his fidgeting on the drive to Arizona Charlie's was any indication.

"So, it's just breakfast? Like, then you all leave, or what?"

"Breakfast, yeah. Then usually they look at the lines for the day's games, talk about them and stuff."

"That'd be what, NBA? NHL?"

"Whatever's in season," I said. "So yeah, those, and of course college basketball right now."

"Right. Yeah," he said, and stopped fidgeting. He knew if put to the test he'd pass on that particular subject.

"WELL, YOU'RE A NEW FACE," Grace said as she came to our table, a full pot of coffee in her hand.

"Grace, this is Raymond, a friend of mine," I said. Raymond looked at me as I used his real name. "Grace is one of us," I said to him, which made him relax. "She doesn't remember names."

Grace studied him, then looked at me and nodded knowingly.

"That's right, sweetie, you're just a cute, bald black kid today. Order the same thing twice and your order becomes your name to me."

Raymond nodded and studied the menu, ordering the special. Jimmy ordered the big breakfast, Gus half of that, and I went with the French toast.

"Missing your boys?" Gus asked, winking at me.

"Like you wouldn't believe," I said truthfully. He placed a hand on mine and squeezed, then pulled it away, took some sugar packets from the holder and started adding them to his coffee. Which he would do several times throughout his meal.

"I'm sure they miss you too, honey," he said, concentrating on his sweetening mission.

But they have each other, I wanted to say. *They left me*, a voice inside me cried. I stifled it, not liking that voices were speaking to me.

I knew that bitch, and she needed to just shove it.

I scarfed down my breakfast, trying to drown my very raw feelings—and JoJo's voice—in maple syrup.

As Grace cleared the table, Jimmy and Gus pulled out odds sheets that they'd grabbed from the book room on their way in. Raymond, feeling unprepared, jumped up and left the restaurant, returning a few minutes later with copies for himself and me.

I set mine to the side, trying not to look at it, even ordering chocolate cake, which got me a look from the men at the table. Grace raised an eyebrow, but only wrote it down and nodded.

"Sublimation," I said to the guys, who nodded at me.

"Big fucking word," Jimmy added. He waved a hand in my direction. "You are who you are."

"Yeah, but cake isn't going to land me in jail, or have me lose my house."

He snorted at that. Gus winked again. Raymond had already dropped his head and was studying the odds sheet.

As I downed my cake—which only made JoJo laugh— Jimmy and Gus gave Raymond a crash course on odds setting, telling him how they would come up with point spreads back in the day.

"Now it's all computers," Jimmy said. A refrain I'd heard many times.

Pushing my empty plate aside, I sat back in my seat as they were wrapping up.

"So, kid, what do you think is the best bet on the board? Where did the computer fuck up?"

It was a test of sorts, and I thought Raymond knew it, if how long he took coming up with an answer was any indication. Finally, he raised his head from the sheet and said, "Kansas giving fifteen."

"Taking Kansas?" Jimmy asked. He seemed a little disappointed, and I wondered if Raymond had failed.

"No. Taking the points. Taking Butler."

Now Jimmy sat up in his seat, his attention—and his estimation?—piqued. "Yeah? Think so? Butler's only got that one player. No depth. They're out of their league against Kansas."

"Oh, Kansas is going to win. Just not by fifteen points. Butler will keep it closer than that," Raymond said. "I played AAU ball with the Kansas center. He's way overrated."

"Jamison? Really? He's been averaging twenty-two a game."

"He hasn't had anybody tough guarding him all year. The

Butler center will shut him down," Raymond said.

Jimmy and Gus looked at each other, then Gus shrugged a little and Jimmy nodded, and they both circled something on their odds sheets. I'd have bet the farm they were circling Butler and the points.

Raymond noticed too, and quickly added, "But, you know, shit happens. People play past their potential all the time, or not up to it."

"Kid, do you know who you're talking to? We get that. We made our lives on that."

Raymond sat back, nodding. "I just don't want that coming back on me if it goes south."

Gus took a drink from his coffee, then added more sweetener as he addressed Raymond. "Bets go south every day. For a multitude of reasons. A true gambler takes responsibility for the bets they make. No blaming it on a bum tip. No bitching about a bad call. You make the bet, it's done the minute you walk away from the counter."

He was right. There had been plenty of times a questionable ruling, or a too-close-to-call buzzer beater, had turned a bet so badly that JoJo had needed to make an appearance.

Like I'd earlier thought with Carla—live by the sword, die by the sword.

If you were going to gamble, then by the very nature of the word, anything could happen—and most of those things were bad.

They finished up their bet picking, and I nearly had to sit on my hands not to pull a pen out and make circles on the one in front of me that I tried to ignore.

We paid the check, gathered our things, and walked out of the Sourdough toward the book room. I wondered if they'd think I was a total pussy if I said I'd wait for them outside while they went in and placed their bets.

Saved by the bell—literally, when my phone in my pocket

went off.

"Jack," I said to the others, motioning for them to continue while I sat at an empty slot machine bank. I watched their retreating backs and answered, "Hey."

"Hey," he said. His voice sounded different. More relaxed, softer. I didn't kid myself that talking to me was what had created the mood.

"How are things going?" I asked.

"Good. Really good. Ben and Casey are getting along really well. We took him to dinner last night and explained it all to him. He was a little confused about a grandfather he knew nothing about, but Ben was great explaining it all to him. The whole Rachael thing. As much as you can explain that to a kid."

"Right," I said. The relaxation in his voice morphed into something that sounded remarkably like happiness.

I smiled thinking about it, but then a childish side of me felt tweaked that he didn't—couldn't?—have that happiness with me.

Could he *ever* have that with me?

"We're picking him up from school today, taking him to a Blazers game tonight."

"Do you think Ben is up to that?" I asked.

"A friend of mine has a luxury box. Easy access; shouldn't be a problem. But we'll play it by ear, make a decision after dinner."

"That's...that's great. I—"

"Where are you? Sounds like a casino," Jack said, the warmth in his voice edging away.

"Just got done having breakfast at the Sourdough," I said. I didn't tell him that I was watching with a gnawing in my stomach as Jimmy, Gus, and Raymond stepped to the counter in the book room to place their bets.

"Is that wise?" he asked.

The gnawing turned to something else, something darker. "I haven't placed a bet in a month. I have to still be in casinos to make my—"

"I meant because of the media. Because of the Lion case," he said.

"Oh," I said, my shoulders sinking.

There was a pause. "You okay?" he finally asked.

"Yeah," I said. "I just miss you both."

He chuckled. "Christ, I just saw you yesterday. I can go days without seeing you if I'm on a case, or you're hot at a table."

"I know." I didn't want to keep on this topic. It wasn't helping the emotions that were bubbling just beneath my surface.

Emotions that fueled JoJo's voice. "Speaking of the Lion case," I said, "have you spoken to Frank?"

"No, why?" he said, his voice giving away the fact that he was feeling some of his own raw emotions, too.

"He called after I dropped you two off, and I went to the station. I answered a few questions, but they didn't tell me much."

"They?"

"He was working with Peter Faxon."

Nothing from Jack, which told me all I needed to know about how he felt about his fellow detective. "Like I said, they didn't tell me much, but then Carla came over last night. They'd called her too. She said that she found out—"

"Stop," he said abruptly.

"Why, what's wrong? Is it Ben?"

"No, he's fine. I just…I just don't want to hear all this."

"Seriously? I thought you'd be pumping me for any detail I'd heard."

He sighed, and I knew the relaxation I'd heard in his voice would be gone when he answered. "I thought so too. But no, I don't want to know." I was right…tired, weary Jack was back.

I could have cried, but I couldn't have told you whether from sorrow or happiness.

"Okay," I said.

"I'm just really enjoying my time here. Spending time with Ben and Casey. Lisa's been really cool about the short-notice visit."

You'd think I'd feel a pang of jealousy over Jack seeing his ex-wife Lisa, but I didn't. She was married to his former partner, and on some level I knew she was not a threat to what Jack and I had.

I couldn't say the same thing about the thought of Jack, Ben, and Casey having family time.

Irrational, sure. And I truly was happy for them all that they'd found each other—especially Ben.

And yet...

Gus, Jimmy, and Raymond walked from the book room, the two older men waving at me and then leaving the casino through the front door. Raymond motioned to the men's room on the other side of the casino floor, and I indicated that I understood.

"Jack," I said, "I have to go. The boys are waiting for me."

"Okay. Stay out of the high-profile places, yeah?"

"Yeah," I agreed, knowing that was the smart move. I watched as Raymond entered the men's room on my far right, then my head swiveled to the book room on my left. "Okay," I said in a wrap-it-up voice, starting to walk. Not toward the restrooms. Not toward the front door to pull the car around.

I walked to my left. To the book room.

"I'll call tomorrow," Jack said.

"That'd be great," I said, my brain fuzzing on what he was saying, his voice getting softer in my head.

JoJo was getting louder.

I had Carla's money on me. A day early. If I doubled that today with a bet, I could pay her off tomorrow and have back the original money that I started with Friday night before the poker game.

I couldn't give it back to Lor; she'd wonder where I'd gotten it.

"Okay, then, take care of yourself," Jack said, concern in

his voice.

"You too," I said, disconnecting as I stepped into the book room area, quickly making my way to the counter.

JoJo's voice again made her case. *Even if I didn't give it back to Lor, I could hang on to it as a buffer. It wouldn't be too long before it'd be okay to go back to playing in casinos—that money could be my stake.*

"Twenty-two thousand on Butler," I said as I got to the counter. I looked over my shoulder to make sure Raymond hadn't come out of the men's room yet, which he hadn't. I took the money out of the envelope Lor had given me. It was a twenty-thousand-dollar bet, with the ten percent "juice" of two thousand. If I won, I'd get forty-two thousand back.

The cashier didn't blink an eye, just made my bet and handed me my ticket.

It wasn't any kind of specialty paper, was quite small in size, maybe two inches by two inches. But oh, the weight of it in my hand, the tingling of it as I held it between my fingers.

The Hummer.

I turned quickly and headed out of the book room, wanting to fondle it longer, but shoved in my jacket pocket so Raymond wouldn't see it.

He came out of the restroom looking to the area where I'd been on the phone, which bought me the few seconds needed to veer to the entrance area.

"Yo," I said, not using his name, but getting his attention through the banks of slots. He saw me and headed over.

We walked out of the casino and to the car in silence.

On the drive home, Raymond said, "They meant what they said, right? They wouldn't hold it against me for that tip if Butler doesn't cover?"

"They meant it," I said. I headed down Charleston toward Summerlin. My heart was beating faster, and I tried to control my breathing so Raymond wouldn't think I was having a heart attack or something.

The Hummer often resembled a heart attack—internally, anyway.

"You make a bet, and it turns out to be a bust, you only have yourself to blame."

Thirty
❖❖

I TOOK A NAP WHEN WE GOT HOME, even though I'd just gotten out of bed a couple of hours ago. I could have blamed it on the big breakfast (and chocolate cake!), and that was what I told Raymond and Lor when I headed to my room, but that wasn't what dragged me under. Wasn't what made me curl up in my covers, after only kicking off my shoes, and pull them up and over my head.

Shame. Guilt. Disgust.

Yeah, that was what drove me to bed. That was what I had to take a three-hour nap to avoid feeling.

They were all still there when I woke up, of course, but by then some of my survivor skills had come back, having been dormant for a month.

It was just this once. JoJo's voice, feeling free and relaxed now that she'd gotten her way.

I numbly acknowledged that JoJo's voice had the same easy quality to it that Jack's voice had had when he'd first called me.

You went a whole month. That proves it's not really a problem, that you can quit at any time.

Yeah, maybe. Maybe not.

Probably not.

Obviously it's not a problem if you can go a month without placing a bet. No worries.

I splashed water on my face in my bathroom, turning away from my reflection in the mirror, fearful of seeing JoJo.

I made my way to the book room and joined Raymond and Jimmy, who had apparently come over while I'd been sleeping.

"No Gus?" I said, half kidding.

"He's in the kitchen flirting with Lorelei," Jimmy said.

"Oh," I said, wondering if I should go run interference. But whom I would be protecting, I wasn't sure. Besides, walking to the kitchen was just too much effort, so I crawled onto the leather loveseat at the front of the room, pulling one of the throws from its back down on top of me.

Butler and Kansas were in warmups, and part of me wished I'd just slept through that game and found out the final score later.

But the other part of me—the part that had me sneaking into Arizona Charlie's book room while Raymond was in the john—knew that my internal clock—my gambler's clock—would never have let me sleep through a game on which I had a bet placed.

And no twenty-dollar bet, either. (Though I'd have to think back to maybe my first few months in Vegas to remember placing a bet as low as twenty dollars.)

"How you doing?" I asked Jimmy, not bothering to look over the back of the loveseat to see him on the top row of our little theater.

He knew I wasn't asking about his health, or how his day was going. "I'm up," he said, and I nodded, though he couldn't see me. "Barely," he added.

"Still…" I said, and heard a snort.

"Raymond?" I asked.

"Up," he said. I didn't ask how much either of them had bet—that wasn't kosher in gambling circles. I knew Raymond would have had the money from Carla's game in his pocket, but wasn't sure how much he'd had when he'd left Chicago. My guess was he'd given whatever he'd had from his point shaving to his mom. But obviously he had some he was willing to bet on college basketball.

Besides, what? I was going to give him advice on money management? I was going to tell him to start putting that away?

Gus poked his head in the doorway. "Lorelei's taking a head count for dinner. And suggestions." He looked at all three of us. I raised my hand, and hoisted myself enough to see Raymond and Jimmy do the same. Gus nodded. "Requests?" Jimmy looked down to me, a brow raised.

"Go for it," I said, waving my permission to him, then sinking back into the soft leather and warm chenille.

"Italian," he said, surprising no one in the room. "Specifically her ziti," he added.

I smiled, probably for the first time since dropping Jack and Ben at the airport.

And then the game started and the Hummer took over.

How to describe watching a game on which you've bet a tremendous amount of money—money that was to be given to someone else the next day—and have absolutely no control?

Exhilarating. I felt like I was flying—no, skydiving. That kind of rush.

Though my body never moved an inch, and I made no sounds.

Lots of gamblers reacted during their games—it was only natural, and book rooms could be a really fun place to watch a game just to hear the cheers and groans.

You'd be watching a game on one screen, hear a collective cheer from somewhere around you, and your eyes would dart from screen to screen, looking for the touchdown/goal/home run/three-pointer.

But that had never been my style—vocally or bodily showing signs that I had money on a game. I think it was probably because early on I knew it was going to be a problem for me, and the feeling of shame quickly became a part of the Hummer.

As if not letting the guy sitting next to me realize I'd made a compulsive bet the amount of a small car would somehow negate the fact that I had.

So shame, sure, was part of the Hummer, but so was certainty, and a smugness—*hey, I was smart enough to see this ending coming.* And then just the thrill of the game, the not knowing, rolled all into one big emotional roller coaster.

And I'd forgotten how much I loved it.

Yeah, I was disgusted with myself for caving, for pissing away a month of non-betting. But the bigger part of me—the *truer* part of me—was in absolute heaven watching the game. Even when Kansas was up by twenty at the half and covering the point spread—meaning I was losing—I couldn't help but feel the best I had in thirty days.

Sick, yeah, I knew that. It was the stuff interventions were made of.

And I loved it.

"No more breakfasts for you, kid," Jimmy said, rising (no small task) from his seat at halftime. He made a motion of ruffling Raymond's nonexistent hair as he passed him coming down the three steps.

"Just wait," Raymond said.

Jimmy put a hand up as he left the room. "What every gambler says, kid."

Gus once again popped his head in the doorway. "Taking orders for anything. Beer? Something else?"

I sat up on the loveseat and stretched my arms. "Are you watching the game?" I asked, wondering about his perfect halftime timing. And also not able to wrap my mind around the idea of being in a house while a game was being played on which you had money and not watching it.

Gus nodded. "I've got it on in the kitchen. Keeping our girl company while she makes Jimmy's ziti."

Raymond and I exchanged glances at the "our girl" comment, but I only said, "I'm good, but thanks."

Raymond left his chair (with much more agility than Jimmy had), and said to Gus as he passed him, "Think I'll take a look at what's in the fridge."

Gus nodded to Raymond and started to follow him out of the room but turned back to look at me. "Sure you're okay, doll?"

"Yep, good, thanks." He studied me for a minute, gave me a wink, then left. Jimmy came back in and took his seat. I turned around and watched the other game that was being played the same time as Kansas/Butler. UConn and UCLA. I didn't have money on it, thus I barely registered that UCLA was winning. Their second half had already started, and Jimmy and I watched in silence as UCLA went up by another three.

Raymond came back in with a loaded plate and a Gatorade. "Want some?" he asked first me, then Jimmy. I shook my head. Jimmy asked, "Lorelei making Italian?"

Raymond nodded. "Yeah, the kitchen smells awesome."

Jimmy said, "I'll wait, then." I hoped Lor made a big batch—which she always did. Raymond's heaping plate of last night's leftovers was a testament to that.

It seemed Raymond would be invited to breakfast again after all, because the Butler center began to wear down Jamison, the Kansas big man. And even more so on the defensive side, where they went at him again and again, causing the coach to take out Jamison due to foul trouble. Kansas was up by seventeen at that point, with two minutes left to play.

There was no chance Butler would win, but other than the Kansas center being pulled for foul trouble, both coaches kept their starters in.

I was losing by two (to push/tie) or three (to outright win) points and the Hummer was in full…hum.

Now being guarded by a second-stringer who didn't get much playing time, the Butler center was fed the ball every chance they got, and Butler cut the deficit to thirteen over the next minute and a half.

Thirty seconds left to play and I was winning my bet with a basket to spare. At the last time-out, with fifteen seconds to play, and the trading of a three-point shot by Kansas and a two by Butler, the coaches pulled their starters and let the scrubs in. In Butler's case to say they had played in the tournament. In Kansas's case as a show of good sportsmanship—or one-upsmanship, depending on how you felt about Kansas.

Kansas was up by fourteen points. Butler was covering by one point. Kansas would get the ball when the time-out was over.

I held my internal breath, wondering if you'd get some gung-ho kid from Kansas who wanted to take a shot, or if the guard would just dribble around the top of the key and let the clock run out.

When it became obvious that the guard had been given instructions not to shoot and just let the clock run out, I let out my breath gently.

See, that was easy. Carla paid back, slush fund once again intact. And no one will be the wiser.

I could even bet on tomorrow's games with my winnings, after I pay Carla off, and double up again.

"Dumb motherfucker," Jimmy boomed from behind me, and JoJo shut up while my eyes focused on the game.

An overzealous scrub for Butler had tried to steal the ball and had fouled the Kansas guard.

The Butler coach was shaking his head, but in their scheme of things it didn't really matter.

In the scheme of things in the book room in a lovely home in Summerlin…it meant a lot.

Raymond's groan had joined Jimmy's outburst, and I

watched, paralyzed, as the Kansas point guard walked to the free throw line with one second left.

He sank the first one and my gut plunged like the ball did through the net. Fifteen points. A push. I'd get most of my money back, losing just the two grand juice.

Okay, that was okay. I could scrounge the juice from funds somewhere around the house where I'd dropped a few hundred here and there. That would give me what I needed to pay Carla off.

No harm done.

Except I had bet again, but that fact was not relevant right now as the Kansas guard lined up to take his second shot.

You would think I'd close my eyes or something, but no, that wasn't part of the rush, the feeling. You had to *see* the free throw, the blocked extra point, the power-play goal with seconds left. It was part of the exquisiteness.

Part of the madness.

It went in. Butler took the ball out and didn't even get a desperation shot off before the buzzer sounded.

Anticlimactic in the arena, where the game was never in doubt.

Cataclysmic in my arena.

"Can you *believe* that?" Gus said from the doorway.

"No," Raymond said, disbelief in his voice.

"Fucking freshman," Jimmy said.

Gus was shaking his head. "March Madness, all right." He rapped his hand on the doorjamb as if slamming down a gavel to end the proceedings. The sound made me jump a tiny bit—the only movement I'd made in the past twenty minutes, though I had lived and died twenty-two thousand times in that short while. "Soup's on. Lor says five minutes."

We all nodded and started moving around. Whoever was holding the remotes turned the televisions off.

I made sure there wasn't a look of panic on my face as I

got up and folded the throw and returned it to the back of the loveseat.

And it really wasn't panic I felt.

The thing was, the feeling wasn't all that different with losing than it was with winning. You felt a weird sense of relief when you lost a bet too, as if to say it was finally over. That maybe it was truly over this time, that you'd just lost your last bet.

But the relief, in both instances, was quickly replaced with dread. Dread, guilt, and—most overwhelmingly—the deep-seated craving to bet again as soon as possible.

I was the last one out of the room, and as I made my way to the kitchen my phone chimed with a text. Hoping it would be Jack, I laughed when I saw who it'd come from. Was she psychic or something?

Carla: *Will be in Summerlin tomorrow morning. Meet at Biscuits at ten for $$?*

Oh, I'd meet her at Biscuits for breakfast at ten, and I texted her as much. But she might be a tad upset when she walked out with only one of their famous cinnamon rolls in her bag.

Thirty-One
❖❖

AFTER THE FABULOUS DINNER, the gin rummy game following, and Jimmy and Gus had left, I let Raymond and Lor know I was going to play cards for a while.

"Is that wise?" Lor asked.

Not wanting to jump to the same conclusion I had with Jack, I said, "Because of the whole Lion thing?"

She looked at me like I was crazy. "Uh...*yeah*."

I shrugged, but made my way to the foyer and the closet there. "It's midnight on a Thursday night. It'll be games that go late into the night. Those are played by locals, real gamblers, not tourists."

"Real gamblers know who you are even more. You just know there'll be pictures of you on Instagram and places of you out playing poker while Lion hasn't even been buried yet."

It was true—Lion had not even been buried yet due to the coroner hanging on to the body and then having to fly it to Florida. It would be a private ceremony, and I certainly wasn't expecting an invitation. They were going to do a larger memorial for him on the Tuesday of Masters week, which was a couple of weeks away.

Didn't think I'd be invited to Augusta, either.

"I'll play in the high rollers' room at the Bellagio. Nobody in there is going to snap a photo of me."

"I don't know," she said. "You're still a hot topic. Somebody would pay to get a photo of you gambling, I'm sure."

"Get out of here," I said, brushing her words aside with a wave of my hand as I put on my jean jacket. I felt around in the pocket and touched the envelope meant for Carla, which was now heavily depleted and going to be used as a stake in a poker game.

I can win it all back tonight. No worries.

JoJo was close to becoming the Robert Evans-esque character Dustin Hoffman played in *Wag the Dog*. "This is *nothing*!"

"No, seriously," Lor said. "You asked me to keep you in the dark, but you've been offered everything from centerfolds to deals for insecticides."

"Insecticides?" both Raymond and I said. I noticed he'd stayed silent during Lor's protest of me playing cards. But he'd been watching. Watching me.

Lor looked at us both, then ducked her head, embarrassed. Finally, I got the connection.

"The Black Widow. Spider killer?"

She nodded, and I couldn't help but start laughing, which seemed to piss her off. "Seriously, Jo, just keep to the house for a while longer. Some celebrity is bound to OD or get caught cheating or something, and your fifteen minutes will be over. Hang on until then."

It was smart advice, of course. Though it was weird to wish for bad news to displace Lion's death. To want the footage of Lion getting out of my car relegated to page two of all the main news sites.

But Carla needed to be paid tomorrow, and I had four thousand dollars to turn into twenty-six.

And no games between now and then to bet on.

Not that I would. No, it was a one-time deal, betting on Butler. And look how that had turned out.

Maybe, like, a bet every thirty days? To feed the Hummer, but knowing that I can stop for a month (not plural as of now) at a time?

"I'm going stir crazy here," I said to Lor. "And the Marathon is coming up, and I was supposed to be logging lots of playing hours to get ready for that tournament," I added. Both statements true, but neither the real reason I needed to play tonight.

She started to balk at those points, and I held up a hand. "Lor, I'm going. I'll try to keep a low profile, but even if a pic is snapped, so what? I'm doing what I do for a living—playing poker—in a legal setting." I jammed my hand back into the pocket and felt an old ponytail holder underneath the money envelope. Pulling it out, I stuck my hair into a ponytail then went back to the closet and grabbed a Packers ball cap that my mom had given me for Christmas last year. Sticking it on my head, I looped the ponytail through the back and pulled the brim down. "Better?" I asked.

She sighed and shrugged. "Play well," she said, and turned around, walking down the hallway to the wing that held her bedroom.

I turned to the side table and grabbed the keys to my Porsche. Probably safer to take the Lexus, but I missed my baby as much as I missed poker, and the media was now gone from the gate permanently. (Not sure how that happened, but I was thinking Jack and/or Frank.)

"You good?" Raymond asked me. Turning to him, I was about to answer yes, but I saw the look in his eye. Knowing. Concerned.

"Working on it." It was about all I was willing to give him.

He took it. I left the house and drove to work.

Where I needed to have a very good shift.

I TAPPED A FINGER ON MY horseshoe pendant three times,

but I knew it was too late. The dealer turned the river card and made it official. I had just lost my last chips.

At least I'd only lost four thousand dollars.

Yeah, that was the fucked-up logic I used. It was *only* four thousand dollars.

And, oh yeah, the twenty-two thousand lost on Butler.

So, not a good day.

At least nobody took my picture. That I knew of.

"That's it for me," I said, rising from the table. I hadn't really brought enough cash to play in the high rollers' room, but based on my past experience, I was invited to join that game. And as I'd told Lor, it was mostly pros, guys I saw all the time, and they'd been cool, not bringing up the Lion stuff.

At least not to my face.

I didn't kid myself. They'd all be jawing the moment I left. Which was now.

Instead of going to the parking deck, I veered to the book room and took a seat on one of their leather loveseats—not unlike the one where I'd watched Carla's money go through my hands like that Kansas guard's shot went through the net.

It was five in the morning, eight in the east, and no games were on yet. There would be college basketball games played later today to get the rest of field of eight set for Saturday and Sunday. Now all the monitors were on different sports channels and their morning news shows. Turning from those to the right and the big board, I saw they'd just posted the day's odds, and I studied them.

Not that I was going to bet. No, just so I'd be prepared to talk about it at breakfast later, if we did breakfast again with just Jimmy and Gus. Oh crap, I couldn't meet them for breakfast—I was meeting Carla at ten at Biscuits.

At least I could treat for breakfast. That was about all she was going to get out of me.

I thought about Jack and Ben in Portland and wondered

if they'd all gone to the Trailblazers game. The score on the big board showed that the game had been a close one that the Blazers pulled out. It would have been a good one for the family outing.

I desperately wanted to hear Jack's or Ben's voice, but knew they'd both be worried if I called at this hour.

"Hey," I heard a man say as he sat in the club chair next to my loveseat. It was fine that he sat there, but there were a lot of empty seats in the deserted room, so it was odd that he'd chosen to sit so close to me.

I nodded at him, not wanting to encourage him, but then did a double take. "Hey," I said to the man who'd been our dealer the night of Carla's game. The night Lion died.

I sat up higher in my seat. "Hey," I repeated. "You work here?" I asked. He wasn't wearing a Bellagio dealer uniform, just civvies—very similar to mine, actually.

"No," he said, shaking his head. "Can't play where you work. I deal at the Venetian."

I nodded, and did a head tilt toward the poker room. "How'd you do?"

"Won a little, not much. You?"

One small head shake and he got it. "I saw you come out of Bobby's Room. Hope it's cool I came over," he said.

"Yeah, sure," I said.

"Sean," he said, reminding me of his name, though I wasn't sure I'd been told it last Friday night. "Goodson," he added.

"Anna Dawson," I said.

He smiled wryly. "Uh, yeah, I know."

Duh. "Right. And yeah, it's cool you came over. I'm glad you did, in fact."

"Yeah?"

"Yeah," I said, leaning forward. "How has your week been? I mean, with the police and everything?"

He leaned forward too so our heads were only a foot or so apart. Looking around before he spoke (though the room remained empty; even the cashier counter was closed up), he said, "I spent *a lot* of time there on Sunday, answered everything I could. Then again on Thursday, after they had a time frame and knew that the game was somehow involved."

I nodded. "Saturday and Wednesday for me."

"Wow, that was fast. Saturday."

I sat back a little. "Yeah, well, it didn't help that the detective on the case knew I was playing cards with Lion that night even before it happened."

A puzzled look crossed Sean's face. Yeah, it was all puzzling, that was for sure. "How'd that happen?"

"Personal connection. He's not on the case anymore," I said.

"Yeah, it was a different guy there today—yesterday, technically—for me."

We discussed what we'd been told by the cops, much like Carla, Raymond, and I had done yesterday. And speculated at all that we did not know. Which was a lot.

Sean didn't know the bartender either, and hadn't recognized Brandt or Calvin from anywhere.

"Something wasn't right with that game," he said after we'd wrapped up our briefing.

"Yeah, someone died right after it," I said.

He shook his head. "No, I mean during the game. *With* the game."

I leaned forward again, elbows on my knees, hands dangling in front. "How so?"

He looked away from me, down and in front of him, as if he was trying to picture something. "I can't really place it, but something was off. There were too many hands that I couldn't call."

"Call?"

He looked at me from the corner of his eye, but his head was still pointing down at his imaginary table. "You deal all the time like I do, you start playing games with yourself, in your head, you know?" I did it all the time too, and I nodded. "So, I play along in my head, guessing who has what, who will win, who's bluffing, stuff like that."

"Basically being another player but without chips in front of you."

"Yeah, exactly."

"I imagine you get pretty good after a while."

He nodded once. "Yeah."

"Must help when you actually play."

"It can, but you're not as objective when you play with your own money. Plus, then you're focused on you first, the table second. When I deal, all the players are the same to me—they all get the same focus. Plus, no matter how good you are at reading tables and probability and people, there's always the luck factor."

"There is that," I said, and we both chuckled, knowing that the luck factor had worked both for and against us. Sometimes during the same game.

His eyes slid back in front of him and his hands moved a little, almost like he was dealing cards, but not quite that precise. "But that game, I was thrown a lot. Way more than normal."

"Off night?" I asked, not really sure what he was getting at.

He left his imaginary table and sat back in his seat, looking at me. "Maybe. Or..."

I bit. "Or?"

"Or somebody—or *sombebodies*, more likely—was cheating."

Thirty-Two

❖❖

I SPENT THE NEXT HOUR after Sean left replaying every hand of Friday night's game. I'd asked him if he'd told the police his suspicions, and he'd said no. That he wasn't sure on Sunday (still wasn't *sure* sure), and yesterday he'd been pissed off enough by Peter Faxon to not want to be overly helpful. Apparently Jack wasn't the only one who didn't care for Faxon's brashness.

If Sean was right—and the more I thought about it, the more I knew he was—Lion had cheated.

But he hadn't been alone.

Normally if someone was cheating it would be with the help of the dealer, but Sean was the one who thought something was amiss.

Of course, that would be a great way to throw suspicion off yourself.

Another way to cheat in poker would be to chip replenish. Meaning you brought in your own matching chips and snuck them into your pile. But that would only work during a cash game at a casino, where it would be impossible to track chips to one game. Players came and went during those games, taking their chips with them. Recently a pro had been arrested for bringing in outside chips during a tournament. He'd saved them from previous tournaments (they used a different chip for those than cash games) and snuck them from his jacket pocket into his stack at future tournaments. But that was tournament play, not cash like we'd played.

Plus, Carla's rack had been full when I'd left that night. I remembered watching her carefully stack them as I waited for Lion to come out of the bathroom. There were no extra chips.

Another way to cheat, though it wasn't really considered cheating because it was a skill, was edge sorting. A player could tell by the printing on the back of cards—at the edge where the pattern would be cut while printing the big sheet of cards—what certain cards were.

But that was a very sophisticated skill and done mostly at blackjack and baccarat, where fewer cards were in play at any given time.

I didn't think Lion had edge-sorting skills in him. And if he was on coke, there was no way his focus would be sharp enough to do it.

Which left collusion with another player.

Signs between the two to let the other know when they had a good or bad hand. A system in place so that the other could either build up the pot for the other, or drop out.

Yeah, that was the most likely route Lion had taken.

Thinking about all the pots Lion pulled in, quite a few leaving my head spinning with a "what just happened" feeling, I was now convinced Sean was right. They were good, but I wondered if I hadn't been so caught up in my dislike of Lion—and wanting to beat him—would I have figured it out myself? But that had been part of their plan, having emotions come into play so maybe you'd miss a thing or two. And it had worked.

Lion had cheated.

And he'd had a partner.

I was pulled out of my reverie by a cup of coffee coming into my eyesight, being held by a black hand. Before I could look up to Raymond, he added another hand to my line of vision, this one holding a bag from the patisserie at the Bellagio.

"Chocolate croissants," he said. I wasn't sure which to reach for first.

He made his way around the furniture and sat next to me on the loveseat, placing his offerings on the little coffee table in front of us.

"Not that I'm not grateful," I said, taking a pull of the strong coffee, "but what are you doing here?"

He had one for himself, and positioned the sleeve collar on the cup as he pulled it from the cardboard carrier. "You told Lor where you'd be playing. Figured you'd be wrapping up pretty soon, so thought I'd meet you for coffee." He motioned to the bakery bag. "Found that place, and by the size of the line, I figured their shit was good."

"It's amazing." It was now nearly six in the morning, and at that weird time in casinos where a few early risers—and those from other time zones—were up and about, and yet there were still some diehards at the poker tables, playing blackjack and slots. I turned back and saw that the poker room was nearly deserted, and what players remained were all on one table. Bobby's Room, the high-roller area where I'd played earlier, was dark behind the crystal walls.

"Thanks," I said as I ripped open the bag and pulled out a flaky, buttery croissant, hints of chocolate peeking out at the ends. We ate in silence, trying to keep the flakes and crumbs over a couple of spread-out napkins.

When we'd finished, I sat back in the seat and sipped what was left of my coffee. Raymond stayed leaning forward, both of us looking straight ahead at the row of television screens. He didn't even look at me when he said, "You made a bet yesterday, didn't you?"

I kind of knew it was coming. There was no reason for Raymond to drive from Summerlin to the Strip at five in the morning just to get me a croissant—fabulous though they were.

"Yeah," I said.

"And you lost."

"Yeah," I answered, though he really hadn't asked a question.

He sat back, his body even with mine, and stretched out his leg, slumping low in the comfy furniture. "I'm not judging, know that. But, I mean, why?"

I thought about trying to explain it, but how could I when I couldn't explain it to myself?

"You ever do Weight Watchers?" I asked, then snorted with my obvious stupidity. "No. Of course not. But see, I've known women who go to Weight Watchers, or other weight-loss places, and they're doing great, really great. Go to the weigh-in, hit their target goal for the week, maybe do even better. Have a great meeting where they get helpful hints and inspirational stories. Then they walk out, get in their car, and go right to the bakery for a huge cupcake, or to McDonald's drive-thru for supersized fries."

"Yeah?" he said. "Again, why?"

I shook my head. I was tempted to scrunch down with him and lay my head upon his shoulder. I *wanted* to lay all of this upon someone else's shoulders.

But I couldn't. It was all on me.

"I don't know," I said finally. "I know I made it to thirty days with really no problems, no dire urges, and"—I snapped a finger—"just like that, I placed a bet. *Needed* to place that bet."

He kept quiet, his hands, deep ebony on top, a lighter mocha on his palms, resting on his abdomen, fingers laced.

"And I'll tell you something else," I added. At that he looked up at me, his body being lower in the loveseat. "It felt awesome," I said. "Even when I was losing. Even when I lost. But especially when I made it. That moment at the counter? Even knowing I was trying to do it on the quick so you wouldn't see? Fucking amazing."

He studied me, then nodded once. "I imagine those supersized fries taste fucking amazing to those Weight Watchers folk too."

"I'm sure they do. Saltier, hotter."

"Greasier," he added.

"Yeah."

Good thing I'd just had that huge croissant or I'd probably be hitting a drive-thru of my own soon.

"Was it the Butler game?" he asked, still watching me. I nodded, and he sighed, turning his head back to the front.

"Again, not on you," I said.

"I know," he said. "I can't not speak up when asked just 'cause you're a degenerate gambler who can't keep her money in her pocket."

I croaked out a laugh and elbowed him. "Hey!"

I saw him smile and was glad we could joke about this mess. And a mess it was.

"I suppose that was the money to pay back Carla?"

"Yep."

"What are you gonna do now?"

I sighed, slouching down a little myself, but still not as low as Raymond. "I have no idea."

"Can you just ask Lor for more money? Do you have it?"

"I probably have it. I think I have it. Though it's not likely that it's liquid. It took her a few days to get this." Then I thought about it and made up my mind. "I'm not going to ask Lor for more."

"Why not?"

I didn't go into how it'd made me feel to go to her for this, or how…useless I'd felt when Lor had handed over the money. The self-loathing and how it would be even worse to admit to Lor that in one blink of an eye I'd lost the money for which she'd juggled accounts around (or cashed in some stocks or whatever the hell she'd had to do) for three days to acquire.

"She'll know I'm gambling again."

"You say that like it wasn't a one-time slip."

I realized I'd clenched my hands into fists, and I slowly loosened them, laced my fingers together, and laid them on my stomach, mimicking Raymond. Yeah, just having morning coffee with a bud, sitting and yapping. Not discussing my fundamental breakdown of being a good person.

"I know myself," I said. "I can't say it was a one-time slip, because I don't know that for sure."

"So you don't want her knowing you're gambling again. Why? You're an adult. It's your money."

He was right. But… "Shame. Embarrassment. Not to mention she'd be really worried about me, and I hate to do that to her. And Ben."

He nodded, but didn't say anything.

"Plus then there'd be more interventions," I said, trying to keep a jokey tone to my voice.

"Yeah, I'm not sitting through one of those again," he said, and I laughed.

"And you were at the happy one! You should see the ones she throws for me."

"No thank you. You're right, keep it on the down-low."

"Yeah," I said.

After another couple of minutes, he nudged my knee with his. "But know that I know…case you need to talk shit through or anything."

"Thanks," I said.

I had cursed myself over and over for involving myself in Raymond Joseph's life. But right now, my belly full of croissant and someone sitting next to me—not judging, not scared for me, just…sitting with me while we finished our coffee—I was glad JoJo had chosen him.

Thirty-Three
❖❖

"I NEED ANOTHER WEEK," I said to Carla when I met her at Biscuits later that morning.

Intellectually I knew syrup couldn't freeze mid-pour, but it seemed to when Carla looked up at me from pouring it on her stack of pancakes.

"I need another week," I repeated. "Add the vig."

"That's not an option," she said. She set the syrup down and looked at her well-saturated stack, then back at me.

"What do you mean, not an option? It's always an option."

"It wasn't always with Vince."

My foot tingled where Paulie had broken it ten years ago. Another one of Vince Santini's options.

But that wasn't the option Carla was thinking about. Still, I said, "You don't even have muscle. And Raymond isn't going to do anything beyond working a door for you, so—"

"That's not the kind of option I was thinking of," she said, and began cutting up her pancakes.

"I know," I said softly, and took a drink of coffee. I'd declined breakfast, still being full from the croissant, and, honestly, I was feeling a little queasy about having this conversation. Somewhere in the back of my mind I had to have known it was going to turn out this way.

I probably knew it when I stepped up to the counter at

Arizona Charlie's yesterday and placed that bet.

"I can't," I said. "Not…not now." *Not ever* I had told Jack, and all those who loved me, once. Done with that. She'd never make another appearance.

Carla shrugged and chewed. After swallowing, she said, "I need money, Anna, and a lot more than your twenty-six K. I need JoJo kind of money."

I was shaking my head before she'd even begun. "JoJo money is just even money. You'd have to have a huge stake to get a huge payout. And if you have a huge stake, you can wait a few more weeks for my twenty-six K."

"Not if it's the money line," she said, and I knew that either Vince had told her, or she'd figured it out that Raymond had not only shaved points to cover a spread, but had outright lost a game in order to win a money-line bet, which could be anywhere from one and a half to five or six times your original bet.

And that would mean buy-in from a player, not just someone playing badly because of a chance meeting with JoJo. Still, I didn't need to give up all my secrets.

I leaned closer to her, happy that no other booths around us had any patrons. "I can't JoJo now. Do you know what would happen if I got caught slipping a roofie to a couple of college kids?" She opened her mouth to speak, but I barreled on. "Not only repercussions from that act, and people putting together point shaving, but the implications in Lion's death." I sat back in my seat. "No. No way. You add the vig and I pay when I can."

She sat back in her chair, put her fork down, and wiped her mouth with a napkin. "You won't need to roofie anybody, and you know it."

Yeah, she'd called my bluff. She knew it would take player (or players—plural) involvement.

"It's JoJo. That's the only option available to you."

I looked her up and down, like a boxer sizing up his competition. "I'll take my chances with your nonexistent muscle."

A small smile came across her face. A smirk, really, and I knew I wouldn't want to hear what she said next.

Not that I'd wanted to hear any of it.

"I may not have an enforcer, but I have something better. Raymond Joseph's balls in a vise."

Shit. She was right. Still, the poker player in me came out and I snorted, seeming to relax in my seat. "Please. You don't have anything. Nothing can be proven about those games."

"Maybe not. But if I come forward and name him as someone who was at Lion LaGasse's last poker game, it's going to start a whole lot of questions about why he was even in Vegas and just what, exactly, his ties to gambling are. I know that, thanks to Vince, he has the goods on those two Feds that had previously looked into him, but there is such a thing as being tried in the court of public opinion. Or different investigators taking on the case. If not charges, then at least the world will know what he did. I'll make sure the press knows what games he threw and that he was there the night Lion died. You think people are gunning for the Black Widow? What do you think they'll do to Raymond?"

"Bitch," I said.

She seemed hurt by that, and leaned forward. "Vince played hardball with you all the time, and you took it as your due because you were desperate enough to place a bet that you borrowed his money. But because I'm a woman doing the same thing, all of a sudden I'm a bitch? That ain't right."

I sat taller in the booth, letting her words sink in. Shit, she was right. "You're right. Sorry. Lean in and everything, Carla. Hear you roar. You can extort just as well as any man."

"And you can rack up gambling debts as well as any of them too."

Ouch. But she was right again.

She took a sip of coffee, keeping her hand on the rim of the mug when she'd placed it back on the table, her nails a blood red. "Well," she said, "aren't we a couple of pioneers."

"Yay us," I said.

Thinking of Detective Faxon now being on the case, I played my last card. "His name could come out at any minute about being at the game. Lion recognized him. Jack's off the case. You might not have the hole card you think you do."

"I like to gamble too. I think his name stays buried. They're not going to release names and say they have no idea who three of the other people in the room were—that works against them while trying to find Brandt, Calvin, and the bartender."

Right again, and I hadn't thought of it that way.

"Clock's ticking," she said. "Not only on this one-time offer, but on the college basketball season. And that does seem to be your sport of choice—or is there more to JoJo than Paulie told me?"

Paulie, right. So Vince hadn't given away my secrets. Paulie had. That made more sense. I didn't bother answering that last question, just concerned myself with the ticking clock, looking for other answers.

"Let me have today. Look at the games, the bracket. Guess what odds would be. I'll get with you tomorrow."

She nodded. "Tomorrow, with a JoJo plan. A money-line bet plan. Or the *Review-Journal* is going to get a call about Raymond."

I nodded and started to leave, rising from the booth. I stopped and leaned down to her. "You're right—calling you a bitch was wrong, but I would have called Vince—at least in my head—a complete asshole for doing this. So, as not to be un-feminist…you're an asshole."

She raised her brow and pursed her lips, then said, "Fair enough."

I walked out of Biscuits and got in my Porsche, wanting to drive it straight to the mountains and off a cliff.

Instead, heading back to my house, I thought about how damn good the Hummer had felt yesterday, and how I wished I had some money on me to stop at the Red Rock casino and place a bet.

Bitch. Asshole. Yeah, I was both.

And worse.

Thirty-Four
❖

"PLAY AAU BALL with any of *these* kids?" Jimmy said that evening as we watched college basketball at my place.

He was yanking Raymond's chain, which Raymond knew, if the bird he flipped Jimmy from his chair was any indication. Jimmy guffawed from behind me.

"Actually, yeah," Raymond said, pointing at the screen on the right, where Lamont University was warming up to play Maryland. "DeShaun Rogers for Lamont. We did three summers together in AAU."

"Shit, now you tell me," Jimmy said. "And is he overrated too?"

"Nah, he's the real deal. Purest three-point shooter I ever saw."

I heard rustling behind me and knew Jimmy was probably looking at an odds sheet, seeing what the spread was on this game, which told me he hadn't taken it—he would have remembered it.

The scene was much like it was last night—Jimmy, Raymond, and I watching games in my book room, though this time I was in the second row in a recliner and Raymond was in the loveseat in the first row.

And instead of making us dinner, tonight Lor had gone out…with Gus. I made myself a mental note to touch base with

Lor in the next day or two to get the scoop on what was going on with her. With the whole Lion thing, and now the Carla thing, I had missed a couple of steps in there if Gus and Lor were actually going out on a real date.

Had Jack and I ever actually gone out on a date? I didn't think so.

He'd called earlier, but I didn't stay on with him long, guessing he might be able to tell I'd slipped just by my voice.

Paranoid? Maybe. But Jack Schiller was one good detective, whether he was on a case or not.

I'd told Raymond about my conversation with Carla. It was right when Jimmy had joined us and known something was up, so I let him in on it.

It was weird that I could tell Jimmy and Raymond about messing up and betting money that was earmarked for someone else, but couldn't say any of that to Jack, Ben, or Lor.

For one, Raymond knew me as JoJo first, so there was no hiding her from him. And Jimmy? I knew I'd get no judgment—or pity, which was just as important—from him.

And I didn't. He shrugged a big shoulder when I told him, and reiterated what he'd said to me before: "You gotta be who you are, Anna."

I didn't think they'd be putting that on any posters at support group meetings.

But it did make me feel a little better.

We watched Lamont warm up, and damn if the kid Raymond knew didn't hit everything he aimed for. Plus, it looked like he was playing point, so he'd control the ball, not be at another player's passing mercy to be able to take a shot.

That was JoJo thinking. Sizing him up. He'd be the one she'd go after if she were...*working* this game.

I gotta work some game. And soon.

Raymond sat up and flung his arms over the back of the loveseat, placing his chin on top, facing Jimmy and me.

"Why me?" he asked. I didn't pretend to misunderstand him. I knew what he was asking. It was as if he'd just been in my head—in JoJo's head—while I'd summed up DeShaun Rogers.

"You controlled the ball. You set the tempo. You were the coach on the court. You could shoot, but you also knew what other players were hot and could get the ball to them." He was nodding, but he knew that was true of most point guards. "But to be safe, I did Lurch too. You could be off and somebody else might still get the ball to Lurch. With both of you off your game, no way would you cover the spread. Might still win, but that's not the same thing—not to gamblers."

He waved his hand in a "hurry up" motion. "Yeah, I get that's why you came after us the first time—when we didn't know what was happening. Why'd you come to me...after?"

We'd had variations on this conversation before, but emotions were gone now. It felt like he was asking in a purely analytical way.

I held up a hand and ticked off my reasons as I listed them. "You're unbelievably smart. You control the game. You needed money. You hadn't said anything to anybody about the first time when it was obvious you'd figured out what happened—and probably why." He nodded at that, confirming what I'd already surmised. "And you're unbelievably smart."

"You said that already."

"It bears repeating," I said, and smiled.

He returned my smile, his a little larger. Not quite the trademark grin he flashed when his team was winning, but close. Close enough.

"DeShaun Rogers has all those qualities," Raymond said softly.

My eyes went back to the screen. I heard more rustling behind me, and soon the Lamont game was on the large center screen. Jimmy had put it on.

"His sister need to get into rehab too?" I asked with

skepticism in my voice.

Raymond rolled his eyes at me. "No. But from what he told me, he's shit-ass poor. A bunch of younger siblings. Scary-ass neighborhood in Cleveland. It ain't no South Side, but I guess it ain't no Summerlin neither."

All the reasons I gave Carla as to why JoJo could not make an appearance rushed back to me. They were all valid, and they all still stood.

"I can't show up at a regional tournament and talk to some kid. There's too much going on around those hotels where the team plays. Press, fans, parents. It's not like just a regular season away game. This is the show."

I didn't even mention the repercussions of slipping something into his drink, but it sounded like Raymond thought of this as more of a player-involved buy-in situation, not a regular JoJo scheme.

I could see wheels spinning in Raymond's bald head, and a tiny part of me felt a sick anticipation to hear what he would come up with.

"What if it was me?" he said.

"Uh...no. You, more than me, can't go anywhere near college basketball right now. Bald head or no, you'd be recognized in a second." I didn't tell Raymond about Carla's threat to expose him—no need to worry him needlessly. I'd just told him that she was adamant that she get her money back and suggested my old habit as a means to get it. The way Jimmy had looked at me when I'd told him the story had me suspecting that he knew there was another, deeper reason I was even considering doing this to pay Carla back, but he didn't say anything.

Though he probably guessed what that reason was.

"I don't mean going there. I mean if it was me who reached out to him—offered him cash to keep Sunday's game close enough that Wichita State would cover the spread."

I pointed to the screen. "Lamont has to win right now

before they'd even get to play Wichita State on Sunday."

"They'll win," Jimmy said from behind me. "And they'll be favored by at least eight against Wichita State. Money line will probably be plus three hundred." That would be winning three times your bet—which would make Carla happy.

My mind was shifting, liking this idea, and weighing out the risk to Raymond getting in touch with DeShaun versus the risk Carla was to him. But the shifting stopped at Raymond shaking his head.

"No. Unh-uh. It can't be money line. They still gotta win."

"It's got to be a money-line bet," I said, recalling Carla's strict edict.

More shaking of the head. "Nobody—least of all DeShaun—is going to give up getting to the final weekend of the tournament and a shot at the championship. Ain't gonna happen."

Yeah, he was right. Much like the activities at a hotel during the tournament as opposed to a regular road game were vastly different, so was throwing a game—losing the game—during the regular season versus getting to be one of the last four teams remaining.

"She'll take the even odds on using the spread," Raymond said, referring to Carla. "It's better than nothing. She gets her money back. You scrounge together any loose change you've got and bet it too so you'll make up some of what you lost."

I was shaking my head. "What? What's wrong with that?" Raymond asked.

"I can't bet on it," I said.

"I know you lost the big chunk, but I'm sure you have some—"

"That's not it," I said. "I don't bet on games that I'm... involved with."

"What?"

I shrugged and sank into the recliner, suddenly wanting to

hide. "It was the two rules I had. That JoJo had. Never have a player be knowingly involved—they always had to be innocent victims." I ignored Jimmy's snort and Raymond's raised eyebrow. "And never bet on the game myself. It was always to pay back a debt, never for personal gain."

"Although…" Jimmy said.

I held up a hand. "I used that money to buy earrings for Lorelei, who deserved them with all of my shit she puts up with."

"But still, it was a bet for you," Jimmy pointed out.

"Yeah," I said, sighing.

Raymond had compassion in his eyes, but laid it on the line when he said, "Bitch, the boat done sailed on both of those rules."

"I know," I said, sighing again. "But Raymond, you asked me not very long ago to watch out for you getting too caught up in this. You said sit on you. Hard. This is definitely getting too caught up."

He waved my words away. "It's just a phone call. A one-shot deal. I'm not past the line or anything. No need to sit on me yet. Besides, I'm thinking it's time for me to get off the bench and into the game."

Thirty-Five
❖❖

LAMONT WON EASILY, making us all think that the spread for Sunday's game with Wichita State might even be more than Jimmy's estimated eight.

I called Carla, and we met late that night at the Cold Stone Creamery on Sahara. I wasn't sure where Carla lived, but she seemed to be out in my neck of the woods a lot, so if it wasn't Summerlin, it was close.

We each got our ice cream in silence, then went to her car and sat, eating our food. It was a shiny new Cadillac ATS, which she'd probably bought pre-will reading. Bet she wished she'd waited on that purchase.

I explained my plan, and as expected, she balked at it not being a money-line game. I explained to her what Raymond had said about no college basketball player willing to lose their shot at a national championship. She thought the right person would jump at the chance to sell his soul. She was probably right, but I told her we didn't have time to go soul shopping with only seven games left in the whole college season, including two of those being played the next day.

We went back and forth as we ate our desserts. She threatened again to out Raymond. I suggested she may want to keep that ace in her hand a bit longer, since she had a way to get back her money and at least double what she did have, if not triple it or more.

She finally caved, and we made a deal that she'd put up twenty thousand to pay DeShaun Rogers. The "finder's fee" for setting it all up and being the go-between was the closing of the twenty-six thousand-dollar debt I had with her. The same deal Vince and I used to do.

Just like old times.

When I got home from meeting with her, Jimmy and Raymond were still up waiting for me. Somehow Jimmy had procured a phone number for DeShaun Rogers so Raymond wouldn't have to go through channels (channels that might remember Raymond searching out DeShaun) to get it.

"How'd you come up with his phone number?" I asked Jimmy, knowing however he'd done it, it would never get traced back to him—or Raymond and me.

A shrug and an "I know a guy" was his only answer, which made me smile.

I found my old burner phone and gave it to Raymond to use. We only heard his side of the conversation with DeShaun. He wanted us in the room, though we both offered to leave. I was guessing he wanted some sort of illegal point-shaving guru advice at his fingertips if needed.

But he didn't need us.

"DeShaun. Yeah, I ain't gonna say who this is. And I don't want you to say my name when you guess. That cool?"

It must have been cool, because Raymond went on. "Yeah, so think back. Remember 'Ain't that the Shizzle, my Grizzle'?"

A pause. "Yeah, you got me? Know me? Good. You somewhere alone? Good." Raymond sat up in his seat at the dining room table. "You know the shit they were saying about me?" A pause. "Thanks, man, 'preciate it. Anyway, what would you say to twenty large on Sunday to make sure you boys win by less than eight points?"

Raymond waited, looking from Jimmy to me, then back

again. Jimmy and I leaned forward, our arms and elbows on the table.

Then it came. That wide, ear-to-ear Raymond Joseph smile. Like he'd just sunk a three-pointer at the buzzer to win. A small nod. "That's great, man. Here's the deal…"

He went on and laid it out to DeShaun, but I barely listened, sitting back in my chair, relaxing. At least until the game on Sunday.

And just like that, JoJo was back in business.

And I knew if she was going mess with my life I was damn well going to make some bets and get the Hummer out of the deal.

I DROVE AROUND THE LAMONT *campus because I had time to kill before meeting DeShaun in the agreed-upon McDonald's parking lot.*

Funny, I'd been joking with myself that I'd be spending a lot of time in McDonald's lots for Ben drop-offs with Jack.

It hadn't come to that. Yet. But here I was in an affluent suburb of Dallas, Texas waiting for a drop-off of a different kind.

Lamont was a small, elite school with a perennial powerhouse basketball team. They didn't compete at a high level in any other sport, but always showed up in March with their eye on the prize. The buildings ranged from state of the art on one side of the compact campus to historic brick on the other. The McDonald's was across the main street from campus on the newer side.

I had on a JoJo wig, but the most subdued one I owned. No need to go for a hooker look here, but really no need to be recognized as Anna Dawson, Lion LaGasse's last hurrah.

Though, looking around at the Dallas airport this morning, I would have blended in with the big blonde wig I had first worn with Raymond and Lurch.

I saw DeShaun before he saw me. He came out of the McDonald's, a paper cup in one hand, and folded-over bag in the other. It was Monday afternoon. He'd be heading to practice now. The team would be heading to Indianapolis—where this year's championship would be held—probably on Wednesday or Thursday for all the press hoopla leading up to Saturday's two games. A week from tonight would be the championship game.

I watched as DeShaun scanned the parking lot, and when his eyes came to me, we locked gazes. He made his way to my rental car, sliding into the passenger seat and shutting the door.

"I'm JoJo," I said, so he wouldn't have to ask.

He nodded. It was the name Raymond had given him as the courier.

Courier. That's basically all I was at this point, and though I wasn't happy that Raymond had thrown himself into the fray, I was happy to have a lesser role this time around.

"Pleasure doing business with you, JoJo," he said when I handed him the thick envelope with his winnings.

Like Raymond had, DeShaun had opted to have his payoff bet for him. So instead of twenty thousand dollars that he'd earned by missing some three-pointers and making a few bad passes, he was getting forty thousand because Lamont had beaten Wichita State by only five points.

Jimmy, Gus (on a "tip" that we'd given him), and Raymond had all bet on Wichita State. As, of course, had Carla. Raymond said he bet the thousand dollars he had from working Carla's game plus whatever winnings he'd made since. I didn't ask Jimmy or Gus how much they'd bet. Carla, I imagined, bet everything she could get her hands on.

I had come up with five thousand between some old envelopes I had lying around, desk drawers, jacket pockets, and the like.

But in the end, I couldn't bet it. Yeah, it was different than not betting on a game because JoJo had roofied a college kid. DeShaun was knowingly—willingly—involved with us.

But still…I just couldn't do it.

Which wasn't to say I didn't bet—just not on the Lamont game. I took that five grand and bet it against Kansas, still pissed at that point guard who made the free throws against Butler on Thursday. Kansas won the game, but they didn't cover the point spread this time (because Jamison fouled out of the game—proving Raymond right), and I won my bet.

"Anytime," I said to DeShaun as he counted the money. I breathed deeply the smell of his food. I hadn't eaten since the tipoff of his game yesterday—I'd been too nervous.

Even collecting his money from Carla this morning on my way to the airport, I had declined her offer to join her for breakfast.

No need to make that a regular thing.

"Want some fries?" DeShaun asked. Guess my deep breath had been a little too deep.

What the hell, I had just given the guy forty thousand dollars. I could steal a few of his fries.

So I opened his bag and helped myself while he continued counting.

"You may need to head back in there," I said, sheepishly, when he'd finished. "There are, like, four fries left."

He bobbed his chin at the bag and the drink, which he'd placed in the console cup holder. "Keep it. Just got it for show. I don't eat that shit. I'm in training."

I nodded. "Yeah, okay. Thanks."

"Thank you," he said, tapping the envelope before putting it in his backpack.

"Good luck on Saturday," I said, meaning it.

He nodded and reached for the door handle. I willed him to pull it. To get out of the car and walk away, never turning around. But his hand slid off the handle and my heart slid down to my gut.

"What do you think the spread will be for us against Gonzaga?"

I shrugged. "As of this morning it opened at Lamont being a three-point favorite."

He shook his head. "No, that's too close for comfort."

I totally agreed, and told him so. "And if Kansas beats Wisconsin, you'd be the underdog in the championship game. If Wisconsin wins, you'd be the fave, but it'd probably be an even closer spread. Maybe two," I said.

His head moved a little as he thought about it, coming around to the point I was making.

This was a one-shot deal.

"Okay then," he said, his hand once again reaching for the door. "Been good to know you, JoJo."

"You too," I said. He shut the door behind him and I started the car.

I ate his Big Mac on my way to the airport.

And had indigestion the whole flight home.

Thirty-Six

❖

IT WAS AFTER NINE WHEN I FINALLY pulled into my driveway, but I immediately perked up seeing Jack's car was there.

He hadn't told me that he and Ben were coming home today—I would have picked them up at the airport. Except no, I couldn't have, because I was in Dallas seeing to JoJo business.

I left the wig I'd worn in a duffel bag in my trunk. Checking my phone as I made my way into the house, I was happy to see that I hadn't missed any texts or calls from Jack. But that had me really wondering why he hadn't let me know his travel plans.

Was he trying to surprise me?

Or catch me?

Shaking that thought, I went down the wing of Ben's room when I saw the dining and living rooms were both empty. Seeing his light on through the crack in the door, I knocked softly, not wanting to wake him up if he'd gone to bed early.

"Come in," he said, and my throat clenched up at hearing his soft voice. "Hannah darling," he said, his brown eyes lighting up when I walked into his room. "It's so good to see you."

"You too, Ben," I said, walking over to the chair he was sitting in and bending down to give him a hug. He dropped the book he was reading to his lap and returned my hug. I kissed the top of his head—getting mostly bald spot, but a few wispy hairs—and pulled away, plunking down in the chair opposite him in the little sitting area of his large room.

"How was your trip?" I asked, then sat back and listened for the next half-hour as Ben extolled the intelligence, kindness, and all the other great features attributed to his newly found grandson, Casey.

My chest hurt with happiness listening to Ben, and also with despair that he'd almost been robbed of this—his son and grandson. And *had* been robbed of Jack for forty years and Casey for eight.

Damn Saul.

"And we have lots of pictures, too," he said as he finished up. "Jack took them on his phone and Lorelei printed them out for us when we got here."

"I can't wait to see them," I said, meaning it. Funny, but since making a bet the other day, it was like a dam had broken and the petty, childish feelings of exclusion I'd been having had drifted away.

Or maybe it was just having Ben home again that did it.

"Have you seen Jack yet?" Ben asked.

I shook my head. "No. Nobody was in the main living area, so I thought I'd head here first."

That pleased Ben, and he smiled. "It was a good trip for Jack, I think," he said. "He was able to relax. Didn't have a drink once in Portland that I saw."

That was interesting. Well, all of it was. That Jack had not taken a drink while gone (and away from me!), and that Ben had noticed, and felt it was important enough to mention.

I tried to recall if I'd ever discussed Jack's drinking with Ben, and was pretty sure I hadn't.

"That's good," was all I said, trying to keep my voice neutral. "He needed a little relaxation," I added.

Ben nodded, his brown eyes studying me. "He did. And of course seeing his son helped quite a bit. But once we got back…" He sighed. "Well, I think he called into the office and maybe that didn't go so well. He was very quiet at dinner, then he's been in your room most of the evening."

I rose from the chair and placed my hand on Ben's arm, giving a soft squeeze. "I'll go say hi to him, then."

Ben patted my hand with his free one, then dropped it to the top of his book. "It's good to be home, Hannah darling."

"Good to have you home," I said, and left the room.

As I made my way over to my wing of the house, I realized Ben hadn't asked me where I'd been. Probably thought I was out playing cards; maybe even Raymond told Ben and Jack that. As I passed Raymond's room, I thought it might be wise to check in and see if he'd mentioned anything, but his room was empty, the light out. Which meant he was either out (though all the cars were accounted for) or he was in the book room. Not wanting to make the effort to double back and check (because that much effort *would* feel like I was trying to get our stories straight), I continued on to my room.

The lights were on, CNN was on the television, though it was on mute, and Jack was sitting in one of my chairs, just like Ben had been. But instead of a holding a book and placing it on his lap, Jack was holding a glass of bourbon, and he didn't set it down as I came in, just took a deep, long swallow of the dark, smoky booze.

I tried not to look at the glass, and it was easy to do because Jack's eyes were intent on me and his voice was weary silk when he said, "Missed you."

"Missed you too," I said.

"Shut the door, lock it, and come here and show me how much."

I shut the door, locked it, and made my way to Jack's chair. He spread his legs, and I walked into the space he created. The hand holding his drink stayed on the arm of the chair, but his other one slid up my outer leg to my waist. He leaned forward, his mouth at waist level, and gave me a small kiss through the cotton Henley I was wearing. My hands went to his hair, sifting, feeling the softness, then drifting down to his shoulders.

"Johanna," he whispered, then leaned his head back, looking up at me. Wordlessly, he rose, tugged my hand, and pulled me to the bed, never spilling a drop of his drink.

It wasn't until I woke up at three in the morning, my body weak and sated after showing Jack just how much I'd missed him, that I realized he'd never asked where I'd been.

And I'd never said.

SHOW AND TELL AT THE SOURDOUGH that morning was less odds sheets and more family photos from Portland.

Gus made a show of looking at them all, commenting on how much like Ben that Casey looked. Jimmy looked at the first few, saw the large stack that Lor had printed out from Jack's phone, and returned to his coffee.

Not a sentimental one, our Jimmy.

I had looked at them all that morning at home when I'd first gotten up, and then again after breakfast with the boys.

Raymond hadn't expected to join us, and was gone with Lorelei when Ben and I had left the house, probably to avoid any awkwardness.

So it was just the four of us, like it had always been, even though we'd been six with Danny and Saul not that long ago.

God, that seemed like years ago, not just months.

Gus was right: there was quite a bit of Ben in Casey, maybe even more so than Jack. If I'd seen pictures of Jack's kid earlier, it probably would have saved me a trip to the DNA place to have paternity confirmed.

I didn't think too hard about the fact that I *hadn't* seen a picture of Jack's kid before then. And that he'd never offered to show me.

No Mrs. Brady, me, that was for sure. But I didn't think I'd have any problems adapting to a life where Casey visited often, perhaps even living with us for summers. (Not that any kid would want Vegas in the summer over Portland, but whatever.)

All assuming, of course, that Jack and I went the distance.

Which meant I had to tell him I had placed a bet. And that—I took a big breath internally as I even thought this—I would probably bet again.

Maybe even this morning after breakfast, if my eyes straying to the odds sheets lying on the table were any indication.

I had no intention of telling Jack about JoJo's trip yesterday. That wasn't my story to tell, affecting others much more than me. There were only so many times Jack could overlook a crime—whether in his jurisdiction or not.

But yeah, I didn't like him thinking I was still on the not-betting wagon when I'd stumbled off. It felt like...cheating.

So, as we were leaving the Sourdough, I left Ben at the bank of slot machines where I'd taken Jack's call last Thursday, and made my way to the book room.

"Hang on, I'm going to make a bet," I said to Ben, like I'd said to him after breakfast a hundred times. (Probably thousands, but I didn't want to deal with that math with the amount of breakfast I'd just eaten.)

He didn't say anything, just sat at one of the slots and waited.

I didn't have much money, a couple hundred dollars, and the only games on the board were NBA or NHL, which was good enough for me, though not my preferred college games. But the Hummer didn't care; it just wanted to come out and play. To soar. I bet on the Cavaliers, and the bet slip again felt like silk in my hands.

On the drive home Ben patted my hand as it sat on the gearshift, but didn't say a word.

Thirty-Seven
❖❖

THAT NIGHT WHEN JACK GOT HOME, I led him to my room before dinner and showed him my bet slip.

"I made a bet last Thursday," I said. "And one today. I just wanted you to know."

He studied the slip like it held my secrets, when I knew full well it didn't—for I didn't even know them myself.

He sat in the chair I'd found him in last night when I'd gotten home, still hanging on to the slip. When he looked up at me, he asked softly, "Are you showing me because this is an iceberg moment and you want me to let it float, or is this…I don't know, a warning or something?"

I wasn't really sure. Taking a deep breath then letting it out, I walked to him and was pleased he moved his arms, indicating I should sit in his lap, which I did. "I guess an iceberg."

"Not a cry for help?" I shook my head, but the movement was small, almost undetectable. Except for a detective. "We could get some help if you want," he said, and I shook my head again.

"I just wanted you to know that my iceberg was still out there, somewhere, floating in the ocean."

He looked at me for a long time. His hand came up and he placed a warm finger on top of my horseshoe pendant, sliding it into the little dent at the top of my clavicle. His eyes were on his finger when he said, "Knowing there's an iceberg out there, not knowing how deep it runs, how big, can make it pretty fucking hard to steer the ship." He looked me in the eye as he finished, and I had to swallow down the lump in my throat.

Placing a hand on his cheek, I quietly said, "I'm not asking you to steer the ship. That's not on you."

He nodded, leaned forward, and kissed my neck just where he'd removed his finger. "Good," he whispered, "Because I'm not really sure I have any lifeboats left, you know?"

I knew. Oh, how I knew. It seemed I'd used up all my lifeboats too. And if my ship hit my iceberg, there would be no hope of surviving.

"Yeah," I whispered, and bent my head, giving him a soft, closed-mouth kiss.

We held each other's gazes for another few seconds, then smiled as we heard Lor call from down the hall that dinner was ready.

I rose from Jack's lap and we walked, hand in hand, down to the dining room to join our family for dinner.

Trying to put thoughts of navigating our private oceans behind us.

THE NEXT FEW DAYS had me believing that life might become normal again. Jack was back at work, and though he wasn't involved with the Lion case, he seemed content to be back to his routine.

The police had released no new updates on the case.

According to Lor—though I wanted no details—the fascination with the Black Widow was waning.

And I bet. Not a lot. But after breakfast each morning Ben would wait for me at the slots while I went with Jimmy and Gus into the book room at Arizona Charlie's. Winning most of the bets I made, I had a nice nut of several thousand dollars on Saturday morning, a day we typically didn't go out for breakfast.

This Saturday Jack had the day off, and suggested a late breakfast buffet at the Red Rock casino. I texted Jimmy and Gus that we'd be there at eleven if they wanted to join us, and Jack, Lor, Ben, Raymond, and I headed over—the three of them in the Lexus, Jack and me in my Porsche.

After the buffet, we switched up and Lor went home with Jack, and Ben and Raymond and I made our way over to the book room. I nodded to the poker room manager as we walked by, and he gave me a wave. The Red Rock was my neighborhood casino, and I played there from time to time, but I mainly went down to the Strip for the bulk of my poker playing.

There were a couple of leather chairs empty, and Raymond and I claimed them, our eyes going to the board to check out the spread for the day's main games: Lamont against Gonzaga and then Wisconsin against Kansas. Kansas and Lamont were the favorites, Kansas by five, Lamont by three, much as I had predicted to DeShaun on Monday when I'd seen him in Dallas.

"Wanna watch here, or go home?" I asked Raymond after a few minutes. Minutes in which the Hummer washed over me, making me feel light and alive, though nobody would have known it to look at me.

"Home," he said, and I nodded, then made my way to the counter and placed half my money on Lamont. I was about to put the rest on Kansas—they'd been pretty stellar the whole tournament, covering the spread in every game except one, especially against Butler, when I'd lost twenty-two thousand. "Eleven hundred on Wisconsin," I said. Except it wasn't my voice. It was JoJo's, and she had changed the bet at the counter, like a quarterback not liking what he saw at the line of scrimmage and calling an audible.

The Hummer flowed through me, pure and clean. This was the best, having done all the figuring, looking at stats and how teams had done against the spread, knowing the absolutely right pick.

And then picking the other team.

I couldn't even hide my smile—me, a seasoned poker player!—as the cashier handed me my bet slip.

The thin paper rustled as I looked at it, then added it to my Lamont slip and put both of them in my jacket pocket, taking my hand quickly away lest my palm become sweaty and smear the print.

As I walked away from the counter, Raymond was stepping away from it as well, a couple of cashier slots down from mine, and he did a chin nod in the direction of the parking deck. I nodded my agreement.

We drove home in silence, me in my euphoria and Raymond, I suspected, in what was quickly becoming his version of the Hummer.

I didn't know whether to feel sorry for him or glad.

WISCONSIN UPSET KANSAS. Not only covered the spread, but actually beat the number-one-ranked team in the nation.

And here's the whacked part, the part that made me know—deep, deep down—that I would never truly beat this thing. Instead of basking in my win, in my last-minute decision that had me up a thousand dollars instead of down, I immediately inwardly groaned that I should have bet Wisconsin on the money line and doubled my winnings.

Yeah, twisted, I know, but there it was.

"Damn, I should have bet the money line," Raymond said from the top row, where he had joined Jimmy, leaving the bottom row available for Ben and his bad hip.

I turned around and smiled at him, nodding, then stopped as I saw the look on his face. It was an outward visage of what I'd felt internally just seconds ago.

And it broke my heart.

"Don't go that way, kid," Jimmy said next to him. "That shit'll drive you crazy. You can't worry about the bets you coulda made, only the ones you did."

I could see Ben nodding from the front row, and I added mine as well, even though it was advice I obviously needed to heed myself.

Jack got a call and had to go to a crime scene before the Lamont game started, and I was secretly a little bit happy about that. I didn't want to watch DeShaun Rogers with my head leaning against Jack's chest, or him holding my hand or anything. Not that we sat like that while watching games very often, but I was afraid that if we did I'd give something away, something to let Jack know that DeShaun Rogers was more than just another college kid out on the floor.

Jack had told me from the start that I had a tell, and I didn't want to test that out today.

And though I didn't wish violence on anyone, I also hoped that the scene Jack had been called to would be something juicy that he could sink his teeth into and get his groove back, as it were.

I mean, if there *had* to be a murder in Vegas—and I didn't wish it, or anything—let it be something good my boyfriend could solve.

Yeah, I know, I know—be careful what I wished for.

In the second game, Lamont won easily, making me two for two in my bets and a happy camper.

"Red Rock for brunch tomorrow?" Raymond asked with a smile on his face. He'd have bet slips to cash there as well.

"You got it," I said.

"Jesus, kid, that must have been some AAU team you had that summer. You, Rogers, Jamison."

Raymond nodded. "Yeah, we smoked everybody. Even our

scrubs went on to play at big schools. I think—" He stood up and made his way down my row and to the doorway. "Just a sec."

Ben told us he was going to get a snack, and left the room. We'd already been told by Lor that we were on our own for dinner, as she and Gus were going out.

Again.

Being that her room was in the other wing, I didn't know if Gus was staying the night—and didn't want to—but Lor seemed happy this past week, so I didn't ask her if she knew what she was doing.

Besides, like I was one to give relationship advice.

"Yeah, here," Raymond said, walking back into the room holding what looked like a large scrapbook. Raymond hadn't brought a ton of stuff with him when we'd gotten him out of Chicago, but I knew he would have taken anything of value to him because at the time it didn't seem like going back would be an option.

It probably still wasn't.

"My mom made this for me," he said, sounding a little embarrassed, as he brought the scrapbook to Jimmy's row. I climbed up on my knees on my recliner and leaned over the back of my chair so I was on the same level as Raymond when he bent down in front of Jimmy's chair.

"That's sweet," I said, realizing it was a scrapbook of Raymond's basketball achievements. He had it open to a team photo taken ten summers ago of an AAU team. The boys were mostly black and looked to range from about nine to eleven years old, though there were a few giants in there with baby faces, one I recognized right away as Kenny Jamison from Kansas. "Awww," I said, pointing to a cherubic-faced Raymond, his smile wide and adorable, his hands behind his back like the other players. His hair was in a small, tight cut, his braids not to come for several more years.

"That's DeShaun," Raymond said, pointing to the player

two down from him in the photo. I wouldn't have necessarily recognized him, but once he'd been pointed out, it was obvious.

"Let's see…that kid is playing for Kentucky. That one is at North Carolina. Richardson is at Louisville," he said, pointing to the only other player as tall as Jamison.

I studied Carl Richardson. A younger version of the guy I'd "encountered" a couple of months ago in Pittsburgh. Well, JoJo had encountered him. And by encountered, I mean roofied and made sure he'd be unable to play at his high level the following day.

That had been for a debt payback for Vince.

Richardson. Vince.

Rogers. Carla.

The players changed, but it seemed the game remained the same.

JoJo's game.

Disgusted with myself, I started to move back down in my chair when a face in the photo snagged my attention.

Not another player with whom I'd come into contact. No, it wasn't even a player, but a manager or trainer or someone. Not a coach—they were all seated at the back of the team. This guy and another were on the side, and seemed like definite afterthoughts in the line up.

"Oh my God," I said, rising again and pulling the book closer, nearly tearing it out of Raymond's hands.

"What?" both he and Jimmy said.

"Him. It's him," I said, pointing at the man. It was a man of probably around mid-forties, but looked quite a bit older due to a head full of beautiful silver hair.

"Who is it?" Jimmy asked.

"Do you know who this is?" I asked Raymond.

He shrugged. "I think he was a trainer or something. Yeah, he was. I never had to use him, though. I can't remember his name."

"I know his name," I said.

"Yeah?"

I nodded. "Or at least I know the name he gave at Carla's poker game. The night Lion died."

Raymond looked at me, then again looked at the photo, mentally adding ten years, and maybe ten pounds, as I just had. "Holy shit," he said, meeting my shocked expression with one of his own.

"Who the fuck is it?" Jimmy said.

"He said his name was Brandt Whitaker, but that was a fake name, because the cops never found him."

"Seriously?" Jimmy said.

Both Raymond and I nodded. "It's him, all right," Raymond said. He sat back on his haunches, letting the scrapbook fall to his lap.

"What does this mean?" he asked me.

I shook my head and whispered, "I have no idea."

Thirty-Eight
❖

JACK TEXTED LATER NOT TO WAIT UP, that he would be on the job most of the night.

When I got up Sunday morning he still hadn't showed, which wasn't unusual. Ben didn't feel like going back to the Red Rock, so he and Lorelei had breakfast in while Raymond and I met Jimmy at the Red Rock, having the buffet twice in as many days.

Afterward we all walked over to the book room and cashed our winning bets and made one (okay, a few) for NHL games.

The board showed Lamont as a two-point favorite tomorrow night over Wisconsin. I didn't touch it, it was too close, and both teams were hot.

I told Raymond that I was going to tell Jack about Brandt being in his AAU photo, and I had the opportunity to do so when we got home and I saw Jack's car in the driveway.

Raymond brought me the scrapbook while I asked Jack to join me in the dining room. There was a "careful, now" look in Raymond's eyes when he handed it over, and I gave a small chin nod, letting him know that I had DeShaun's back.

No need for that to come out—it wasn't in play as far as Brandt being at Carla's game the night Lion died.

"What's going on?" Jack asked, as I motioned for him to sit beside me. Raymond opened the book to the right page then left Jack and me alone. Jimmy had followed us back to the house from the Red Rock and was now with Ben somewhere in the house—my guess was the book room watching games.

Jack was looking at the book in front of him, easily concluding what it was, then looked up at me.

"Yesterday, while we were watching college basketball, Raymond mentioned that he'd played AAU ball one summer with a couple of guys whose teams were doing really well in the tournament. Jimmy said that must have been quite a team. So Raymond goes and gets the scrapbook that Halia made for him when he was a kid." I pointed to the book, like it was exhibit A—which it kind of was. Jack nodded, becoming more interested, scanning the open page. He knew I wasn't someone who just told idle stories of how she'd spent the previous day.

If I was telling him this, it was for a reason. His eyes came up blank on the page—because he didn't know what he was looking for.

"So he's showing us this picture. It's from ten years ago, a summer league, but quite a few of the players are doing well in college right now. But what I notice is this," I say, putting my finger directly on Brandt in the photo, just at his shoulders so his face was still visible.

"Yeah?" Jack said.

"*This* is Brandt Whitaker."

He straightened in his seat, looking more closely at the photo. It was ten years ago, but I knew it was the same man, and told Jack as much.

"Did Raymond remember him?"

I shook my head. "Not really. When I pointed him out, he agreed it was the same man from Carla's game. He didn't know him well that summer—he wasn't a coach. Raymond thought he might either be a trainer or an equipment guy. Never knew his name."

"So…he's… I don't get it," Jack said.

"Brandt—or whatever his name actually is—was or is involved in basketball," I said.

"So?"

"I've been…involved with basketball players."

He looked confused—I didn't blame him. I was too. "So?" he said again.

I shrugged. "So, maybe nothing. But you're the one who said something about there being too many coincidences around me. That maybe they weren't coincidences at all."

"You think, what? This guy heard you were playing cards that night and…somehow knew you'd messed with college players and wanted to…frame you for murder?"

Yeah, when he said it out loud like that, it did sound pretty far-fetched. Like, why even involve Lion? Why not just expose me?

"Maybe it has nothing to do with me and basketball. Maybe it's all about Lion? Ralph said he'd played in a pro-am with Lion once—maybe Brandt had too?" But why kill him? Which was what Jack was thinking, his eyes going from the picture to look at me, then back at the picture.

"There were steroids found in Lion's system, right? And beta blockers? If this Brandt guy was a trainer, maybe he, I don't know, had some connection to Lion through that?" I said.

I could see his brain was in detective mode, and I wondered if he had more pieces that I wasn't aware of that were now sliding into place for him. Or if Frank would have those pieces and not have told Jack since he'd been off the case?

"I don't know," I said, thinking maybe there was nothing to any of it. "It may have absolutely nothing to do with Lion's death. But at least you can probably find out his real identity now. I'm sure AAU would have that kind of stuff on record, right?"

Jack was already rising as he nodded. "I need to take this. Think Raymond will care if I remove it?"

The picture was slid into a paper frame and would be easy to take out, but my stomach tightened when I thought of a photo with Raymond and DeShaun in it hanging around the desks of the police station.

"Can I make a copy of it, blow up Brandt, and keep the kids out of it?" I asked.

Jack looked at me, then back at the picture. I knew it would probably be better for them to have the whole photo for purposes of tracking down Brandt. But he knew why I'd asked—to protect Raymond.

He just didn't know there was another kid in that photo that also needed protecting.

After studying me for a few moments, and a deep sigh, he nodded, slipped the picture out of its holder, and handed it to me.

"I'll just be a sec," I said, and headed out of the dining room, moving toward the office Lor and I shared.

I made the copy, blowing up the original a few times, making sure the rest of the kids were cropped out.

Coming out of the office, I nearly had a head-on with Raymond, who was coming down the hall at a fast clip.

His eyes were huge, and when I looked down I saw my old burner phone in his hand.

Oh, shit.

"I just got a call…from Indianapolis." I nodded, and he went on, "He'd like to talk about doing…a job Monday night."

Oh, double shit.

"Anna?" Jack called from down the hall.

Like two kids caught stealing candy, Raymond and I both jumped. I motioned with my head for him to go into the office while I made my way back to Jack.

Whom I would need to quickly get rid of.

So JoJo could take over.

♠ ♥ ♦ ♣

"HE SAYS HE'S WILLING to do it for forty thousand," Raymond said when Jack had left the house, the cropped picture of Brandt in hand. I'd joined Raymond back in my office, closing the door behind me. He was sitting on Lor's side of the desk, and I moved over to mine and took a seat. "Half of which he wants up front. The other half he wants to bet on the game."

"But the point spread is too close. I told him it would be when I saw him on Monday in Dallas."

"It's not to cover the spread. It's to lose outright. A money-line bet."

Staring at Raymond, I wrapped my head around what repercussions this could have—to DeShaun, Carla, Raymond, and me.

"Are you serious? He said he's willing to throw the national championship?" Raymond nodded. "But...we both thought he'd never do that. Not when he'll be in the pros soon, making money. I mean, I can see a college kid at a clean school like Lamont, where there isn't anything shady going on, needing the money, but..."

Raymond and I, as well as Jimmy, Ben, and Gus, had had several conversations on whether or not college athletes in top-tier, revenue-generating sports should be compensated. We all felt they probably should be. And some of those kids, coming from very poor backgrounds, really *needed* to be, even though their school costs were covered with scholarships.

But DeShaun was a senior and was only months away from signing with the NBA. He was probably too small—like they'd said about Raymond—to become a huge star, but he'd be drafted for sure. Plus, he had the winnings I'd given him on Monday to easily see him through until a contract was signed.

But if there was one thing I'd learned from my gambling life, it was you never really knew about another person's money.

Still, this felt wrong. It seemed like he'd have mentioned something about a possible next time when I said on Monday that the point spread against Wisconsin would probably be less than the three it was when they played Gonzaga. "Do you think he's setting us up or something?"

Raymond thought about this before answering. "Nah. He'd be in just as much trouble as we would be. He already shaved points."

"Maybe he got a conscience about it. Maybe he went to the feds out of remorse. He's forgiven if he brings them us."

He leaned back in the chair, reaching out over his head. When he righted himself, he was shaking his head. "I don't think so. It just felt…real when he was talking."

Gut instinct. I trusted mine, and now it looked like I was trusting Raymond's as well. Then I remembered I had trusted Raymond before, to get me out of a major jam—and debt—with Vince.

"I think we have to bring it to Carla," Raymond said, and I knew he was right. It was just enough to bargain with Carla for her word (which may or may not be worth anything, seeing as she loaned me money when I'd asked her not to) that Raymond's identity and past deeds stayed with her. And a money-line bet would help give her the capital she needed to take over Vince's client list.

Their debts may have been paid off with Vince's will reading, but deadbeat gamblers were always looking for money to borrow to place their next bet.

As well I knew.

"Besides," Raymond added, "if it's a setup—and I don't think it is—I have Vince's information as a trump card to be played if needed."

I nodded and wondered if Vince, smart as he was, could have foreseen this all coming to fruition?

Were we being played from beyond the grave?

"Okay. I'll take it to Carla. She's not going to want to touch it herself, so we're the middlemen again." He and I both knew how we'd get paid for sticking our necks out for DeShaun and Carla.

"You're going to bet it this time, right?" he asked.

"Oh, hell yeah."

Raymond smiled, nodded, and said, "He wants half before the game. Tonight."

I looked at the clock. Noon here in Vegas, three in Indianapolis where the tournament was being held. "How's that going to happen? It's not like I can deposit it in his PayPal account or something."

Raymond shrugged. "Feel like going to Indianapolis tonight?"

I thought about the wig and false ID that were still in my trunk from my Monday trip to Dallas. With a heavy sigh, I nodded. "Let me call Carla and see if she can meet up."

He leaned across the desk and placed a hand on mine as I reached for my phone. "Why don't I do this one? There's no reason you need to do it. Yeah, stuff has died down out here a little on the Lion thing, but still…"

Shaking my head, I said, "It can't be you. There's even more chance of you being recognized in Indy. That place will be nothing but basketball people. This is me sitting on you, hard." I pulled away from his hand and started scrolling through recent calls to Carla's name and number. "And I don't trust it to be anybody other than you or I. The less people involved, the safer we all are. Besides, I've got stuff to hide my identity—you don't."

"Oh, I know," Raymond said. "I can't quite forget you in that tube top and miniskirt, blonde hair out to there." He made a motion with his hand. I rolled my eyes.

"Yeah, try a little harder to forget, will ya?"

He laughed at that, but let me make the call.

Thirty-Nine
❖❖

I GOT BACK FROM MEETING WITH CARLA a couple of hours later. There was no way I was going to discuss DeShaun's offer with her over the phone. She'd been overjoyed to hear the plan, and agreed immediately, telling me she'd have DeShaun's front end—twenty thousand—to me later that night, and bet his other half herself.

I'd already checked the flight schedules and told her to meet me at the airport, in the short-term parking at Terminal One, at seven.

I called Jimmy and Gus separately and told them I had a good feeling about Wisconsin in tomorrow night's game. Taking the money line. Gus thanked me and asked no questions. Jimmy asked if I needed any bets placed or if there was anything he could do for me.

He knew I'd be taking a trip.

Ya gotta love Jimmy.

I was happy to see that Jack's car was still gone when I got home. He'd probably be pulling an all-nighter with the picture of Brandt in play. I figured they'd have to let him be involved if he was the one bringing in the new information. I wished I could've been there to see Peter Faxon's face.

As it turned out, it was a blessing that I'd given Jack that photo today—little chance of him being around when I left for the airport tonight. If I got really lucky, I could do Indy tonight, back to Vegas in the morning, then to Dallas and back late Monday night or Tuesday morning, and he might not even know I'd left town.

I wouldn't outright lie to Jack, but we didn't typically keep each other apprised of our every waking moment's whereabouts, either.

Lorelei was out and Ben and Raymond were watching golf in the book room when I joined them. "Golf? Really?" I asked, taking my seat. The two men just shrugged.

"Are you in for the evening, Hannah dear?" Ben asked. He was sitting in the first row, where he usually sat due to the steps. Every once in a while, he'd get to feeling spunky, and he'd climb to the higher seating areas.

"No, Ben. I'm meeting a friend later."

He didn't ask more, and I didn't offer. I'd been in a weird place with Ben lately. Partially due to the shit storm that had descended, ending with Vince dying and Raymond living with us. Also partially because of his growing relationship with Jack. He knew Jack and I had a rocky foundation, and I was sure he didn't want to be the person who shifted the sand on which our house of cards was built.

Smart man, Ben.

I zoned out while the final holes of the golf tournament were played. The games Raymond and I had bet on this morning were on the smaller screens, and I tried to let the Hummer wash over me, but it was hard as I thought about the little trip JoJo would be making later that night.

When the golf ended, as often happened in Vegas due to being on the West Coast, a rerun of *CSI* was showing until network coverage would come on at seven. I was about to turn it when I realized Ben was watching, and I kept it on, continuing to zone out.

Something permeated, though, and I sat up in my seat.

"Holy shit," I said, and Raymond sat up, scanning the smaller screens, looking at games, trying to figure out if I was winning or losing.

I shook my head and pointed to the screen showing the *CSI* rerun.

"Can you back that up?" I asked as I looked around for the remote. "We've got that, right, where you can replay stuff?"

He nodded and looked around for the clicker for the main screen. Neither he nor I had it, but Ben did, and he handed it to me. I wasn't sure how to do it, so I passed it on to Raymond. "Go back about four minutes," I said.

It was near the end of the episode. The part where they explained how it all happened. If it were a Scooby Doo episode, it'd be the part where they unmask the ghost to find it had been the museum curator all along.

Believe me, living with an eighty-two-year-old man, I knew the setup of every CBS procedural show there was.

Anyway, the gang on *CSI* finally figured out that—and this was probably why it caught my attention—during a card game, somebody had slipped a couple of drops of Visine into the victim's drink. That was what had killed him.

"I'm not getting it," Raymond said as I had him back up and watch it again.

"The eye drops," I said, already on my phone Googling *Will swallowing eye drops kill you?*

"Yeah? So?"

I scrolled through the top hits. "Says it can wreak havoc on your system—give you diarrhea and other ailments." I scrolled through some of the other hits. "In larger doses it can do more harm. A couple of people arrested for trying to poison people with them." I looked up from my phone, meeting both Raymond's and Ben's blank stares.

"You didn't see Brandt use eye drops?" I asked Raymond, who shook his head. "He pulled them out at the table, used them at least once that I saw. We talked about how dry it was out here, allergies, stuff like that."

"I heard a little of that conversation, but I didn't see him use the drops."

"You know how many times everybody used the john, but didn't see somebody tipping their head back and dropping liquid into them?"

Raymond shrugged. "That was at the table. I didn't really pay attention to what was going on there. When everybody was moving around… I guess I paid more attention to that."

I read some more entries about eye drops being used as poison—whether accidentally or not. "I'm sure this is crazy, but if it were the drops, mixed with the other stuff that was already in his system…"

My mind whirled with whether or not to call Jack and tell him this information. Part of me thought it would be good to give him more information so that he'd have more to follow up on, which would take more time. Less time for him to be here and realize I wasn't.

The other part of me was thinking that if I called Jack now, there was an off chance that he'd ask me to come to the station to tell Frank and Faxon about Brandt's eye drops.

And I had a flight to catch.

The decision was made for me when Ben clapped his hands. "Hannah darling, you may have cracked the case! I can't wait for Jack to hear this."

I DIDN'T EVEN GET TO TELL HIM why I called before Jack broke in.

"It feels so good, to be back in this," he said, and I smiled, thinking about how the light was probably shining in his brown eyes. And I had made that happen.

"I'll bet Faxon is shitting a brick," I said, and Jack laughed.

"A big brick. But the lieutenant is keeping me in this thing. At least while we run this Brandt lead."

"That's why I'm calling," I said. I told him about the *CSI* episode and the fact that Brandt had used eye drops that night. "I mean, it could be crazy, but if they still haven't fully identified everything in the toxicology report…"

"They haven't. I've gotta go, babe. I want to call the lab about this."

"You don't think it's crazy?"

He chuckled. God, I loved that sound from him. It came so infrequently. "Christ, everything about this case is crazy. Why would using an old crime show to solve it be any less weird?"

"Okay, well, good. I hope it helps."

"Yeah, here's hoping. Oh, probably don't need to tell you this, but it's unlikely I'll be coming home tonight. I want to stay, and—"

"You don't need to explain," I said. "Do what you have to do," I added, hoping that would take him well into the next day, and possibly even Tuesday, when, in all likelihood, JoJo would be done with her sightseeing tour and be retired.

For good this time.

"Thanks for understanding, babe," he said. "You're the best."

"Remember that," I said, and he laughed. I savored the sound as I disconnected, hoping I'd get the chance to hear it again.

Forty

❖

I WASN'T GOING BACK *to Vegas that night.*

I met with DeShaun in his room while his roommate was at dinner, to give him the front end of his payoff and a few tips on how to control the game and let Wisconsin win.

But something was off. I could feel it. He was nervous, and he seemed like a different kid than the one who'd been in my rental car in Dallas just a week ago. Looking around the room, I tried to find anything that might be taping us. He was holding his phone and I asked to see it, but nothing was recording. Still, I made sure all the apps were closed, and hung on to it.

"You seem a little nervous," I said, wondering if the information on the federal investigators that Vince had given Raymond would be enough to get me off the hook if the door burst open and I was placed under arrest.

DeShaun let out a small snort. "Yeah, I guess I am. Wouldn't you be?"

I would be. Or maybe not. It seemed like JoJo had nerves of steel.

Still, I didn't like it. Something was definitely off. But what? Would the kid take the money and screw us? I motioned to the door of the bathroom. "Okay, if I…" He nodded, glancing at his phone that I still held. Which I took into the bathroom with me, closing the door, and locking it.

I looked around the small room, but didn't see anything amiss. Pulling the envelope with DeShaun's twenty thousand out of my money belt, I took half out and put the rest away, pulling my shirt back down over it. I put the ten thousand in an envelope I had in my jacket pocket.

After I flushed the toilet I hadn't used, turned the faucet on and off, I returned to DeShaun. First handing him his phone, then taking the envelope out of my pocket and giving that to him.

"It's only half," I said as he tossed his phone to the bed and opened the envelope.

"Yeah, that was the deal. You were going to bet my other half."

"No, I mean, this is only half of that. Ten thousand."

His head came up from counting as my words sank in. Suspicion clouded over his eyes. "What the fuck?"

Holding up a hand, I said, "You'll have the second half right after the game. The other twenty thousand is being bet for you. Last I looked, the money line was plus one twenty-five, so you'll win twenty-five thousand, collecting forty-five."

"Why after the game for the other ten? Half before, half being bet that I'd get after, that's what we said."

"That was the deal you made with Raymond. I'm just making an amendment. If the game goes as planned, you're only waiting twenty-four hours for the other ten."

He came close to me. Too close, but JoJo didn't back down. He was a point guard, not a center, but he was still several inches taller than me. "That's the deal now. Take it or leave it," I said. "I can walk out of here and we can pretend we never met. You go on and win by twenty for all I care. Nobody's hurt."

Sort of. If DeShaun kicked me out, I'd be hurriedly making calls to see if Carla, Jimmy, Gus, and Raymond had already made their bets on Wisconsin, and if they hadn't, not to.

He was frustrated, thinking I was playing at some game. I wasn't; I just wanted a little extra insurance that he was in this with us. Finally he nodded and stepped back. Again, JoJo showed no emotion.

"Deal," he said.

"Let's talk about tomorrow night," I said, moving further into the room and sitting in one of the side chairs.

After leaving DeShaun's room, I drove back toward the airport and had to go another twenty miles outside of Indianapolis to find a hotel with an available room. I called Raymond and told him what was up, that I was staying until after the game. Then I sent Lor a text saying I couldn't get away, and asking if she could take Ben to breakfast the next morning.

She texted back of course and wished me luck. It was clear she assumed I was in Vegas playing cards somewhere and didn't want to leave the table.

I let her think that.

Checking flights, I found a red-eye that I could take after the game tomorrow night, getting me back to Vegas in the wee hours Tuesday morning. Then I called Carla and brought her up to speed, making a meeting time and place at McCarran Tuesday morning before I'd fly to Dallas with DeShaun's winnings.

I would end up being gone from around dinnertime Sunday until dinnertime Tuesday. It was possible nobody would put it together that I hadn't come home in that time frame. Given Jack's busyness, Ben's routines, and my oftentimes being at tables for hours, going home to crash, then back at the tables, it was possible.

But I'd have to get very lucky.

THE NEXT MORNING *I slept late, had a big breakfast, and read the papers. Jack hadn't called, and I took that as a good sign— that he was so caught up in finding out Brandt's identity and the possibility of eye drops being given to Lion, he wouldn't be coming home. Wouldn't notice I wasn't there. Then I took a nap until it was close to game time. Donning a JoJo wig and some Wisconsin gear*

*that I'd picked up at one of the street vendors last night, I made my
way downtown.*

DeSHAUN MISSED *the third free throw.*

*There was a beat of stunned silence and then the red section—
half the stadium—erupted in pandemonium. The Lamont blue side
of the building moved in one motion as everybody dropped to their
seats, stunned.*

The Badgers ran to their bench, embracing their fellow players.

*DeShaun crouched, still at the foul line, and held his head in
his hands.*

I WAITED IN THE SPOT *DeShaun and I had agreed upon last
night. It was two hours after he'd missed his shot. He'd had to do
interviews, of course. Solemn, stoic interviews of the defeated. His
coach spoke in his defense, stating that game should never have come
down to those last free throws anyway. That DeShaun was not to
blame.*

*DeShaun's face showed a different take, but that was fine—it
played well that he couldn't seem to forgive himself and sat in a near
silence. Numb.*

I knew that feeling, too.

*But the backpack I now held, waiting for him to show, would
help assuage that numbness.*

*Ten thousand worth of de-numbing. With another forty-five
to follow.*

*He finally came out of the locker room, his backpack, identical
to the one at my feet, slung around his shoulder. Most of the other
players were already out, being consoled by their family members
and friends who had been at the game.*

DeShaun nodded to his family, then pointed to the small group of people that were around me, though I was set apart as much as I dared.

The folks around me were not affiliated with any particular player, but were there to encourage their team and to ask for an autograph or two.

DeShaun walked to us, turning his back to me. He pulled his backpack from his shoulder, in theory to give himself a free hand to sign, and set the bag down on the hard concrete next to mine. The group of people was thick enough that it wasn't obvious that there were two identical backpacks next to each other at our feet.

He signed every slip of paper that was handed to him. He nodded, his head bowed, as people tried to encourage him, tell him he played a great game, stuff like that.

Finally he turned to me, and I handed him my program and a Sharpie. He wouldn't meet my eye as he signed, just looked a little lower than my face.

Which put him staring at the top of the Wisconsin sweatshirt I'd covered up with my fleece after I'd left my seat. Mostly covered up. DeShaun saw the tiny bit of red peeking out from under my fleece and flinched. He looked up to my eyes, taking in the different hair than he'd seen last night (a different wig). His eyes were full of indignation, and a little bit of hurt, about the red sweatshirt. Like I was pouring salt in his wound.

Which I guess I was, but when he bent down and picked up my backpack and not his own, I figured the salt was just a sprinkle. Like the kind you threw over your shoulder for luck.

He handed my program back to me, turned, and walked toward his family, waving over his shoulder as the group of people once again lauded him.

I reached down and picked up DeShaun's backpack and walked through the maze of people toward the place I'd parked my rental. A face in the group of people heading toward the team bus stopped me. It was the silver hair amongst the more youthful ones was that did *it. But the quick glance turned into a full-blown jaw-dropping stare as I watched a man I'd sat across from at Carla's game a few weeks ago get onto the Lamont team bus.*

Holy shit, Brandt Whitaker—or whatever the hell his name was—was with the Lamont team!

I COULDN'T TELL JACK that I'd found Brandt—that he was a trainer (or something) for the Lamont basketball team. At least not yet.

As we'd agreed, Carla met me at the airport with DeShaun's second half and his winnings. I ducked into the women's room and strapped it into my money belt I wore under my clothes. I was going to turn right around and catch an early morning flight to Dallas.

"Well, he certainly took it down to the wire, didn't he?" she said when I returned to her.

"That's what you want. Throws off any suspicion."

"I guess. But I was about to shit myself. I had a million riding on that game."

I knew she'd put everything she had on it, but she would have had to borrow to get that kind of money.

Ironic—going to loan sharks for money to place a bet so that you had the capital to…loan shark.

"Got time for breakfast?" she asked. I probably did, but I shook my head. I was tired and felt grimy, and not just because of trying to sleep on a plane.

JoJo being back was messing me up.

"Okay," Carla said. "Safe flight. Talk to you later."

"We're done."

"Yeah, we're even," she said.

"No," I said, leaning in closer to her, "we're *done*."

She looked at me, then a slow smile came across her face.

"How many times did you say that to Vince?"

She had me there. Still… "I mean it."

A shrug from her. "How many times did you say *that* too?"

"Don't contact me," I said, and turned, walking as quickly away from her as I could.

I texted Raymond and asked him to take a picture of the Brandt picture and send it to me, which he did. He said again that no one was aware I wasn't at some casino playing cards into the morning. Lor and Ben were out at breakfast, and Raymond said he was going to shut my bedroom door like I did when I was napping, just in case someone went looking for me.

That wouldn't stop Jack if he came home, but there'd been no sign of him so far.

I had breakfast alone in the airport, waiting for Jack to come strolling in and bust me any minute. Or worse, federal agents that DeShaun might be working with to swarm in and *really* bust me.

Neither happened. As I pulled out my wallet to pay for my breakfast, I saw the slip for the bet I'd made on the money line before leaving town for Wisconsin. It felt light to the touch, and a bit of the Hummer washed through me just seeing it.

So much for not breaking my own rules.

Forty-One

❖❖

IT WAS THE SAME MCDONALD'S *on the edge of the Lamont campus that I'd met DeShaun at the previous week. This time instead of fries and a burger, he had a breakfast combo meal. Even though I'd eaten at the airport before my flight, I dug into the bag when he offered it to me.*

We switched back our backpacks and he started counting out his winnings while I ate.

I still had half an eye open to the parking lot around me, waiting for the feds to move in, but my suspicion was waning as DeShaun's eyes got bigger and bigger counting out the money.

He was all in.

When he was done he nodded, stuffing the envelope into the top compartment of his backpack and zipping it up. He reached for the door, but I put a hand on his arm.

"Hang on a second." I took my phone from where it rested on the console and called up the photo Raymond had texted me. "I'm assuming you know this guy? The pic is ten years old."

"Yeah, that's Doc. Why do you have a picture of him?"

"Don't worry, it has nothing to do with..." I motioned to his backpack and the envelope inside. "Totally unrelated. He's the, what? Trainer at Lamont?"

DeShaun shook his head. "Team doctor. He travels with us, but has his own practice here."

"What's his name?"

"Hey, is that from an old AAU team photo?"

I nodded. "His name?"

"Where'd you even find—" He stopped when he remembered our mutual friend.

"Name?" I asked again.

"Bruce Williamson."

Initials B.W.—not that that fact alone necessarily meant anything. DeShaun reached into his backpack and pulled out a business card from one of the small zippered compartments. "Here you go."

It was the business card for Doctor Williamson, complete with phone, email, and office address. Well, that was way too easy.

"Why would you have this on you? Do you all carry the team doctor's info around?" Maybe they did. Maybe that was standard for a program like Lamont during a national championship run.

DeShaun looked out the window, then he sighed and poked a finger into the McDonald's bag and pulled out the hash browns that I'd left for last. He took a big bite of them, chewed, and swallowed. Guess he wasn't worried about being in training anymore.

"Nah, I have the card 'cause I'm...seeing him."

I didn't think he meant it in the romantic way. "Everything okay?" I asked, wondering if he'd answer me. We weren't exactly besties, but did share a kind of...intimacy.

He polished off the hash browns and then gave his head one small shake. "Nah. My knee's fucked up. Hurt it during the Gonzaga game on Saturday. He looked at it that night and said I was probably going to need surgery."

"Meniscus?"

"ACL."

"Ouch."

"Got that right."

I was thinking back to the coverage over the last three days. News like this would have been all over the place, and certainly would have affected the point spread. "You kept it quiet," I said, and he nodded.

Things fell into place for me quickly. Why the call on Sunday to Raymond. Why DeShaun was so nervous Sunday night.

Why he'd go for the money and throw the biggest game of his life.

His future income was disintegrating, so he was cashing in. Creating a nest egg. Smart.

"NBA isn't going to ignore major knee surgery right before the draft," *I said, telling him something he had already figured out—and what had made him decide to call Raymond.*

"Got that right, too."

He was never going to be a star in the NBA, but now with a bum knee, his chances of making a decent living in the league—hell, making a team at all—had lessened considerably.

"I can't believe you were able to keep it quiet," *I said. Another reason he was probably so nervous Sunday night—if word got out, the point spread would have shifted to Wisconsin being the favorite. Money still could be made, but it would have been a much longer shot.*

He shrugged. "It didn't happen on a particular play or anything, so nobody knew. And it wasn't like I couldn't play on it, it's just... We knew it was going to have to be looked at. And Doc felt it wasn't going to be good. I head to his office tomorrow for an MRI."

"Good luck," *I said, meaning it. He nodded, and I added,* "With all of it, I mean. NBA, or whatever."

A wry smile crept across his face. "Yeah, I'm thinking straight to med school for me now."

"Med school? That's great." *Raymond had said DeShaun was smart. I had thought he didn't have Raymond's cunning, but book smarts and streets smarts weren't always the same thing.*

"I was going to try the NBA first, get, I don't know, a couple years at league minimum, and use that for medical school. Now"—*he tapped his backpack*—"I'm thinking it'll be straight to med* *school."*

We said our goodbyes. It wasn't tearful, or joyful—it wasn't really anything. How could it have been? He let me keep Bruce Williamson's card.

I was beginning to think that maybe, in this one instance, JoJo knowingly involving a player wasn't so bad. The kid made his choice, was the benefactor of his own future. He wouldn't have had that otherwise. He might still have gone straight to med school, but he'd be taking out thousands of dollars in debt. In two instances of doing business with me, he had made over a hundred thousand dollars.

A good start in life, to be sure.

As he started to get out of my car, he turned back to me. "You know, I didn't have to keep it so close. I could have let Wisconsin win by a lot more."

"I know," I said. "But you made it look great. So close, and you made some clutch shots at the end."

But not the very end. Not when it counted most.

"Yeah, but I didn't do it for that—not to keep it close, not so there wouldn't be any guessing."

"No?"

"No. I...I wanted to know myself that we could win. I wanted—at least in my head, in my heart—to prove that we were national champions. At the wire I let it go, but we would have won. We would have been the ones cutting down the nets last night."

There was a hollow look in his eye, and he seemed to look right through me. My thoughts, only a moment ago, of JoJo doing some good this time slammed shut like DeShaun slammed shut the car door as he left.

Forty-Two

❖

BRUCE WILLIAMSON—a.k.a. Brandt Whitaker—made a good living as an orthopedic specialist, if his beautiful office building was any indication. In fact, with all the glass, it kind of reminded me of Marvin Harrison's law offices.

No view of the mountains in Texas, though.

The reception area was empty, and I wondered about my chances that he'd even be in today, with the team flight probably not touching down in Dallas until the wee hours of the morning. But if they'd won, there probably would have been a lot of celebrating, so maybe they'd canceled all appointments for today already.

There would be no parade down the Lamont campus in the coming days.

I'd bet a hell of a one in Madison, though.

"May I help you?" the receptionist asked. She wasn't wearing scrubs like a lot of nurses and doctor's assistants did. She was strawberry blonde, in her late forties, and dressed professionally in a pantsuit. Definitely an office manager of some sort.

"I'd like to speak with Doctor Williamson if he's available."

"Do you have an appointment?" she asked. The tone of her voice confirmed my thoughts that no appointments were scheduled for today. It also gave me hope that he was in the office.

"I don't. It's not for medical reasons, but personal."

She looked me over carefully—probably not something she heard every day. "Can I tell him to what this is pertaining?"

I weighed out giving her my real name versus getting in to see Brandt/Bruce without it. "As I said, it's personal. But you could tell him that Anna Dawson would like just a few minutes of his time."

The name meant nothing to her, I could tell. She looked me over once more and finally made her way down a hallway and around a corner. I didn't bother sitting down. If Brandt was in the office, hearing my name would provoke some kind of response from him.

Yep. Within a minute she was back and motioning me to follow her. I let her lead with her back to me as I took out my iPhone and opened what I hoped was the voice memos app. I'd seen Lor use hers tons of times to leave herself a note about something or other. It hadn't quite replaced her omnipresent notebooks, but she'd use it in a pinch.

I didn't have many apps on my phone—by design—so hopefully I got the right one and it was recording. I slipped it into my jeans back pocket—no time to check it to be sure, since the receptionist was now turning to face me at an open door.

"Here you go," she said, and I thanked her. She closed the door behind me as I entered.

And there sat the man who had played poker with me the night Lion LaGasse was murdered.

He waved me to a seat in front of him, but did not stand. Dressed casually as he was, he still exuded money, just like he had the night of the game. The gorgeous dark wood office and expensive furniture around him didn't hurt, either.

Going for my inner Jack, I took a shot, aiming for the element of surprise. "I know you put the eye drops in Lion's drink."

I watched him closely. Like, poker opponent closely. No

flicker of recognition of any kind, no fear, no calculating going on in his mind.

Just confusion.

"What?"

"The eye drops."

His eyes moved to a corner of his huge desk, where a bottle of eye drops sat near a box of Kleenex. There was a little candy dish there too, but instead of candy it held wrapped Halls cough drops. Apparently Bruce *did* have some allergy issues. "My...eye drops?"

Again, just confusion.

And just like that, with the surety I used when raising somebody or folding a good hand, I knew he was telling the truth. Or not so much telling the truth, as having absolutely no idea what the hell I was talking about.

He hadn't slipped the drops into Lion's drink. (If there had even been drops slipped into Lion's drink—but I was becoming more and more convinced that that was exactly what had happened.)

Gambler's intuition.

I sat in the chair and told him my theory about the eye drops being an element in the cause of death for Lion.

"Wait," he said, holding up a hand. "First of all, how did you even find me?"

I took a leap. "You were shown behind the bench during the game on Saturday. I went from there."

He bought it. Maybe he'd already thought about the possibility of being seen and recognized during the tournament.

"Second," he said, "you've come to Dallas to...*question* me, based on an old *NCIS* episode?"

"It was *CSI*, actually," I said. Again, living with an octogenarian male, I knew the difference.

He leaned forward, elbows on the table, lacing his fingers. "Whatever. Do you know how...outrageous this all seems?"

I nodded. Oh, I did. But given the past few months in my life, and the funerals I'd attended (and those I hadn't), I was living with my fair share of outrageous.

"I know. But I think it's a good hunch."

"Just like your good hunch to bet the farm with king/ten?"

Ouch. He didn't have to throw shade about my poker playing. I didn't address the fact that he was sitting in an office making his living while I made mine—a very good living!—sitting at poker tables.

"If you think it's such a preposterous idea, you won't have any problem with me taking those eye drops back to Vegas with me. Give them to the cops. I will, of course, be giving them your name and location as well."

The expression on his face told me he'd already figured that part out. And was annoyed, sure. But again, no flash of fear or real concern. Looking at the bottle of eye drops on his desk, I wondered if he'd loan me some plastic gloves and a baggie to wrap the bottle in.

"You can take it, but that's not the same bottle I had in Las Vegas."

I read his face again, and came up with the same conclusion—he was telling the truth.

Grasping, I asked, "Do you still happen to have that bottle? At your home, perhaps? Traveling kit of some kind?"

He was shaking his head before I even finished. "No. I mean, I didn't have the bottle the next day. I couldn't find it in the morning. I had to go out and…"

His eyes met mine as a piece of the puzzle fell into place. Ha! *CSI* detecting didn't sound so stupid to him now. And it solidified the thought that I didn't need to bother taking the bottle on his desk back with me.

Whoever put the drops in Lion's drink had the bottle—or more likely had already disposed of it.

And that man wasn't Bruce.

I started to rise from my seat, but he waved me back down.

"Listen, I don't know if it has anything to do with Lion, and the damn eye drops, or whatever, but there was a guy there, the black kid who was working the door."

I sat back down, putting my own poker face in place. "Yeah?"

Bruce scratched the top of his head, like he was thinking, remembering. Was it all now just coming to him who Raymond was? I didn't think so. For the first time since I'd walked through the door, I got the impression he wasn't being, let's say, completely forthcoming with me.

"He is—was—a college basketball player. Had some trouble a month or so ago and went off the grid. That he turns up in Vegas at an unlicensed poker game, one where someone is killed…I don't know, but he's someone I'd take a look at if I were the cops."

Was he trying to deflect suspicion? He wouldn't need to if he'd had nothing to do with it, which was what I'd come to believe.

But Raymond's appearance at that game *would* seem out of place, given his recent history. Which was exactly why I made the deals I did, with the cops and with Carla, so his name wouldn't be released—because everyone would think just like Bruce was now.

And he'd be the one being crucified in the press and on social media instead of me. Not to mention having the feds knocking on our door.

Thank God for Vince Santini's gift from beyond the grave, if it came to that.

I nodded like he made good sense. And if I didn't know Raymond, it would have been true. "Did you tell anybody about that? Seeing that guy at the game?"

Bruce shook his head, his hand dropping to his desk. "Hell no. Nobody knows I was there. A golf god is dead. You think

I'm going to say anything to anybody? I'm just happy I had the foresight to give Carla a fake name."

"Yeah, why did you do that?"

He shrugged. "It's an illegal poker game in Vegas. I'm a consulting physician with a top college basketball program. I was lucky I made it back here in time for our Saturday afternoon game. I'm sure half the people there gave fake names."

Not half. Only two. Well, who knew about Mr. Chow? Okay, the bartender made three, but he wasn't playing cards. I nodded like he had a point. He did.

"Okay. I'll pass that on to the investigators." Yeah, like hell I would. Still, maybe it would cause him not to tell the cops about Raymond once I told them where to find Bruce. A slim chance, but one worth taking.

"Thanks for your time," I said, attempting to leave again. There wasn't anything more I was going to get out of Bruce, and I didn't want him going deeper on the whole "Raymond did it" angle. Also, I wasn't sure about the voice app on my phone. Would it beep after a certain time? Was it still going even if there were periods of quiet? Had I even turned the damn thing on the right way to begin with?

I left my chair and turned toward the door, walking as Bruce said, "Yeah, he was sure something on the court, that kid. Nothin' but net for days every time he touched the ball. It's a shame what happened to him."

Nothin' but net for days every time he touched the ball.

Not an entirely original statement about a good shooter, but the phrasing was too unique to be a coincidence.

And certainly too unique for Lion to have said those exact words to me on our way to the Wynn after the game without having heard them from—or given them to—Bruce.

Now, they could have been talking about Raymond during one of our breaks, and Bruce had used the phrase, and Lion repeated it to me a few hours later.

Or...

I turned back around, returned to my chair, and sat down. Praying the recording app was still going, I again went for the straight-shooter routine.

"I believe you about the eye drops, Bruce, I do." He nodded once, but watched me warily. "But you can see why I'd be hesitant. I mean, a man who will cheat at poker? Who knows what else he'd do?"

Forty-Three

❖❖

THERE. YEP, THERE. A tiny flicker in his eye, the smallest of movements of his jaw. If he'd done either of those during the poker game I probably wouldn't even be in Dallas this morning. I'd have taken my poker winnings and paid Carla back that night.

Then I remembered that Bruce had paid Carla back within hours of the game, and I became even surer that Bruce and Lion were working together to rig the game. But to get his payout, he would have had to see Lion again.

"Was there any sign that he was in...distress when Lion gave you your share of the winnings?" I asked.

Another flinch. Instinctively, I raised my hand and tapped my pendant three times.

I had him.

And he seemed to know it too, sitting back in his chair, shoulders slumping. His mind was working, chewing on how much to say—I could see that too.

Shit, how did I miss any of his signs to Lion at the game? The guy was an open book!

Or maybe just when he was ambushed. He'd known what he was going to do at the game, could have prepared for it.

Me walking in here and accusing him of cheating? Didn't see that coming, did ya, Bruce?

"He was...sweaty, and a little out of breath, but I assumed that was because he'd taken the stairs in the parking deck up to meet me. After he'd taken the elevator down for the cameras. And I guess I thought that perhaps you and he had...um..."

"Had a quickie in my Porsche?" I—literally and figuratively—shuddered at the thought.

Bruce shrugged. "He can be quite...persuasive when he wants to be."

I figured he was right if Lion had persuaded Bruce (if that was how it had happened) to help him cheat at cards. Still, no means of persuasion were strong enough for me to be the cause of Lion's breathlessness.

"Spill, Bruce," I said, sitting back in my chair, arms crossed against my chest, waiting.

He went through how he and Lion colluded, almost hand by hand, which, as a player at the game, was satisfying and humiliating. Again, I was shocked that I hadn't seen it.

"But that was part of his game, his plan. He had pissed you off at the event so you were predisposed to want to beat *him*. Me, you probably assessed early on as no real threat and mentally dismissed me."

Yep. That was exactly what I'd done.

"So, Lion being an asshole was just to get all the venom at the table directed at him? So no one would know how you were helping him? Folding when he had good cards, raising pots that he would then win?"

"No. Well, yes, it was part of the plan. But let's just say Lion didn't have to work too hard at being an asshole."

It turned out that Bruce had done a knee surgery on Lion years ago (I vaguely remembered Lion having a surgery during the golf off-season maybe seven or eight years ago), and they'd remained friendly. Poker buddies from time to time, though Lion lived in Florida and Bruce in Texas.

When Lion agreed to play in the game, he called Bruce and

came up with his plan.

"But why?" I asked. "It's not like he needed the money." I waved my hand around the well-appointed office. "It's not like *you* needed the money."

"He didn't do it for the money. In fact, that night in the stairwell, he gave me all the money he won, not just half. Even though I didn't want it." He looked away from me, down at his desk. "Didn't want any of it, really. But I did have to pay Carla back."

"So, why? Why would Lion do this if not for the money?"

Bruce shrugged. "It was part of the thrill for him. He wanted to see if he could do it. He isn't—wasn't—much of a poker player, and knew that. So when the opportunity came for him to play against the best? Well…he didn't want to be embarrassed, was my guess. Especially with you playing. He followed you a little bit—you were his favorite pro." Another shrug. "He thought it was all in good fun. He knew only people who could afford to lose played in those games."

Could afford to lose? I wondered what Bruce would think if I told him that if I had been playing a fair game that night, and hadn't borrowed money from Carla, that there was a very good chance that instead of sitting in his office right now, he would be sitting on the back of a convertible being driven through a celebratory parade for the Lamont basketball team.

But of course I couldn't tell him any of that. Couldn't let on about the chain reaction he and Lion LaGasse had caused simply because Lion didn't want to be shown up. By a girl. By the Black Widow.

But it was even clearer now why he'd given Carla a fake name—he didn't want anyone to make the connection between him and Lion, small as it was.

I felt like I did after playing poker for twelve straight hours. Yeah, I'd been up a long time, and hadn't slept well on the flights, but the knowledge that someone of Lion LaGasse's stature and wealth would cheat at cards?

It felt like a weird betrayal to me. And yes, I saw the irony that I, someone who had a hand in fixing college basketball games, would be so taken aback by mere cheating at cards, but I was.

"Are you going to tell the cops about Lion and me?" Bruce asked.

I was tempted to bargain with him, tell him that I'd not mention it if he didn't say anything about Raymond being there, but I didn't want him to know there was a connection between Raymond and me. Plus, if it was Frank and Jack questioning Bruce, they already knew about Raymond. I just hoped it wouldn't be Faxon, who might really like the idea of a disgraced basketball player being one of the men in the room. He might even become a dog with a bone about it.

Because even though one mystery was solved—with whom and how Lion had cheated that night—I was still no closer to knowing who had slipped Lion the fatal drops.

Forty-Four

❖❖

THE BOTTLE OF BOURBON was two-thirds empty, but Jack's eyes were clear and focused.

On me.

Raymond had given me a heads-up call that Jack had returned to the house Tuesday morning. When Lor had taken Ben to breakfast for the second morning in a row, Raymond said that Jack questioned him about where I was, but Raymond had said he wasn't sure. Not quite a lie—I could have been in the airspace over a few different states at that time.

He said Jack spent Tuesday afternoon with Ben, then after dinner had taken a bottle of bourbon to my room and shut the door.

Which had been about four hours—and apparently two-thirds of a bottle of Maker's Mark—earlier.

I'd decided I had to give Jack the information about Bruce. I could come up with some elaborate lie about how I'd found Bruce (and why I'd gone to Dallas myself and not just called Jack like I had with the eye drop/*CSI* revelation?), but that wasn't how I wanted to play it.

I had tried very hard not to outright lie to Jack since we'd met, and it was probably the only reason he was still sitting in my room now, waiting for me.

So I brought in my overnight bag with me, opting not to

leave it in the car. Jack didn't say a word as I wheeled it in, pulled it up, and opened it on the bed. He only took a drink when I pulled out the two JoJo wigs and moved them to a different bag at the back of my closet. The rest of the stuff in the bag I threw in my hamper. I'd trashed the Wisconsin sweatshirt in the Indianapolis airport bathroom, so at least I didn't have that to pull out in front of Jack.

Unpacked, and still both of us silent, I reached into my jacket pocket and pulled out Bruce's card and my phone, before taking the jacket off and throwing it on the empty chair next to Jack's. I slowly made my way to him, standing in front of him just like I had only a week ago, when he'd been thrown off the Lion case. This time he didn't lean into me, didn't touch his head to my stomach, didn't look for comfort.

And I probably didn't have any to give him.

Not the kind he needed. Not the reassurance he needed.

To his credit, he didn't say any "I thought you said it was over" kind of words. And for that I loved him. Or at least finally knew that I loved Jack Schiller, though of course I'd known it on some quiet, soft level all along.

But know I *knew* it.

And it was the absolute worst time to say it.

I handed him the business card. "This is Brandt. His name is Bruce Williamson and he's a doctor near Dallas." I set the phone on the table next to him. "I have him recorded saying he and Lion colluded to cheat during the poker game. He says that he doesn't know anything about his eye drops being used to poison Lion, but that he didn't have his drops the next morning. And I believe him."

He flashed his hand toward my closet, toward the suitcase and wigs. "You mean all this, where you've been, was all related to the case?" A flash of hope crept into his tired face. And I could hear it in his voice—he wanted to believe. I hated myself even more knowing I was going to burn that hope up into my flames.

The flames of JoJo.

And yet if you asked me if I regretted placing that bet on Butler last Thursday, I would have said no. Or I would have said yes, but not really meant it.

Because…the Hummer.

"No," I answered. A small nod from him. Down deep he knew the answer before he asked the question. I absently wondered how long there would be that glimmer of hope for me in Jack's eyes.

"It was just coincidence that I found Bruce," I said.

He raised one eyebrow at my use of the word *coincidence*. "Actually, it was," I said, and he didn't ask me any more about how I came to be in Bruce's office.

Sitting down in the chair opposite him, I played the recording and told him my observations about my meeting with Bruce. He listened intently to both. Whatever Jack's issues with my gambling—and so far they'd been back and forth, as had my gambling—he seemed to value my opinions on the cases he worked.

Afterward I asked if he needed to go back to work, or call Frank. His eyes slid to his near-empty glass and the near-empty bottle and he shook his head. "Tomorrow," he said, rising from his chair. He held out a hand to me, and the relief I felt was almost as sweet as the Hummer.

Almost.

I took his hand and he led me to bed. Our lovemaking should have felt like making up for lost time, like saying hello again after a few days apart. It didn't.

It felt like saying goodbye.

"WE'RE NO GOOD FOR EACH OTHER," Jack said in the morning. He was sitting on the edge of the bed, legs over the side, his finger tracing the empty bottle of booze that he'd brought to the bedside table with us last night.

"You mean I'm no good for you," I said, my voice holding no attitude, no accusation. Just stating the facts.

His shoulders slumped a little, and it was all I could do to not reach out and run a hand down his strong back, across those broad shoulders. They had to be broad with all the shit he carried on them.

"No, that's not what I mean," he said, rising and sliding his boxers on from where they'd been tossed to the floor last night. He turned and looked down at me, wrapped up in the sheets that we'd thoroughly disheveled. "I know you feel pressure to not gamble because you think that's what I want. I don't think that pressure's good for you. If you want to quit, you need to do it for yourself. Not Lor. Not me. Not even Ben."

I kept quiet. He was right. And I wasn't sure I really *wanted* to quit, to give up the Hummer forever, even though I knew what it was doing to Jack and me. This very moment was proof.

Jack walked to the table and brought my phone to me. "Send that recording to me, yeah?"

I nodded and opened the voice memo app. I had stayed gadget ignorant for a reason—so I wouldn't start betting, or playing poker, online. But at times like this, I wished I had the tech savvy of the average ten-year-old. I handed it to Jack. "Here, you do it."

A few flashes of his fingers later, he handed my phone back to me. He dressed in silence, and when he was done he looked at me then headed for the door. I couldn't help myself, though I felt like an eighteen-year-old girl doing it—I asked, "So, if we're no good for each other, where does that leave us?"

He turned and looked at me, no emotion on his face, but maybe just a tiny, *tiny* bit of pain in his eyes.

"I don't know. This is now affecting my job. The one thing I know I'm good at. However else I fucked up my life, being a good detective was always a constant. I've looked the other way lots of times because it was penny ante type shit. But it's wearing on me. And I know it's wearing on you, too, trying to shield me from stuff. I don't want that for you." I didn't say anything, but I knew he was right. He sighed, then continued, "I know we said we'd let each other's icebergs float. But I've got to tell you, babe, I'm feeling like I'm on the *Titanic* and going full steam ahead, you know? The *Titanic* didn't see it coming, not in time. But to me, it's a clear, sunny day and I have vision for miles."

"You'd be a fool not to steer clear, then," I said.

"And I'm not saying that you're not in your own boat, too. It's just…"

"I know, Jack."

He nodded, and his deep voice turned soft and low as he said, "I love you, Johanna, but I don't think we… I don't think we're going to make it."

It was the first time he'd said he loved me. And would most likely be the last.

I swallowed the lump in my throat, nodded, and said, "I love you too. And…you're probably right."

He looked at me for another few seconds, nothing left to say. Then he turned and walked out of my room.

Most likely out of my life.

Forty-Five
❖❖

A WEEK WENT BY. The Masters was held and they had a lot of coverage on the special tribute to Lion. It was a good thing they had those tributes before the final toxicology report came out a few days later.

The final report stated the official cause of death was heart failure brought on by the mixture of cocaine, sustained use of anabolic androgenic steroids, beta blockers (both of those banned by the PGA Tour), and tetrahydrozoline (most commonly found in eye drops). Police were investigating the possibility of eye drops being administered to Lion unknowingly.

Yeah, like he was going to knowingly slip himself a chemical cocktail while also snorting coke.

No names—other than mine, of course—had been released as those who had played cards with Lion hours before his death. The timeline of the eye drops entering his system was not made public, so as far as the world knew, it could have been anytime that night, even at Lion's own foundation event.

A day after that announcement, a rock star died of an overdose—while in bed with a fifteen-year-old girl—and the fickle spotlight of the press and social media turned to that, and the focus on Lion—and me—thankfully dimmed a bit.

Frank and Jack had gone to Dallas to question Bruce and came away feeling the same way I did—that Bruce and Lion cheated, but Bruce had not slipped the eye drops to Lion. The cheating at the poker game had not been made public. Once they knew where to look, the cops found snatches of Bruce and Lion (their backs and a glimpse of Lion's shirt) meeting in the parking deck stairwell at the Wynn for the money exchange. But that wouldn't have been enough to prove cheating. And why bother? Charging a dead man for cheating at an illegal poker game? Didn't seem worth their trouble.

They wanted to find a killer, not unmask card cheats.

With Peter Faxon, they continued to look for the bartender and Calvin, while—I assumed—re-looking at all the others that were in the room that night. Raymond and I were basically left alone, not questioned any further. There wasn't anything left to say.

Jack told me about the Dallas trip over the dinner table when he'd gotten back. He'd been to the house a few times since that Wednesday morning a week ago, but only to have dinner and visit with Ben.

He had not returned to my bed.

And though I was crushed, I didn't ask him back. Didn't tell him I'd stop gambling or anything like that. I'd done that once, and look how that had turned out. Another body. Another investigation with me smack dab in the middle of it.

So I just tried to hide my hurt when he was around.

Ben, poor Ben, was torn, and I tried even harder for his sake to pretend it was cool that Jack and I were quits. We went to breakfast each morning, and most days I placed a bet or two afterward, as did Jimmy and Gus. Ben, as always, never bet. But he didn't say a word about me betting.

Carla tried to contact me once about a game and I hung up on her, though I told Raymond it wouldn't bother me if he continued to work for her, but I don't think he did.

Life went on.

The Hummer got me through the heartbreak, fleeting as it

was.

In fact, I was trying to ease my pain by staring at the odds board in the book room at the Red Rock when I heard a sneeze and sniffle from a few rows behind me.

A very distinctive sneeze and sniffle.

It sounded like a dog trying to suppress a bark while his tail was stepped on, then whimpering about it.

Where had I heard that sound before?

At Carla's game.

Calvin!

I didn't turn around, and silently said thanks that in my rush to get to the casino (get to a book room) I hadn't showered and had just thrown my hair into a ponytail and put on a baseball cap. It would be hard to recognize me from the back, but had he been there when I sat down? My eyes had been on the board, not paying any attention to those around me, just finding an empty seat.

"Do I say 'Bless you' or put you out of your misery?"

Two men chuckled, and I knew for sure that one of them, the one who sneezed, was Calvin. "I'll be damn glad when the pollen count goes down," Calvin said.

"I never had that problem, but Ruth is having a hell of a spring. I guess it's really bad this year. That's what they said on the news too."

Nothing else from either one as they, presumably, watched the games on the screens. I gauged they were two rows behind me and about three seats down, over my left shoulder. Still I didn't turn around, not wanting to draw attention to myself.

After about ten minutes I started to get twitchy. Maybe they'd already left and I wouldn't have even known it. Should I just turn around, and not care if Calvin saw me? I could just go up to him and say hi, couldn't I?

In theory there was no reason why he should freak out to see me.

And yet I stayed in my seat.

"That's it for me," Calvin said. "I need to check in at the site."

"Make sure to crack that whip," his companion said.

A chuckle from Calvin. "Something like that. My foreman does a good job, but nothing like the owner showing up unexpectedly at the end of the day to keep workers on their toes. No cutting out ten minutes early or that kind of thing."

"Good practice."

"It has its advantages."

"See you, Fritz," the man said to Calvin. To Fritz.

"Have a good one, Gordy. Breakfast tomorrow?" His voice moved as he spoke. He must have been getting out of his seat.

"Sounds good."

Nothing after that. No mention of time and place where Fritz would be the next morning. (Damn!) Apparently Fritz and Gordy had a standing breakfast date. Kind of like the Corporation.

I waited a few seconds until Fritz would have cleared the book room, then rose from my seat and scanned the perimeter. He could have gone left, past the poker room, to the outdoor street-level parking. Or he could have gone right, toward the parking deck.

I saw his thinning hair rounding the corner by the poker room. As he made the corner and I could see through the glass walls of the poker room, it was obvious I hadn't come across Calvin's sneeze doppelgänger—it was definitely him.

Left—he'd gone left. He'd parked outside, just like I had. Typically I parked in the deck when I came to the Red Rock so my car didn't get stiflingly hot from the desert sun. But it was a cloudy day today, and cooler, and I didn't think I'd be staying long. Zip in, look at the board, feed the monster by making a bet, and zip out.

Little did I know I would stumble upon one of the two

people still unidentified from Carla's game.

Fritz. I knew his name was Fritz. And he owned a construction company. Or at least something that used a foreman, workers, and a "site." I could just call Jack with that information right now, sit back down, and watch the games. Let them figure out the rest.

Yeah, right. Like I could do that.

I walked briskly to the exit, watching from just inside the tinted glass doors as Fritz walked down a row of cars. He got into a red Audi, and when he started to back out, I left the building and sprinted to my own car, parked a row over from his. The row he would most likely drive past to leave the parking lot.

I had a spot closer to the casino, so I was in my Porsche by the time the red Audi drove past. Because of all the pedestrians, and it being a busy casino, cars crawled through the parking lot, which allowed me to easily get into the flow, two cars behind Fritz.

At one of the three-way stops in the parking area, I grabbed my iPhone and, for the first time ever, used Siri.

"Call Jack Schiller," I said, hoping I was doing it right just from watching Lor. "Speaker."

"Calling Jack Schiller," she said back to me, and I set the phone on my dash, keeping a hand on the gearshift in the stop-and-start traffic of the parking lot.

Instead of turning to get onto Charleston, Fritz kept going through the parking lot to the east side, coming out on Pavilion. At that light, he kept going straight, taking the smaller street, Griffith Peak, again instead of turning to get on the main thoroughfare, Charleston.

"Anna," Jack said came through after a couple of rings. "Is Ben okay?"

Cutting to the chase—no time for chitchat with an ex. "He's fine. That's not why I called. Jack, I'm—"

"Not really a good time," he said.

"I found Calvin," I got out quickly, before he could disconnect. I didn't think he'd outright hang up on me, but I couldn't be sure. I wasn't sure just how deep Jack's anger/disgust/love/exhaustion with me went.

"What?"

As I followed Calvin across the light at Pavilion, I gave Jack the lowdown on where I was, what kind of car Calvin was driving. And that Calvin was now Fritz.

"You recognized him by his sneeze? Are you shitting me?"

"It's a very distinctive sneeze," I said, a little defensively.

A sigh from Jack. "Jesus, only you." Another sigh, this one more resigned. "Okay, if you can easily do it, keep following him, and stay on the line with me."

"No problem," I said. "We'll be coming to Town Center in a second and— Oh, wait, he's turning."

"Where are you?"

I pulled over onto the shoulder, there not being any buildings on this stretch to have any side streets or driveways.

"He's pulled into the driveway of those apartment buildings going up. You know, the ones by the new shopping center?"

"On Town Center?"

"Yeah, but he went into them off Griffith Peak. I'm not sure if they have a Town Center entrance or not."

"On it. I'm about twenty minutes away. I don't want to spook him with a patrol car. If you can find a place to park where he wouldn't see you, do it. Don't follow him if he goes inside; just wait in your car in case he goes somewhere else. I'll be there as soon as I can."

"Okay," I said, reaching for the phone to disconnect and looking to see if I could pull back onto the road.

"Anna?"

"Yeah?"

"It may be one *coincidence* after another with you…but I'm glad shit like this seems to find you."

I laughed. "You didn't think that the morning after Lion died." Or pretty much any other time in the past few weeks, except when I'd delivered Bruce and now Fritz.

"I don't really think it now," he said, and disconnected.

I was smiling as I pulled into the drive that ran along the back of five large apartment buildings. Each building was three stories high—townhouse-style apartments, it looked like, with garages on the ground floor. Four large units in each building, all with corner views. Two of the mountains, two of the Strip. The first two buildings looked nearly done, with painted facades and windows put in. The second two buildings weren't quite as far along. No windows, no paint, but otherwise complete—at least that was how it looked from the outside.

The last building was the one that Fritz drove to, parked his car, and went into. There were three pickup trucks outside, all with "Stevenson Construction" on their sides. This building was the least completed, with the outside about half done, but you could still see lots of bare beams and studs through the window holes. Two men in hard hats walked past one of the openings on the third floor as I watched.

Parking in the lot of the fourth building, I took a picture of the side of the truck, catching the name. My car was parked facing the building in front of me, and I had to turn toward the passenger seat to see the fifth building. If anybody looked out of the windows they would probably wonder what someone was doing at the next-door building, but I was hoping they were too busy working to look out of the windows for more than a passing second.

Especially now that the boss was there.

Fritz's car was on the other side of one of the trucks. I couldn't get a picture of the license plate without getting out of my car and walking over. But I figured Jack would be there soon, so all I'd need to do was make sure Fritz didn't leave before that happened.

About five minutes after Fritz went into the building, men started coming out, taking off their hard hats as soon as they were clear of the site, rubbing their hands through their hair. (Yeah, it would suck having to wear one of those all day.) As they moved to the trucks, I snapped pictures of them all, not really thinking it would be important, but why not while I was just sitting there waiting for Jack?

I looked at my watch. Ten minutes to five. That was strange. If Fritz was stopping by unannounced to keep workers on their toes, why let them go early?

Soon all the trucks were gone, and I assumed all of the workers. Only Fritz's Audi remained in the lot. Probably checking up on their workmanship. Maybe that was why he let them go early?

A sharp rap on my driver's-side window scared the crap out of me. I untwisted my body, prepared to see Jack at my window, ready to take over the stakeout.

But it wasn't Jack. It was Fritz. He must have gone around the buildings and approached me from the other side while I was watching the workers leave.

I eyed my phone on the dash while he made a "roll down" motion with his hand. I put the window down.

"Hey, Calvin," I said, not letting him know I knew his real name. Though really, Fritz could have just been a nickname the guy at the Red Rock called him. It sounded kind of nicknamey.

"Hello, Anna," he said. No surprise in his voice. He'd made me at some point, either at the Red Rock from the beginning, or he'd seen me sitting here from the fifth building. "I see you're interested in my buildings. Why don't you come on in and I'll give you a tour?"

"Um, that's okay. I was just checking them out from here. I'm set with what I've got."

"Oh, but you haven't seen the inside. They're really beautiful."

"Yeah, but I—"

"Come on inside, Anna," he said. And this time, as added incentive to check out his apartments, he pointed a handgun at me.

"On second thought, I'd love to see them."

Forty-Six

❖

HE DIDN'T TAKE ME to the building where his car was, where the workers had been, but into the one where I'd parked.

When Jack showed up he'd have to guess which building we were in. Assuming he guessed I was with Fritz and hadn't just abandoned my car or something.

Poor Jack—he was going to be both livid and scared to death when he came into that parking lot and saw my empty car and Fritz's Audi.

Fritz had made me leave my phone in the Porsche, but did let me lock it up and bring the keys, which made me believe that he didn't mean to harm me, that he expected I'd be returning to the car at some point. Maybe.

I cataloged all Fritz would have known, and not known, about why I might be following him. He couldn't have known Jack was on his way, or even that I had a relationship with Jack—and therefore the cops—at all.

The media had reported my appearance at the police station after Lion's death, but nothing else. And he wouldn't have known that Bruce had been found, and that I'd talked to him.

And knew that his eye drops had gone missing.

He led me into the building, and I saw that it was less finished than I originally thought. There were some walls that had been finished, and a couple of hallways that went out of sight, but the ceilings hadn't been put in and you could see through to the third floor in some places.

A few places to hide if needed, but a lot of open space too.

And a lot of metal, wood, and other building material shit that a bullet could ricochet off.

We moved into one of the open areas, Fritz pointing the gun at me, while he moved a little away from me, getting his back away from the main door. I moved a few steps the other way, facing him, the main door also to my side now.

Whether or not he knew I was working with the police, Fritz had pulled a gun on me, so he already thought I was a possible threat. He just wasn't sure to what level. Playing dumb wasn't going to work, but would probably piss him off. So, taking the same tactic I took with Bruce, and trying to throw Fritz off a little, I said, "Did you know the eye drops would kill Lion when you slipped them in his drink?"

Without missing a beat, he answered, "Hell no. I just wanted him to puke his guts out later. Spend the night on the toilet. Because he was being such a complete asshole to everyone there. I didn't even know you *could* die from that. Not just the tiny bit I put in."

Well, a confession. And an easy confession at that. Which either meant Fritz thought I'd be on his side and stay silent…or he was going to silence me himself.

"I don't think you normally can. But with the other stuff in his system…"

He waved the gun a little as he moved his hand in an exasperated manner. "Exactly. A cokehead is one thing. But the fucker was on steroids and beta blockers? Total pollution in his body, that's what."

I nodded. "Yeah, nobody knew that. He would have kept it all secret for sure."

"Steroids for golf. Can you believe that? Beta blockers, yeah, I can see, but steroids?" His voice was full of contempt for the man he'd killed.

I shrugged, then held my hands a little out to my sides when he trained the gun on me at my movement.

"A cheater," Fritz said, "with the steroids and beta blockers."

Nodding, I kept my hands still as I said, "Not only cheating there. He cheated at cards that night, too."

The gun hand waved again and I sucked in a breath. "I knew it! I knew there was something off about that game. That cocksucker."

"I talked with Brandt. Remember Brandt, the guy with the silver hair?"

Fritz nodded, and motioned—again with the gun hand, making me more nervous—to go on. "He told me he was in on it with Lion. They colluded. Brandt raising pots when he knew Lion had a good hand, dropping out of others, stuff like that. Lion let him keep all the winnings, but he was doing it more for the win than the money."

"Motherfucker."

"Yeah," I said. I was careful not to use words like "found" Brandt and he "admitted" when telling the story. I wanted Fritz to think that Brandt and I had just talked it out, kind of like Fritz and I were doing now. Two players telling war stories about a game gone bad.

"You were playing well, Calvin, but there was no way you were going to walk away a winner that night."

He shook his head. "It's not even the money, you know?" I nodded. I knew. Oh, how I knew.

Then I thought of something. I was trying to keep him talking anyway until Jack arrived, so I said, "Hey, Calvin, you're a good player." I waved my hand—slowly, no sudden moves—around the building. "And you obviously have the money to play in big-stakes games. How is it I've never played against you before? How have we not met?"

He seemed a little flattered at this—a pro thinking they

should be traveling, playing, in the same circles.

"I play mostly in L.A., where my main company is located. We got the bid for this job as a means to move into the Vegas area. I've only been here about six months."

"Why the fake name that night?"

"To protect the business. I don't need locals knowing how much I win or lose at the tables, not when I have to work with zoning boards and city officials. That's none of their business. Which is why I usually play private games and not at the casinos."

That made sense. "And the story about getting married the next day?"

He snorted, and the hand around his gun tightened. Oops, maybe not a good topic to bring up. "That part was true. But when I came home furious about losing in that fucking game, my fiancée decided she was heading back to L.A. Wedding never happened."

"Oh. Sorry," I said, and he shrugged, like it happened every day. Maybe it did to him. I thought I recalled him saying it would have been marriage number three.

If I made it through this alive I'd be sure to introduce Calvin to Gus—they'd get along great.

Except Gus had never killed anyone.

Part of me knew I had no room to judge Calvin. He had no intent to kill Lion, just to make him sick because he was being such an asshole and had won everyone's money. Just as I'd only wanted to make college basketball players sick enough to not have their A-game the next day. If any of them had heart conditions or had their systems full of shit the way Lion had, it could be me standing with a gun thinking I was cornered.

Speaking of cornered, where the hell was Jack?

"Police, freeze," someone yelled from one of the corners near me.

Jack.

He stepped into the open space, gun trained on Fritz. "Drop

it," he said calmly. Fritz kept the gun pointing toward me, with a look of surprise—and hurt—on his face. "What's going on?"

"Drop the gun," Jack said, stepping in front of me.

I took a step to the side, then another, putting space between Jack and me. "Calvin," I said, my hands in front of me in a "let's just chill out" way. "Drop the gun. You didn't mean to kill him. But you're now entering a realm of something entirely different."

"What, were you wired or something? Was this all a set-up?"

I shook my head. "No, nothing like that. Nothing's been recorded. You can explain this any way you want to the cops."

"Johanna," Jack warned.

Fitz looked between Jack and me, Jack taking steps in my direction and me moving away from him, making Fritz have to choose one of us. I didn't think he'd shoot me, and I didn't think he was stupid enough to point a gun at an armed cop.

A look of panic crossed his face, then turned to resignation. He knew he had to stand down, take his chances. His hand started to lower, but at that moment a crash came from behind him as Peter Faxon stepped on something which sent a pile of two-by-fours that had been balanced against a wall rattling to the floor. Fritz jumped, and the look on his face went from resignation to anger.

"You fucking bitch," he said, and aimed his gun at me.

A series of shots thundered in the cavernous room from both Fritz and Jack, with Faxon joining in at the end.

I dove for the floor, glad I'd stepped away from Jack, since Fritz had been aiming in my direction when his body was riddled with bullets.

I felt a sting in my foot and looked down. Blood at my ankle, but it seemed to be just a graze. Of course it would be on the foot that had been broken years before, and mangled weeks ago on Vince's terrace.

"Clear," I heard Faxon say, and I looked up to see him

standing over Fritz's lifeless body, kicking the gun away from it, still holding on to his own. Faxon looked over in our direction.

"Fuck," he said, running over to me.

"It's not that bad; just a graze. I'm—"

But he ran past me and my eyes followed him to see Jack lying on the floor, a spreading patch of blood blossoming across his chambray shirt.

"Officer down," Faxon was saying into a phone in the short time it took me to crawl (maybe it was more than a graze after all) to Jack.

"Keep your hand there," Faxon told me as he took off his jacket and placed it on top of Jack's wound. "Lots of pressure."

Then he got back to the phone, giving instructions for cops and an ambulance.

I kept my hands on top of the jacket, pressing as hard as I could, willing Jack to open his eyes. "Jack," I said loudly. "Jack, just hang on. Help's coming."

His eyes did open at that. His whiskey-brown eyes, like the color of the bourbon he loved so much.

Ben's eyes.

"Johanna," he whispered, then closed his eyes.

"Shit," Faxon said, dropping to his knees, tossing his phone aside and adding his strong hands to mine.

I put everything I had into keeping Jack alive.

And I prayed.

Forty-Seven

❖

I DIDN'T REALLY THINK GOD would be listening while I prayed at Fritz's construction site. I was pretty sure I wasn't on the Big Guy's good side.

Perhaps it was all the prayers of the others who were with me in the hospital waiting room.

Or it might have just been Jack's stubbornness that saved him.

Whatever the reason, he made it out of surgery. Lost a lot of blood, but the bullet had missed organs and he was expected to make a full recovery.

I missed most of the surgery, having a minor one of my own to remove the bullet, which apparently didn't just graze by me. But it hadn't done a lot of damage either. I had come out of surgery, been well enough to move around (with a boot—again—would I ever get rid of that thing?), and was brought to the waiting room outside of surgery to join Ben, Raymond, Gus, Jimmy, Lorelei, Frank, Faxon, and a couple other cops I didn't know. All while Jack had been fighting for his life.

There were a lot of cops who came in and out, talking with Frank and Faxon, then going to Ben and introducing themselves.

As it should be, with Ben being Jack's father. A fact that apparently had been spread through the department, most likely by Frank.

I noticed all those cops steered clear of me.

Except Frank, who took me to another room to get my statement as soon as I was completely free of the anesthetic. I gave him the play-by-play of what went down. The ending he knew from Faxon, who had followed Jack to the construction site.

When we were wrapping up, I said to Frank, "Listen, I'm not throwing shade, because I know I'm the reason that Jack's in surgery right now." He didn't bother arguing with me, and I continued, "But I think we would have had a different ending if Faxon hadn't been Jack's backup. Just sayin'."

Frank didn't say anything to that, but he did nod that he got me.

Once we got word about Jack's condition, the cops cleared out and it was just "family."

I hobbled over to Ben and sat next to him, reaching for his hand. It was cold, and I knew I wouldn't be spreading any heat his way—I had none of my own to give.

"Should we call Lisa?" I asked. "So that Casey knows?"

Ben pulled his hand out from under mine, making like he was buttoning up his cardigan. Maybe that's all it was, but the gesture still stung. "We did. While you were talking with Frank."

That stung too, but I couldn't say why. It made sense that Ben would be the one to talk to Jack's ex-wife and son. Hell, he'd spent days with them. I'd never even met them.

Hearing from her ex-husband's ex-girlfriend was not quite the same.

"Oh, that's good," I said.

Ben nodded, still keeping his attention on his sweater, not looking at me. "We waited until we knew for sure that he would…" Once more I wanted to reach for his hand, but he fiddled again with his buttons so I didn't. "She asked if she should bring Casey down, but we both thought it would be better to wait until Jack is stronger, so as not to scare him."

"Okay," I said, though it wasn't like he was asking my opinion. "How are you doing?" I asked. "Do you want to stay, or Lorelei could bring you home for a while and back later?"

It was seven in the morning and we'd been here all night, though again, I'd missed most of it. I wasn't even sure when the gang had gotten there.

"No," he said.

"No? But Ben, you've got to be—"

"No," he said softly but very firmly, with steel in his voice.

"Ben," I said. "I know it's scary, but he's going to be okay."

"No thanks to you," he said. My head shot back like he'd slapped me. The sting was the same as if he had. I heard Lorelei gasp. He went on before I'd even recovered from his first words.

"I'm sorry, Hannah, I don't want to hurt you, but it's true." His brown eyes were soft and full of pain as he looked at me and went on, "I thought it wasn't my place to say. You're a grown woman, and it's your money. You've protected yourself—protected me and Lorelei—as best as you can by letting her handle the money. But now it's not just about making sure I have a roof over my head in my old age."

It never was just about that to me. It was about our little family, such as it was.

"It's about my son now. And my grandson. The way you live, the company you keep, almost cost my son his life. He's a cop; it's dangerous. This I know. But him being with you, trying to protect you…"

I felt a stinging in my eyes and willed it away. I could always keep my emotions in check when playing high stakes. But it seemed to me that the stakes had never been higher than they were right now.

"Your life, how you live, cannot cost me my son, Hannah," he said in almost a whisper. "I waited too long to find him."

He turned his body to me, his shoulders hunching more each day, it seemed. Or maybe it was just the weight of his words. The weight of his burden.

Me.

"Hannah darling, I love you. But…"

I held up a hand, not wanting to hear more. Besides, I'd already heard it a week earlier. It was just that that time it came from Jack.

But it was the same message.

"My doctor suggested getting off my feet as soon as possible," I said. "I think maybe I'll go home for a while." I had no idea if my doc had said that, but I needed to get out of there.

Besides, Jack had his father with him, and others who loved him.

He didn't need me.

And he certainly didn't want me.

"That's a good idea," Ben said. "We don't need to talk about this now. We can figure it out after Jack's healthy again."

Figure what out?

But I knew.

Ben would choose to live with Jack over me. He would cut me out of his life to protect his son.

From me.

I nodded and rose. Everyone else came to their feet. Lor brushed by me, whispering, "He's just upset. It'll be okay." I nodded, but didn't believe her.

"Glad you're okay, sweetie," Gus said, and gave me a peck on the cheek.

"Thanks, Gus."

"I'll take you home," Raymond said, and I nodded. I had no idea where my Porsche was—not that I was in any condition to drive it.

"I'll walk out with you," Jimmy said. "Ben, can I bring you anything?"

"Maybe some fresh coffee, Jimmy, thank you." Jimmy nodded, and he, Raymond, and I turned and made our way out of the waiting room area.

Since I was now being officially discharged, they made me ride out in a wheelchair, which, quite frankly, I was happy to do, not sure my body could hold me up too much longer.

Jimmy stayed with me and the nurse at the hospital entrance while Raymond went to get the car. He didn't try the kind words that Lor had of Ben just being upset. Jimmy knew better.

Instead he said words similar to ones he'd said a couple of weeks ago when we were at my place in the book room watching games.

"You might be able to change what you do, Anna," he said, "and only you can decide if you wanna do that. But you can't change who you *are.*"

He helped me get in the Lexus when Raymond pulled up, then leaned forward and, like Gus, gave me a kiss on the cheek.

Shit. If Jimmy was kissing me in sympathy, I must really be fucked.

His words reverberated in my mind as we pulled away from the Summerlin Medical Center. We didn't have far to go; the hospital was near my house. But the drive was still long enough for me to play Jimmy's words over and over.

Did I—could I—deny who I was at the core? Did alcoholics or drug addicts feel like this? Was this rock bottom? And even if it was, would I change? Did I even want to?

For the most part, I was okay with who I was. But it seemed the past few months had shown me that my life was beyond just me. I was endangering the people I loved.

"You might want to do what Ben needs to do and get clear of me," I said to Raymond.

"What do you mean?"

"Given the past four weeks, it's obvious that I can't protect you. It's a miracle your name hasn't been made public. It still might."

He shrugged and continued driving.

"I told your mom I'd keep you safe."

"I'm safe," he said.

"Today. Right now, but who knows. Maybe you'd be better off in Atlanta with her and your sister."

"Enough of this," he said, but I couldn't let it go.

"You asked one thing of me—to not let it consume you. To not let you end up like me. And I couldn't even do that. So much for sitting on you hard."

"I'm not like you," he said as nicely as he could, but still getting his point across. Which he did—he wasn't nearly as bad off as I was. "Besides, if I hadn't gotten involved you wouldn't have cracked the case."

"How do you figure?"

"That picture of DeShaun. That led you to Bruce, and he told you about the cheating and losing his eye drops, which gave Calvin motive and opportunity."

"And led to Jack lying on a concrete floor in a pool of his own blood."

A sigh from Raymond. "Let's talk about my future some other time. Not when you're high on painkillers."

I had refused painkillers when offered hours ago. But I didn't push it.

"Hey," he said after a few minutes of silence, "I finally came up with my superhero name."

"Yeah? What?"

"The Fixer."

"Jesus," I said, and he laughed. I joined him, and even though it was my foot that had been shot, my whole body ached.

"What about you? Still staying with Black Widow?"

No. I was most definitely the Destroyer—that was clearer now more than ever.

"Yeah, I guess," I said.

Raymond came in with me and got me settled in my room, then I shooed him out, telling him to pick up some breakfast somewhere and bring it to the hospital for everyone. He wanted to stay, but I told him I was just going to get some sleep anyway, so he finally agreed.

I tried to sleep, but Ben's words haunted me.

Finally I got out of bed and made my way—with the cane I thought I'd never see again—to the office, going behind my desk and booting up my laptop, thinking I'd catch the coverage about Fritz's death.

But as I waited for the laptop to boot, I saw Vince's letter to me sitting on my desk where I'd thrown it after the will reading.

I had briefly skimmed it that day, but really hadn't registered his words, just noting whether or not he mentioned JoJo and her jobs.

What the hell. It couldn't get any worse. I pulled it to me, dislodging a business card from the edge of my desk blotter as I did. Pulling the letter out of the envelope, I leaned forward and braced myself.

But it wasn't that bad. It was actually kind of Jimmy-esque.

Dear Anna,

You're not going to want to hear this, but there are things I need to say. As I write this you're in Chicago, trying to help Raymond Joseph. I'm sorry I couldn't go with you, but am so proud of you for going.

If you're reading this, it means things didn't work out for us like I hoped they might. It also means I'm not around to tell you how much I wished things could have been different between us. If I could turn back time, I would have cut you off as a customer years ago before JoJo had a chance to be born. That I was a part of her birth in you is something I will always regret.

And yet she is a part of you, Anna. Like the dark parts of me were important facets, too.

Neither of us can deny them. We shouldn't have to.

Unfortunately, it was those parts that led us here—you reading this letter instead of me trying to win you away from Schiller.

I just wanted to let you know that you were always more to me than a customer. And that I wished I'd let you know that years ago.

Take care of yourself. With love,

Vince

P.S. As you no doubt know by now, I have left my estate to a woman who is very close to me—Cassandra Hall. I have let her know that if she is ever in trouble to contact you. Hopefully that will never happen, but please help her if you can.

Though my curiosity was piqued all over again about Cassandra Hall, it was Vince's words of what might have been that stuck with me. What if he'd cut me off before we'd come up with JoJo? Would she never have been born?

Or was she always there and would have come out on her own eventually?

Who cares? I am who I am. Let's see what games are being played today.

A sound between a gasp and a sob escaped from my throat. God, would she ever shut up? I put Vince's letter back on my desk, and pulled forward the business card that I'd uncovered, turning it over. It was for Monty Westerfield, a guy who'd presided over one of Lor's ill-fated interventions for me.

It had been Monty's first intervention and he'd been really nervous. I hoped the past couple of months had improved his batting average, 'cause he'd struck out with me.

I didn't remember him giving me a business card. Oh, I'd walked out, that's right. Lor must have hung on to his card. And, as subtle as she ever was, put it in my desk blotter.

A feeling not unlike the Hummer rushed through me as I ran a finger along the edges of Monty's card. There was a little electric prickle that I didn't typically feel when betting, and it was that feeling that was like…hope. Hope that there could even be a different feeling from the Hummer had me picking up my phone and dialing the number on the card.

"Hello," he answered, his voice a little creaky, and I knew

I'd woken him up. Intervening in Vegas was probably a late-night activity, and Monty most likely slept in.

"Monty, this is Anna Dawson. I'm not sure if you remember me or not, but—"

"Of course I remember you. You were my first intervention."

Apparently you never forgot your first.

"Um, okay," I said, then stopped. What now? I hadn't really thought further than calling Monty. Suddenly I felt like one of those cartoon anvils had been dropped on me, but instead of flattening me like Wile E. Coyote, it was hanging there, pressing down, my head and shoulders keeping it in place. With startling clarity, I knew I couldn't keep it in place any longer. I could either try to crawl out from under it or become road kill.

"Monty?"

"Yeah?"

My voice cracked a little as I said, "I need help."

"Do you still live where you did when we met? Are you there now?"

"Yes."

"I'll be there in half an hour. Are you okay until then?"

"Yes. I mean, it's not urgent or anything. We could make an appointment for later or something."

"No. Hang on, Anna, I'm on my way."

"Okay, Monty," I said, and disconnected.

I sat back in my chair and just tried to breathe.

Acknowledgments

Beta readers Holli Bertram, Liz Kelly, Colleen Gleason and Patti Kearly were invaluable in their feedback. The editing at Twin Tweasks and Editing 720 was, as always, top notch. And a big thank you to my last-look editor, Margo Burrage.

The Anna Dawson Series continues with

AGAINST THE WALL
ANNA DAWSON BOOK 4

Try Mara Jacobs's romantic mystery

BROKEN WINGS

Try Mara Jacobs's *New York Times* bestselling Worth series

Worth The Weight

Worth The Drive

Worth The Fall

Worth The Effort

Totally Worth Christmas

Worth The Price

Worth The Lies

Worth The Flight

Worth The Burn

Find out more at
www.MaraJacobs.com

Mara Jacobs is the *New York Times* and *USA Today*
bestselling author of The Worth Series

After graduating from Michigan
State University with a degree
in advertising, Mara spent
several years working at daily
newspapers in Advertising sales
and production. This certainly
prepared her for the world of
deadlines!

Mara writes mysteries with
romance, thrillers with romance,
and romances with...well, you
get it.

Forever a Yooper (someone who hails from Michigan's glorious
Upper Peninsula), Mara now splits her time between the U.P. and
Las Vegas.

You can find out more about her books at **www.marajacobs.com**

www.ingramcontent.com/pod-product-compliance
Lightning Source LLC
Chambersburg PA
CBHW031657170626
46808CB00005B/1493